DARIEN DOGS

Darien Dogs

HENRY SHUKMAN

Jonathan Cape
London

Published by Jonathan Cape 2004

2 4 6 8 10 9 7 5 3 1

First published in Great Britain in 2004 by Jonathan Cape
Random House, 20 Vauxhall Bridge Road, London SW1V 2SA

Random House Australia (Pty) Limited
20 Alfred Street, Milsons Point, Sydney,
New South Wales 2061, Australia

Random House New Zealand Limited
18 Poland Road, Glenfield,
Auckland 10, New Zealand

Random House South Africa (Pty) Limited
Endulini, 5A Jubilee Road, Parktown 2193, South Africa

The Random House Group Limited Reg. No. 954009
www.randomhouse.co.uk

A CIP catalogue record for this book is available from the British Library

ISBN 0-224-07282-X

Papers used by The Random House Group are natural, recyclable products made from wood grown in sustainable forests; the manufacturing processes conform to the environmental regulations of the country of origin

Typeset by Palimpsest Book Production Limited,
Polmont, Stirlingshire
Printed and bound in Great Britain by
Mackays of Chatham plc, Chatham, Kent

For Stevie and Saul

Contents

Acknowledgements

I would like to thank the Wordsworth Trust, the Royal Literary Fund and the Arts Council England for their generous support.

Thanks to the following publications, in which some of the stories appeared: the *Hudson Review* ('Road Movie'); the *Missouri Review* ('Mortimer of the Maghreb'); the *New England Review* ('Castaway'); *O. Henry Prize Stories 1999*, in which 'Mortimer of the Maghreb' was a finalist.

Darien Dogs

Rogers did not remember coming aboard. He lay on the hard surface listening to the voices swooping round him. Black voices on black wings.

Yeah man, you lucky we pass.

Lucky we stop, man. Ain't easy to stop like that.

They were talking a language he had once known. He didn't know what a language was now. It was sounds made in the back of the head. It was something you heard and you knew you knew why you were hearing but just then you couldn't remember the reason. It was bright light in a steep stairwell. Sunlight on a deck, sunlight in a hatch. The sound of men eating, the clatter of plates, a screech-boom on a television mounted above.

Take a lot a fuel you want to stop fas' like we did back there. You see? So man, where you from?

Leave the man alone, Silas.

Don't talk how that Silas does talk.

Likely the fella could want to know who ship he on. That we ain't no Colombian pirate boat running no drugs or nothin.

A cup a water and a bunk, thass all the fella need.

He need a doctor, man. Look at them scrapes.

Somebody laid a blanket over him. The blanket was night and it was warm. Rogers could feel its weight all over his limbs, light and heavy at once like a fur coat, prickly with stars. The night bled into his mouth. Melted into his throat like ice. Like ink. Could be he was drinking ink. Surely ink would go down the throat like this, slick so it clung to your gullet.

Then he was gone.

I

I

'You want AC?' the taxi driver asked in indeterminately accented English.

What a question. Ten minutes out of the plane and Jim Rogers' shirt was already dissolving into his skin.

'AC twenny-fy, no AC twenny,' the driver went on.

'*Claro que sí*,' Rogers snapped. What kind of country was this? It didn't even have its own language, it didn't care who occupied it. Brits one year, Yanks the next, Spaniards the year after. And the taxi drivers charged for air-conditioning.

The car, a mid-seventies Lincoln, was of the vintage that favoured the colour burgundy. There was a long line of them at the Mario Rosales Airport. Rogers sank into its velvet upholstery and with something like relief felt the ancient suspension sag into the first pothole. The suspension of America, the potholes of Latinismo: two things he thought he knew how to love. Panama lay ahead, a whole week of it, but at least he was out of New York, away from Sylvester Securities. Sylvester's: the seal and stamp of his shame. What a *name* for a bank – you could just hear how shoddy and low-budget they were.

The driver buzzed up the windows and switched on the air-conditioning. A clattering of maracas burst forth under the hood, and steam poured from the vents. Rogers wondered if he ought to have economised after all.

He watched a fan of banana bushes move past, coated in a sheen from another world, and thought: I'm a ruin, a shell of a man. Lately he'd been suffering terrible attacks of panic, misery, dread – he wasn't sure what to call them. The smallest setbacks shook him with annoyance, rattled about inside him. And at the same time, things – objects, sights, smells – could find no purchase in him. There was nothing left in him for them to get a toehold on.

Take those spindly palm trees. They were probably beautiful, their fronds glittered like metal, like knives, in the equatorial sun. But he couldn't say if they were beautiful. He could barely have said if they existed. Maybe they were just figments of a dream. When consciousness was backed into the blackest corner and only the tiniest chink of light still reached you, how did you really know if you were awake or asleep, alive or dead? It was as if he had woken at three in the morning in the depths of the circadian trough, only this trough went on and on. All the bright fields of the mind closed down one by one until all that was left was one gorge, which you gradually fouled with your daily presence.

Now, now, he told himself. Don't go that way, don't let it start.

Maybe the change of scene would do him good.

A bus pulled out in front of the taxi, a big old American school bus painted a riotous mosaic of colours. Smoke billowed from under the fender. At the back window the hairdos of five schoolgirls bounced up and down: ponytail, braids, plaits, all of them black. When the bus braked the heads bowed away from the window, then bobbed back into place. Rogers was cheered by the sight. They were poor, obviously, those girls, but he could see them smile and giggle at each other. There was something obscurely comforting about a land of poverty. Perhaps it reminded you of a simpler way of living.

The taxi driver said, 'You got some pretty girls where you're going.'

Rogers didn't answer.

'Great girls,' the driver repeated, as if Rogers might not have understood. 'Chicas. You looking for chicas?'

Rogers shrugged involuntarily.

The man growled out a laugh. Rogers glanced at the rear-view mirror and saw that the driver was staring at him. 'The Geisha Sauna. Good place. The girls they've got – *good ass*.' He uttered the final phrase in English, with much relish, and a protracted cackle.

These Third World types, they had no concept of personal space. The word *intrude* wasn't in the lexicon. There was nothing remotely embarrassing, apparently, about discussing sex with a stranger.

Yet Rogers found that oddly comforting too.

The city was nothing but concrete. Concrete transmission shops, concrete stalls loaded with papayas, concrete high-rises pale in the distance, and everywhere the unmistakable smell of the cheap Caribbean, a smell composed of rotting fruit, diesel fumes and urine. This was the real Caribbean, nothing to do with beaches and Bacardi. It was a land of Indian businessmen, Syrian traders, Chinese storekeepers, of graceful black cabbies with wrinkled notes wadded in breast pockets, of Range Rovered whites in button-downs, of small-time salesmen prowling the ports with their briefcases of catalogues. It was a world of mildew and oil drums, and concrete. Rogers felt something almost like nostalgia to be back in it.

He surveyed the fetid scene and wondered: could this really be the setting for his great comeback? He had got wind of a chance to steal a march not just on his so-called colleagues at Sylvester's, not just on the market, but on the very multinationals themselves. Rogers had had to visit the desk manager three times in his glass office to get him to listen. Twice he was brushed off with a 'Later, Rogers', like an office boy, until finally the man said, 'We're sending you down to Panama,' as if it hadn't been his idea all along.

And it was a good idea, just the kind he had been waiting for: a chance to lead a consortium of banks. They would finance a new pipeline. The beauty of it was that the line was short: less than a hundred miles. Short, hassle-free, and buildable in less than three years. Yet it would link the two great oceans. All you had to do was look at a map to see its beauty. The Isthmus of Darien, the snake of Panama, the gateway between the two worlds: you could either say that land had been illogically and inconveniently placed whereby all that was rational there ought to have been no country, no land at all, only open sea to allow the passage of free trade. Or else you could seize the opportunity. There was still only one way through. With its choppy blue channel of warm water Panama was nothing but an inverse ferryman, the ferryman's tollbooth.

Pierce it, puncture it, plumb it into the world's oil trade, and you could be picking up fees on millions of barrrels a day. And with the Gulf the way it was, the timing couldn't have been better. It was a miracle no one else had thought of it. But then Panama was a closed shop: you had to find the right way in.

Yet when the taxi man pressed a button on the Deluxe radio and a salsa tune jangled from the speakers, the music's optimism didn't infect Rogers. He felt nothing, none of the spark and clarity that in the past used to presage a good deal. Rogers was unhappy with many things: his age – halfway – appalled him; his marital status – zero – sickened him; and his job – which was all it was now – had shrunk to banana republics, the nowheres, the armpits of the continent. Latin American accounts were the dead end, the sump of the business.

Yet he couldn't help liking Latin music. Every time he heard it he would catch a whiff of his first few months in New York – the odour of traffic, of pizza, of a perfume called Kosaku worn by a girl called Monica, and the detergent smell of the tiny never-used kitchen in his apartment: they all came back to him, together with the tremendous hopefulness of those early days in Manhattan. Surely those had been the best months of his life. Monica had hailed from the upper-upper east side, the Spanish quarter. He'd had his school-dance fumblings before, his moody college loves, but nothing to prepare him for the love of a hot-blooded Latina. On the first warm day of March her many uncles would set out tin tables on sidewalk and fire-escape, and clack down their dominoes, dewy beer bottle between the legs, while their transistors filled the city's hazy atmosphere with a dawn-to-dusk background of Latin rhythm – popping congas, dinging cowbells, screeching trumpets, and above all of it the high-octane, high-stave, highly excitable Hispanic male vocals. Monica taught him the dance steps right out there on the sidewalk, to the amusement of her uncles. She painted her nails and her lips blood-red, and in the bedroom dominated him in every way until the final moment of submission, whereupon she would become a helpless victim of passion. It was very flattering.

But all that was long, long ago, in another life.

The first thing Rogers did in his room at the Hotel Panama was step out on to the balcony and smell the air. It was thick, rich, a balm, full of tropical heaviness. Across the car park sat a squat brown building with a curly neon sign on the roof: 'Geisha Sauna'. He took one look at it and with a heavy heart acknowledged that he would not be able to resist its sordid allure. There was simply no reason to.

The girl said she was called Paulina. She spoke Spanish with a mellifluous accent he hadn't heard before, a flow of words perhaps devised specially for use in the little room where she led him – the death chamber of love, he reflected, with its white-sheeted bench. When she agreed to the acrobatic posture he suggested and commenced to tackle him, the tangle of emotion he had carried with him from New York fell slack, unbinding him. He expected a tremor of vague guilt – this wasn't something he had done in a long while, after all – but felt only a flutter of gratitude. He buried his hungry face in her, mumbling something about 'love'.

And she was lovely. Afterwards, relief administered, he lit them a cigarette each, sighed out a column of smoke and studied her face. She could have been oriental. She had strong cheeks and warm, intelligent eyes, and a smile of curiosity played on her lips as if she were interested in him, as if he pleased her.

He asked where she was from. Sitting on a stool with her bare legs drawn into her chest, she cocked her head, blew out smoke. 'San Blas,' she said.

'San Blas?' He imagined some market town where they grew grapefruits and coffee, somewhere she had gone blind with boredom before delivering herself into this noncity, neither suburb nor downtown, of plastic and concrete. Panama, really, was nothing but a shopping mall, to which the label-struck of all Latin America came for their Dior and de la Renta.

She frowned. 'You haven't heard of San Blas?'

Rogers shook his head. This sort of thing could be a bore – having to hear about My Country, *mi país*, pronounced with an emphatic caesura. Latins could get maudlin about their homeland, he thought, their *patria*. But she was pretty. He propped himself on an elbow.

'Tell me about San Blas.'

She hesitated, perhaps thinking about money.

'I'd like to hear,' he said. 'Charge me whatever.' Yes, he might be down on '90, '91, '92, but he still had deep pockets, he could dip and dip and the well would not at once run dry. The material of his trade, if you could call it a trade, was after all money.

Her cigarette hand rose to her lips and she paused as she inhaled. Then she smiled, revealing good teeth, perhaps a little big in the middle, though that added character.

'San Blas is a different world,' she told him. 'We have no illness, no poverty, no hurricanes. People live a long, long time.'

He raised his eyebrows. 'Like how long?'

The girl whistled and shrugged. 'We have our own doctors, they keep us well with their songs. A hundred, a hundred and twenty, that's normal.'

'With their songs?' She was obviously some tribal girl from the pages of anthropology.

'Our doctors sing to keep illness away. Sharks too. If any shark comes near, they hear the song and go away. Sharks are like dogs, we call them sea-dogs. The doctors know what to tell them, and they stay away.'

He watched her as she talked. She was very watchable. The flare of her cheeks, their copper hue: she must be an Indian, a real native. But a pretty one, nothing like the heavy people he had seen out west in the States. She spoke languorously, crossing her knees, resting her wrists on them, fingertips lifting and dropping as she spoke, like some nightclub socialite. She was lovely, her belief in folklore was charming. For the first time in months, Rogers kept his attention right on what was before him. She was worth it. He felt vaguely sad that she should be living in a soulless city – sooner or later it would infect her and she would forget about the shark-doctors back home –

but he was also excited to be sitting, or reclining, here with her.

One of her shoes dangled from a toe. She swung it about. 'You should go to San Blas,' she said.

'You should take me.'

The truth was, he felt like asking her to dinner. She was bright, he could see that already. Something in her eyes matched what was left of his own intelligence. He didn't know what protocol there might be to seeing a prostitute outside her place of trade, but he didn't care. His heart beat harder as he said, 'I'd like to see you again.'

She smiled. 'Come back later.'

'If I didn't have a business dinner I'd take you out.'

'Another night, hombre.'

He could see her eyes cloud over. Which made him all the more determined to set something up, something other than a further appointment on the white bench. 'How's tomorrow?' he tried.

'I'm here.'

Rogers didn't know if that meant she was busy or available. 'Could we go out for dinner?'

'Why not?' She smiled again.

'Let's make it a date.' He was unexpectedly pleased. Maybe the week wouldn't be so bad after all.

He roused again. She put a finger to his lips and pressed him back down, climbing on board. He trusted her – her turn to show him the native ways, the San Blas formulas. Which she did. She swam over him like a dolphin, roosted on him like a bird, raced him like a pair of horses to the line. She was very convincing.

2

Once, and not all that long ago, Jim Rogers had had everything – a huge income, an office in the sky, a girlfriend whose face graced the continent's highways and its palaces of darkness. His three cars, of German obsidian, Detroit's best chrome, and one piloted by an angel of English gold, slumbered in the underworld beneath his home. His home had been a palazzo hoisted atop a stone-clad pillar of industry in a historic district. From his balconies he could see the light beating off the Hudson River and all the flatlands of America groaning into the sunset beneath their burden of iron.

Nor had he been one of those men imprisoned by their wealth, encumbered by sections of sod, piles of bricks, acres of rippling roof sheltering ranked machinery. He didn't own his wealth, he was paid it. Month after month, in the cheques came. To go every day empty-handed into the office, free on this earth, and emerge with a slip of paper in one's pocket that had the right numbers on it – that was truly to live by one's wits, as a modern-day hunter-gatherer. He made it a point never to put down. The cars, for instance: from the figures that flew in each month lesser figures winged off to take care of them. His life was a flight of figures.

Year after year, he wore his wealth lightly for indeed it weighed little. The crash of '87 saw him sway on his pillar but not topple. He had laughed to feel the breeze of risk on his cheek, then tightened the belt by one or two holes.

Rogers' partner had been European, like him, but of ancient, long-distilled stock. Royalty flickered distantly in her blood. She had fled the Sorbonne after three weeks, hopped on a whim to America, joined a modern-dance studio, and changed her name from Kandele to Candlebury. Five years on, when Jim met her, the lowlands of Benelux still hovered in her voice like an aroma.

Sometimes he wondered if they had treated each other well because they came from different countries and met in a third, never quite shaking off a certain diplomatic protocol.

Somewhere he had read: *a lost soul groping in the darkness of remembered ways*. That was right, exactly. To be lost, as he was now, was to remember the time when you were not lost, and to dream, or despair, of recovering it; but either way to look back. And he had also read about love being a rock, and if the rock is cleaved then either half dwindles, corrodes in the air. You know by that litmus if it has been real love. And he knew that yes, his had been true love and he had thrown it away. Happiness – which was the same as his soul – had shrivelled up in him like a dead spider. Three years had passed since he gave her up, three years of disaster, disaster metaphysical, moral, material. Morgan's had moved him from Far East to Middle East, then London, then Latin accounts. Then they dropped him entirely, and he had had to scramble on to a stool at Sylvester's.

He tried to be a good man, a flexible man. He knew fortune was a wheel and wheels spun. He had had to give up the loft, had moved to the West Village, to a narrow three-room railroad with a strip of a view of the Empire State and a friendly Colombian across the hall who invited him in to watch Mexican football matches on cable. Occasionally they got a UEFA match too. The place was cheap enough that he could save.

In the hotel car park clouds of insects whirled about the lamps, cars gleamed and from a pair of poles two translucent flags hung limply above a coarse lawn. There was something about a lawn in the tropics, and a city of concrete: they acquired glamour in the heat. Here in the warmth you could believe that even if you were no longer the success you had once been, you were at least still a man making his own way, you still had some kind of chance.

An oil-bird flapped out of the darkness, disappeared into a palm tree.

Re-entering the tropics always gave Rogers a buzz, even now, after many trips, after two years of Latin accounts. Every time he came down he still couldn't help enjoying the first fragrance of night blossom in humid air.

The Panama Pipe Corporation had taken a back room at the Casa Frattini. Or rather the company's ghost had. The PPC didn't really exist, it was just a name and an all but empty bank account. That was why they were gathering: to see if they could make it exist.

Rogers' flight caught up with him. When his lobster bisque appeared, dizziness swamped him. He guzzled his

Chablis, doubting it would have the power to inebriate but hoping it might plant his feet on the ground.

The company was what you got at such dinners. A Swedish ex-dish in her fifties with cropped blonde hair, from a Scandinavian bank; a Señor Carreras with bald head and injudiciously solemn countenance who was the official host, being high up in the Bank of Panama; Señora Carreras too, who patted the corners of her mouth with her napkin after every forkful; and a slick young banker with wavy hair and expensive loafers called Jean-Louis Codrin, Carreras's sidekick.

Of the five men and two women who made up the party, Sylvester's would be wanting him to watch the various bank executives, but Rogers was interested in Albert Jones, an improbably named Argentinian with a flushed face and bouffant of white hair. He had put together the consortium of Latin investors and was close to Milagros, a Colombian of immense wealth renowned for his 'clean nose'. Milagros, ultimately, was the man one needed, and the way to him was through Jones. Rogers and Jones had talked on the phone a few times, and Rogers had steered him to a friend on the trading floor for some low-commission sweeteners on the Nasdaq.

Twice Jones sent Rogers a curious look across the table, a smile at once supplicating and smug. Rogers wasn't sure what to make of it.

Jones spoke English fluently, with a richness no native speaker could muster, fluting his way through the syllables as if the language were Brazilian, a delight to listen to.

Tournedos Rossini, Lobster Thermidor, Poulet à la Kiev: it was that kind of place, nothing but famous dishes. The least one could do was bury it with one's credit line. That was the point of a dinner like this, after all: to eat well then be the one who paid for it. Sylvester's policy: it is better to give than receive hospitality. Rogers had the platinum trump up his sleeve. Soon he would excuse himself and slip it into the maître d's palm.

In the lavatory the ventilation hummed. A tiled floor and dark wood cubicles gave an Iberian touch. Rogers looked at himself in the mirror and felt exhausted. He was exhausted. He was approaching forty womanless, childless and not moneyless exactly but with less money, much less, than ever before. He was a man with troubles, a man who needed to sit through dull dinners in the hope of pulling off a deal worthy of his past, worthy of his aspirations, what was left of them. And that was another worry: his aspirations were dwindling fast. All the more need to pull something off now, before they disappeared altogether.

The floor tiles swayed, flexed, became spongey, settled again. He was tired of his aspirations. What was the point of them? So the folks back home could say, My, isn't he doing well? So his one-time fellows in rainy Blighty could look wistfully across the ocean and follow the dazzling trail he left behind him? What was glamour anyway but something you were bound to lose? He remembered the glamorous dinners in the early days in Manhattan, dinners clustered with the up and coming, all attracted to one another by the mutual flicker of success. They were long gone now. Or rather not they, but *he*. He was long gone. Whatever you did, however bravely you swept across the hills and fought your way up the gleaming towers of downtown, sooner or later you started losing your hair, succumbing to male standard pattern, while your stomach swelled and success drained from you like lymph.

Rogers scooped his hands under the tap, not as cold as he'd hoped, and lifted a bubbly handful which defrothed into a tiny dribble before it reached his face. His cheeks prickled.

Albert Jones walked in while Rogers was drying his hands. 'So,' Jones said. It was a question. He looked up from an industrious scrubbing of the hands, the water roaring, and stared at Rogers that way he had, half appraising, half appealing.

Perhaps he was gay, Rogers thought. He didn't know what to do. 'Cool,' he said, to say something.

Jones smiled. 'When in Rome . . . What do you think?' He sniffed, tapped his nose with a knuckle.

'Good idea,' Rogers answered, before he could stop himself. 'Do as the bloody Romans. Wonderful.' He injected a trace of cockney into his voice, a touch of Claptonese. Foreigners sometimes liked that in an Englishman.

'Here.' Albert Jones held out a closed hand. 'Welcome package.'

In a locked cubicle Rogers opened up the little envelope. It was a long time since he had had any cocaine, and for just a moment he considered pouring it down the toilet. Then he thought: Why not? He exercised too much restraint, he had forgotten how to let go and get on a roll. He pulled out a credit card, a bill and stooped to the cistern. Nothing like the good stuff. And these people tonight, they were partners, future partners. He had nothing to fear. They were all on the same side in the fight against moneylessness, against the indifference of the world. Their job was to take a mountain, a cliff, a bay, a forest, and make it *mean* something. It was up to human beings to inscribe their meaning on to the world, and the number-one language was money: sterling, balboa, inti, cruzeiro, whatever you called it it all amounted to the same thing. No one *needed* Tournedos Rossini medium rare, no one *needed* Porsches or Connoisseur Class, except to give a little indication, an index of what they had; except to talk their talk in the one universal language, the *idioma del mundo*.

Rogers' sinuses felt hollow, almost visible they were so happily defined. A smile affixed itself to his cheeks and in the back of his throat the wonderful chalky taste settled in. Why didn't he do this more often?

Back at the table he was aware of a long silence. Finally, when he himself was about to break it, Albert Jones put his hands on the table and said, 'Well, shall we?'

Jones's hands were hairy, and very clean. His ruby-studded ring left a little dent in the tablecloth.

Outside, as the others slipped past car doors being held open for them – '*Gracias*,' '*Tak*,' '*Merci*' – Jones suggested a nightcap. He cocked his head by way of beckoning, and strolled up the road with hands in pockets, expecting Rogers to follow, which he did. Halfway down the block

the high-pitched wail of a locking system rang out and a Mercedes blinked its lights.

They drove fast under high white buildings and palm trees orange in street light. When they stopped, a stiff night wind had got up. Rogers' trousers flapped, the car door sprang from his fingers, slamming shut, and a paper bag raced past his ankles.

Down red-carpeted steps, through a red velvet door. Jones nodded at the doorman. Inside, in dim light, golden flesh strapped with black lace, white nylon. The eye required a moment to adjust, understand.

'OK?' Jones grinned. He led them past the bar, freighted with mirrors and bottles and chrome, to a corner cubicle.

A bottle of dark rum añejo, four bottles of Coca-Cola, their caps snapped off by a waiter, an ice bucket, a packet of Marlboro, unpeeled, half ejected from their cartridge.

Jones said, 'You can do what you like here.'

'In that case . . .' Rogers laughed, then felt a little foolish for laughing. He pulled out his gift pack and cut some lines in the lee of the ice bucket. Jones chuckled in that suave, suntanned way of his.

A second waiter came up and asked Jones if there was to be anything special tonight. Jones shook his head and said, 'Just something nice.'

A moment's unease hit Rogers. They were bankers, throwing a rope of trust from ship to ship on the high seas of business. That was fine. But there was something else with Jones, something Rogers couldn't put a finger on, that wasn't quite like a banker.

They clinked glasses. Rogers took a long pull. 'I have

to tell you, I still don't get why the oil companies won't come on board.'

Jones shrugged, glanced to one side as if looking for someone. 'Like I told you, they've been scared off.'

'But by who?' Rogers' drink was sweet and cold.

Jones shook his head. 'The government doesn't want to rock the boat. You've seen the margins. If the government hikes the canal tolls for tankers, which they've been threatening to do for years –'

'Then the line would be a godsend.'

'Yes and no. We're talking three to five years to build this thing. That's a lot of tolls. But I'm not talking about the Panamanian government. It's the Casa Blanca. No US president wants to risk any commotion so close to the canal. Sixty years ago they had a war on their hands, the Cuna War. They're afraid. The region is sensitive. There's the environment, there's the locals, there's Colombian guerrillas just next door. All that, with the canal right in the middle of it.'

Rogers shrugged. 'So?'

'So you need cowboys to pull off a stunt like this.' Jones raised his glass and chuckled.

Rogers nodded and drained his drink.

'You really can't move this stuff fast enough. Once we're up and running they can't *not* jump on board.'

A girl came over, a dyed blonde whose bottle had managed only a pale rust, the best it could do with what must have been a spectacular oil-black mane. She wore bustier, suspenders, boots, the whole catalogue, and planted a shining black heel theatrically on the table.

Jones hissed in Rogers' ear, 'Colombiana. Pretty, no?' He looked up at the dancing girl, who had pulled herself on to the table top and was swaying to the salsa music.

'The best are the Colombianas,' Jones explained seriously. 'All the pretty ones come here to get their pussies on the Yankee dollar.' He let out an impassioned giggle, his face creasing up.

Rogers was surprised. It was the kind of remark you heard from morose taxi drivers. Rogers felt a certain fondness for Panama. He thought of the country's tenuous 'S' resting under the tropical sun, the link between North and South stretched thin like a piece of taffy. There was surely something romantic about it, it ought to be granted its share of prettiness.

'What about the pretty Panamanians?' he asked.

Jones shrugged. 'What about them?' He cackled, then paused, coughed, realising he'd got the joke wrong, and said: 'What pretty Panamanians?' He laughed again.

Rogers took a long draw on his drink. He would need drink to pull off conversation like this.

Jones leaned close. 'Actually,' he said, returning to a serious tone, 'some of the Cuna girls, they're lovely.'

'Cuna?'

They were having to raise their voices over the music. Jones smiled up at the dancing girl, who moved with bewitching attachment to the beat. 'San Blas,' he explained. 'They're from San Blas.'

Since walking into the club Jim Rogers had been wondering how soon he could plead jet lag and hustle his way back to see the sauna girl. He had already decided he wouldn't wait till the next day. He would propose right now, tonight, that Paulina come and spend the night with him. Maybe he would even try to fix up a *Pretty Woman* deal. Be my wife for the week, I'll pay you handsomely. It wasn't every day you got a chance to hang out with someone who came from the tribal world, if she really did, and who was that pretty. And bright too. He even felt an urgency about seeing her. How much would she want? It didn't matter. He imagined her unfolding his shirts, tutting over his thick socks, snapping out his Italian ties. The important thing was to keep the impulse alive.

'To rum and coke,' Rogers said, raising his glass.

Jones cackled, tapping out a heap of powder from some hidden phial and handing a straw up to the dancer, who squatted, bent to the table, snorted through the straw, then straddled his face. He flicked his eyebrows. '*Sabrosa mujer.*'

Drink slipped down an ice channel in the back of Rogers' head. He reached the cold bloom, the flush, the fresh ice bucket of the high.

On the way to the door Jones took hold of the inside of Rogers' elbow. Rogers liked the mild intimacy. They were two men exploring the realms of pleasure together, of entrepreneurial expansiveness.

'Can you keep a secret?' Jones looked closely at Rogers. 'I think you can.'

'Of course.' Rogers enjoyed feeling close to this man he hardly knew, this bouffanted voice from the telephone.

Jones reached into his jacket and handed Rogers an envelope. 'Look after this. No copies.'

Rogers caught himself frowning. A small frown. He

swept it from his face and slipped the envelope into his pocket. Jones's eyes lit up, a beautiful pale hazel.

Outside, the doorman held open the door of an old white Lincoln. Rogers gave the man a screwed-up five. Panama ran on dollars. It was not a place to be if you were counting your money. He loosened his tie and sank into the sinking velvet of the old seat.

3

The girl at reception brought him a Heineken. She wore a miniskirt that both gave nothing away, and was sufficient advertisement to anyone looking for it. After a couple of swigs, Rogers sat forward in the armchair to which he had been directed and engaged her in conversation. She sat behind the glass counter top filing her nails.

'You should come here carnival time,' she said in a bored voice. 'You know cumbias? Cumbias all over town.'

Rogers nodded and said he did know, and loved, cumbia music, and perhaps she would teach him to dance the cumbia when he returned.

She said of course she would, mustering a ghost of a smile. It was late, the girl evidently could not summon the kind of bonhomie such conversation called for. He sensed she would be happier to sit and file her nails in silence, musing to herself. He imagined that nail-filing must be one of the great muse-inducing activities. He guzzled the beer then went to the bathroom.

Inside the envelope Jones had given him was a single

sheet of paper folded in three on which a diagram had been drawn. Rogers recognised it at once as the intended course of the pipeline, the curves, the straights, the pump stations. Notes had been handwritten beside each section in neat English. The uppermost section, in the north, where the dock and plant would be, was circled.

It was odd to receive such a document on paper, and handwritten. It wasn't good news, he saw that at once. Jones had told him they were clear the whole way, but it was obvious that they weren't. That northern section, labelled '36-A, 36-B', had no deed title written beside it, instead only a big question mark in a square, and a reference to some kind of legislation. *Acto 347IIc de 1939*. He crumpled the envelope and dropped it to the floor, then folded the paper and slipped it into his wallet. He would have to ask Jones about this.

Paulina had changed into an emerald minidress that buttoned up at the front. It suited her. She smiled sweetly when she saw him, coming forward to take his hand and offering her cheek. As soon as they were in the room he knew he had done the right thing in coming back, and also in not coming earlier. He had taken care of business and now he could take care of her.

She held his wrist, looked at his watch and said, 'Hombre, it's late. Just for you I can stay longer.'

He squinted at her. 'Just for me?'

She shrugged and smiled. 'Did you have a good dinner?'

He sat on the edge of the massage bench and took off his tie, then moved to a small yellow sofa he hadn't noticed last time. Words flowed from him, water from a reservoir. 'It's not every day you find someone you can really talk to,' he said. 'You're a fool if you don't see more of the person.' He felt it as he said it. She was beautiful, she came from an unsullied world; he did want to see more of her, badly.

She stood with her back to the door. He liked seeing her standing there against the door, as if she didn't want either of them to leave. It softened the business aspect, which was somehow graphically represented by the door. He was amazed at how being with her sobered him, cut through the drug's upholstery.

He told her he had a suggestion. She looked at her nails and blew on them as if she had been painting them. Which encouraged him. Perhaps she had been sitting here alone all evening doing her nails. 'A suggestion I hope you like.'

She came over and kissed the top of his head, her legs brown and gleaming in the low light. She had beautiful slender knees. She folded her arms against her chest, making her breasts rise under the cloth. 'What is it?'

He felt a light come on in his chest and he told her. He said he'd pay anything but wanted her to quit working for the week. He'd look after her, buy her clothes, whatever she wanted. Already he imagined them going to the Valentino store and abusing the credit cards. People like her, poor beauties in poor countries, always got less than they deserved, and here he was with a chance to redress that. And a chance to be with one more real beauty before he himself finally slumped into hairless, bellied, terminal middle age. It would almost be like an affair, a real relationship.

She stroked his cheek. 'If you would like,' she said. *Sí te gustaria.*

He nodded.

She continued looking at him. '*Yo te gusto?*' You like me?

He nodded seriously.

She said nothing but bent forward and planted a kiss on his lips.

Walking across the hotel car park Rogers wasn't sure whether to put his arm round her. Would it seem sentimental or decorous? She walked confidently beside him, apparently not bothered whether he did or didn't.

It was good to be strolling through the dark at two in the morning beside a beautiful girl while the city sighed around them. For a moment, approaching the marble ocean of the hotel entrance, Rogers felt himself crumpling under the need for more of the drug. But in the confines of the elevator, their voices muffled in the small space, a kind of peace returned. He took her hand – she had slender, long-nailed fingers – and conducted her into the quiet corridor, past the heavy door, which opened with a click, into his quiet room.

She wanted nothing to drink, just Sprite. He didn't even need to call room service. He snapped the tag on the little brown fridge and poured out a glass, cracking ice into it. Then he picked up the half bottle of Moët and raised his eyebrows. She said sweetly, 'Well, if you're offering,' and he was touched to understand she had been holding back, not wanting to be any trouble.

He left his jacket on the desk by the window. She was quiet, perhaps a little overawed by the situation, and was more comfortable once she had him on the bed and had popped off his shoes. She pulled off his socks the long way, by the toe, then kissed his feet.

'How long have you been in Panama City?' he asked.

She knelt by his face. Her thighs golden. The original cigar maiden, native girl from the land of tobacco. Walter Ralegh himself must have rested his cheek on such a thigh while puffing a rubbery roll of leaves.

She leaned over him, hair falling like rain on his cheek. She kissed him, put a finger to his lips. '*Estoy nueva*,' she whispered.

She was unbelievable. The girl from the junction of east, west, north and south. He had heard about Amerindian tribes who taught their girls the full Kama Sutra before they were allowed to marry. Perhaps she had been through something like that. She gathered him into her arms and rolled him like a tobacco leaf, then raised him on her palm, in her fingers, blew smoke through him. His eyelids glittered with sun-strewn water, his skin stretched on warm sand, and his ears filled with the pounding of surf.

At six a.m. there was only one other man in the hotel sauna, a bald-headed guy who sat with his skull lodged into the corner, some victim of sleeplessness hoping to heat himself into a coma, perhaps. He didn't stir when Rogers came in.

The smell of sweat and something sweet cloyed the air.

Rogers had woken into a pool of lucidity. The first thing he had seen, the beautiful face on his pillow, its cheek slightly concave in rest, had moved him inordinately. And dawn had been astir, brushing the fringes of the curtain with snowy light, an untropical light that reminded him of England. A wave of nostalgia had seized him. Perhaps he was finally coming to realise that he was an exile. Perhaps it was time to go home. He imagined how much he would enjoy his native land's soft grey air, walking over its rain-drenched lawns. In some strange way this girl brought it back to him. She too, after all, was from a real place, a real home, San Blas, where the witch doctors kept everyone safe from old age and sharks. He didn't normally miss his homeland. It was one of the successes of his life that he had left it. Yet now he thought of taking her there, of how she would like that. Perhaps what he had been waiting for all along was just this: a chance to go home with a prize on his arm.

The man in the corner of the sauna groaned and shifted his shoulders, adjusting his weight against the dripping tiles. Rogers' nose poured sweat: last night pouring off him, a stream of hygiene.

When he got back to the room he noticed the quiet, the emptiness, at once. The rumpled sheets, the jacket on the blond-pine chair, the quiet in the bathroom, a towel left damp on the sofa. She had gone. No note. He searched the desk, the bedside table, on the TV. Perhaps she couldn't write.

He wasn't worried, all in all. For one thing, he hadn't paid her. She would surely be back. There must be some prostitute's tenet about never leaving the scene of the act without the money. As he thought of her his chest filled with clouds. They had not had sex but made love, slowly, warmly, intoxicated not with drink but with warmth, with mutual fascination. Surely she couldn't have been faking it when she traced her fingers over his torso, down his legs, at a snail's pace. Or when she rested her cheek on his chest reminiscing about her childhood on the lagoons of San Blas, in the hammocks and dugouts and long-houses, confiding in him about the places she wanted to go, the work she hoped one day to get as a location manager for a television station. There was something pretty about that ambition. They hadn't slept till late, very late, talking and making love by turns.

No, he needn't question it – it happened from time to time, a hooker and a client.

His fingers tingled when he pressed a five into the hand of the uniformed boy who brought the breakfast tray. Scrambled eggs, Marlboros, coffee for two. He ate fast. Fruit had come too, wonderful slices of tropical fruit from nature's laboratory. He loved this part of the world today with a new love.

He hung yesterday's blue suit in the closet and peeled out today's Saint Laurent, a relic of his good old days. When he was ready – showered, shaved, tied, shod – and feeling better than he could remember in a long time, he went to the desk to pick up his wallet, then realising he had left it in his blue jacket went to the closet and searched the jacket and found first one inside pocket empty then the other. He checked the side pockets too, and the little breast pocket, even though the wallet couldn't have fitted into it. He took the coat hanger out, slung off the trousers and checked them. Then he checked the jacket again. He looked under the bedside tables and in their drawers – one red Bible each – and under the bed and in the bathroom and behind the mirror – empty glass shelves. Then he checked on the balcony with its bare glass table and two slatted chairs, and in the bathroom again.

He had to accept that the wallet had gone.

He called down to reception and hung up before they answered. He called Albert Jones's office without asking himself why, and hung up when the machine answered. Which gave him the idea of calling Janet at the desk in New York. But he felt that he needed to do nothing, just sit still. Except there was no time for that: seven o'clock: one had to move, move along, if one was an unloved salesman on his way through middle age, with success evaporating from him like dew. The young filched it from your pockets while you weren't looking. While you were worrying about your hairline, your slackening belly, your dwindling gym life, they leapt into the seat you had just vacated.

He left a message for Janet about the credit cards. He could survive off the hotel bill until tomorrow, when replacements would arrive. The cash? Cash came and went. But he would have to try and find the girl. No question about that. He didn't want to think about Jones's damn piece of paper, but it wasn't the kind of thing you let go walkabout.

He snapped open the curtains on a flowing morning. Shadows raced across the city like smoke, the shadows of palms, clouds, buses. A few things were golden: half a building, a flight of high windows, a sapling dying down the block. A vulture went by, high up. The underside of its wings glistened like tinfoil. After all, a man could misspend his years and still recognise beauty when it glided by.

7.30 a.m. The Geisha Sauna's tinted-glass door was locked. He buzzed and buzzed into the darkness within.

4

The Panama Pipe Corporation did not yet have its own offices but met in a suite high in the Bank of Panama. Rogers managed to avoid Jones all morning, even in the breaks. Except once, in the bathroom.

The hiss of plumbing, a faint smell of bleach, a lingering trace of urine – the smell of an institutional toilet. For some reason it brought back a feeling of New York in the early days, when he had first moved there: the morning walks beneath the granite crags, the air like mountain air, the subway vents steaming, the little coffee-and-donut places rattling up their shutters and the water towers of the high buildings catching the sun. He had loved New York then. There had been no better place on earth for him.

Someone walked in while Rogers was peeing, crossing behind his back to one of the cubicles. The lock clicked. As Rogers shook himself, Jones's voice reached him. First a low chuckle, then: '*Qué tal?* Good night?'

'*Excelente*,' Rogers answered, projecting a smile into his voice.

Jones flushed and emerged in one commotion while Rogers was drying his hands. 'You must let me have back the document.' He looked up and pulled a smile. It was hard to say what it meant.

'Of course,' Rogers said. Under that gaze he could say nothing else. This was a man one wanted to agree with. 'We'll have to talk about that, you know. I understood we were clear the whole way.'

'Nearly the whole way.' Jones shrugged like it was no big deal. 'We'll talk. But I must have it back now.'

'After lunch OK?'

'Why not now?'

'It's at the hotel.'

Jones wiped his hands. 'Why jou didn't bring here?' He stepped closer to Rogers, his eyes narrow, then turned away. Jones snapped the towel-roll down and swore under his breath. He looked at Rogers. 'Is not mine. Jou know that. We don't play games.'

Rogers cried off lunch.

A middle-aged woman wearing a black skirt and clinking bead necklace opened up for him at the Geisha Sauna. He reminded himself to be polite and smile at her, but she turned before he could, clinking away ahead of him, revealing an absurdly long slit up the back of her skirt. No one else seemed to be around.

'Is Paulina here?' Rogers tried. 'Excuse me for interrupting, señora,' he added, though he didn't seem to have interrupted anything.

The woman raised her dark eyes and studied him. He felt ridiculous, chasing a prostitute like this. His cheeks burned.

'*Se fue*,' she said. '*Ya se fue*.' She looked down at a diary. 'You want to make an appointment?'

The thought had not occurred to him, and stirred his loins. 'No, that's fine,' he mumbled. The woman shrugged sulkily.

'She went back to San Blas,' she said, vaguely lifting and dropping a hand.

San Blas. Where the hell *was* San Blas?

He told the taxi to stop at a news-stand and jumped out to buy a school map of the country, the only kind the vendor had. Rogers opened it up in the back of the car. It showed none of the terrain, only the administrative regions, all in the cartographer's dreary pastels. San Blas was a pink strip along the north coast.

Panama was a narrow country, and on his map it looked like San Blas could hardly be more than sixty miles away, an hour or so on the road. He had to keep Jones sweet at all costs. Not to mention the risk – which in fact seemed to him remote – of scuppering the deal with a careless leak. All in all, he ought just to go ahead and take the taxi up there right now, and miss the afternoon session.

All they were discussing was the South American loan plan. He knew these small Latin towns. It wasn't hard to find people. Even if Paulina was not her real name, he could probably track her down – the *bella* who works in Panama City. But then again, who knew how many towns and villages there might be in the district called San Blas? One on the map, what looked like the largest, was actually called San Blas. But did that mean she was necessarily from there?

'How long to get to San Blas?' he asked the thick-necked driver, who was busy accelerating past a truck belching smoke.

The driver braked. 'San Blas?' he asked, letting out a long, 'Er . . .' He concluded the sound with a concerned, '*Qué?*' and a frown in the mirror.

The truck roared beside them.

Rogers repeated the question. Only then did he look down at the map again and see that San Blas ran most of the length of the north coast between Panama City and Colombia. It couldn't fail to be the very region where the pipeline's route had run into some kind of problem. Probably just some farmer or rancher who had previously said yes and now changed his mind, or wanted more compensation.

'You mean San Blas *islas*?'

'San Blas. Just San Blas.'

The driver speeded up again, glancing at Rogers in the mirror. 'San Blas is the other side of the mountains,' he said. 'An ugly road. *Muy feo.* You need a Land-Rover.'

'How long does it take?'

'To get to San Blas? That depends. *San Blas islas . . . o toda la región?*'

'Just to get there,' Rogers said.

The driver mumbled to himself, swerving past a school bus.

Jones was waiting in the lobby of the Bank of Panama. He sideswiped Rogers from the elevators and walked him towards the polished black marble of the rear wall, where their two reflections flashed as they approached. Jones fluttered his fingers in the universal gesture for *gimme*.

'It's gone.'

Jones stepped close. 'This is not funny. It doesn't go. It doesn't go anywhere. This stuff is not public knowledge, you know that.' He plunged both hands deep into his pockets and swivelled like a dancer on the polished floor. 'Come on. Enough joking.' His breath was warm and fragrant.

Rogers was familiar with this Latin temperament. He did not like to be its brunt but it didn't scare him. 'Someone stole it. They stole my wallet and went to San Blas.'

Jones uttered an expletive that sounded like *Hotspur*. 'San Blas? Quit joking.'

'I'm not joking. Why would I be joking?'

'Why? *Hotspur*.' Jones pulled a grimace and pirouetted again on the gleaming floor. 'So who was it?'

'A girl.'

'When?'

'Last night. After I got back to the hotel.'

'Why you think they went to San Blas?'

'That's what they told me.'

'Who?'

'The people she works with.'

Jones rested his eyes on him. They sparkled. 'A chica stole your wallet. Tell her she's giving chicas a bad name.' He shrugged, then enunciated: 'Well, we will have to go and get it back, won't we?'

'I'll go. I know who I'm looking for.'

Jones shook his head. 'You don't know who you're looking for. You don't know anything. We both go, there's no other way. Tomorrow morning, first thing.'

'Why not now?'

He inhaled audibly. 'You have to leave this to me, man. You don't know this place. All the flights are in the morning.'

'The flights?'

Jones tutted, examining Rogers' face, then moved away towards the elevators.

Dawn. 5.45 a.m. As the taxi rumbled down a back street Rogers saw a coconut fall, something he had never witnessed before. No wind, no provocation, it simply dropped, a lethal nugget, from a spindly palm in a wasteland between two concrete hulks, landing without a bounce.

Rogers felt strangely excited. Salsa was playing quietly on the radio, soft sunshine had begun to suffuse the city, and he felt unaccountably free. Free, and heading off into the sunny unknown, a million miles from home, wherever home was, with a roll of large-denomination bills in his pocket that Sylvester's had wired through. He remembered how, when he first moved to New York, every morning he had been thrilled to think that while England had already been up for five hours, America like an irresponsible younger brother still had its head on the pillow. He used to walk down through the canyons of the city, the gulfs of shadow, while the high floors of buildings were struck gold by early sun. And all the subway vents would be releasing their bright steam into the morning. And meanwhile his deals had kept getting bigger and better. The only limit to Rogers' achievement had been himself. The world had offered him all its scope and it had been up to him to occupy it. He had never worried, never hurried, just worked the long hours and lived by the law of least effort. And the universe had returned with its abundance. Which was not only financial. He remembered one summer evening meeting a redhead dance student in a SoHo gallery; not three hours later, after a well-sluiced dinner at the Odeon, she was performing the splits on the edge of his Le Corbusier while he knelt before her raising a ruckus of moans. That was the way to live: man the hunter, man the pleasure-giver. Man stomping down the walls of the present to ambush the future. If you didn't live that way – this was the maddening thing – the only alternative was to allow yourself to be led by the nose. It was one or the other: lead or be led. Somewhere deep down he couldn't help feeling that it oughtn't to be like that. Surely it was possible to feel calm, content. Or were those the very feelings nature deployed to keep the followers dumbly following?

'Going to the islands?' the taxi driver asked him. 'Nice place. You're gonna like it.'

'Is there anything to do?'

The driver laughed. 'Man, you don't go there to do anything. There's nothing there but the Indians.'

Rogers arrived at the small downtown airport in time to see a black-windowed Mercedes pull away. The weather was perfect: the tall buildings across the runway orange and beautiful in the dawn sun, the air warm on face and arm. And he still carried an absolving glow of physical satisfaction, even now, twenty-four hours after Paulina had left him.

Rogers clicked his Biro to write a note to himself and noticed that the pen's barrel was stamped 'med U.S.A.'. He had never noticed before: Medusa! He and the Medusa were heading off on an adventure. Coconut and lobster galore, if what the girl had said was true. It was good to be travelling with just a holdall, in short sleeves and slacks, to be getting away from offices and computers and business, getting out into the real world.

The terminal was thronged with twelve-year-olds, all with lank black hair in Beatle bobs, dressed in extraordinary theatrical clothes. They might have been some school drama expedition, except that the female kids, in blue skirts and fluffy blouses, barefoot, their ankles roped with beads, had babies strapped to their backs. They weren't twelve-year-olds at all. The men, in baggy trousers and crumpled bowler hats, pressed at a counter behind which an official paced about, periodically thrusting strips of green paper into the forest of hands reaching out to him.

Despite his white shirt and thick spectacles the official was visibly of the same stock as the rest of them, with his long black hair and modest stature. The place was more like a post office in some Soviet Asian republic than an airport.

Albert Jones appeared, wading through the throng. '*Jose Maria, ven!*' he called out.

The spectacled official came to the end of the counter and entered into a leisurely chat with Jones as if the boisterous crowd in the room didn't exist. Then the two men disappeared through a door.

Rogers waited. The crowd was in fact quite orderly. Everyone seemed to be in a good mood. Rogers couldn't remember the last time he had been in a room full of such good humour. It was like some happy, sober party, filled with a babble of anticipation. Like the last day of school. Albert Jones reappeared in the doorway and beckoned to Rogers.

In a small back office a man with a greasy mane of ashen hair sat at a metal desk. Jones introduced him as Señor Carlos. 'This girl,' he told Rogers. 'Tell Señor Carlos how she looks.'

Carlos didn't look up but held a pen wavering over a table of figures.

'The girl?'

Jones and Carlos chuckled. A third man joined in the laughter. It was the white-shirted official from next door, standing in the doorway, watching with arms folded.

'Average height,' Rogers said. 'Slim, black hair.'

'Pretty?' Carlos asked seriously.

Rogers shrugged. '*Sí*.'

'You think she flew yesterday?' Without waiting for an answer, Carlos brushed back a lock of his grey hair and grabbed a microphone off a radio set, turning up the speaker so it filled the office with a crackle of static. He exchanged some noisy incomprehensible remarks with a man on the other end then hung up. 'It's impossible. None of the pilots can say. Could be Porvenir, could be Tigre, could be El Corbiski, could be anywhere.'

Rogers couldn't imagine how that brief communication could have established anything so categorical. Carlos tapped his pen on the desk in a series of little clicks.

Jones coughed into a fist. 'Well, what are we to do now?'

The official shrugged extravagantly, eyebrows joining in, and sent Rogers a sympathetic look. The clerk from next door, still enjoying the excuse to ignore the crowd behind him, followed the conversation with interest, uttering little exclamations of agreement and concern.

'The greatest volume is of course to El Porvenir,' Señor Carlos continued, running a hand back through his long hair. 'Very few go to Corbiski or further down.'

Jones fiddled with something – keys, change – in his trouser pocket, his knuckles pressing out the cloth.

Carlos asked mournfully: 'You don't have a name?'

Albert Jones said: 'Paulina. So she says.'

'Paulina?' The man brightened, but Rogers could tell that it was only because here at last was one tangible detail, not because he knew anything that would help.

Jones coughed. 'She's his girlfriend.' He glanced at Rogers. 'At least, you understand. A chica.'

Carlos nodded vigorously.

Rogers felt like breaking out in an embarrassed giggle. All of this, this search, this caucus of masculine heads pondering a problem, had been occasioned by his lust. He had been caught with his pants down.

In one smooth, quick motion Jones tucked a folded bill under the writing pad on Carlos's desk. The man picked up his microphone and again filled the room with a roar of static, in the midst of which voices hovered like ghosts. It was impossible to understand what they were saying. After a while he set the microphone down and raised his palms in a gesture of caution. 'No one knows for sure. But maybe, *maybe* Inadule.' He shrugged. 'But it depends how she looks.'

Jones clasped his hand across the desk. '*Gracias*.' He turned to Rogers. 'Dark and pretty, right?'

But Rogers had already let himself out of the office.

As soon as Albert Jones emerged, Rogers seized him by the elbow and walked him out into the car park. 'You want to go a step further with this you're going to tell me what's going on with San Blas.'

Jones spread his arms wide in a Latin gesture of compliance, truce. Hey, the arms said, your call. 'Whatever, it's fine, whatever jou want.' Jones stood like that a moment, defenceless, then cleared his throat and took Rogers by the arm.

'Well, this is hardly the time or place,' Jones said, 'but what the hell.'

Suddenly they were two businessmen again, strolling arm in arm, very Latin, charming and brotherly. They walked among the ailing cars strewn about the lot, which might or might not have been taxis waiting for rides. A few men who might or might not have been their drivers were drinking coffee from paper cups, and a teenage boy was selling fruit juice to local women from a giant plastic cooler.

'I said we were clear the whole way. Well, not any more. Ninety-five per cent of the way,' Jones said brightly, 'there's no problem. We have options on the deeds, et cetera. But ninety-five per cent is not much without the last five.' He contemplated the ground. 'It's complicated. Let me give you an example. You want to drill for oil on one of your Indian Reservations out west. Somehow you have got hold of a good seismic and you want to go in. You think you can just do it?' He shrugged. 'Here in Panama we have something special, unlike anywhere else. The real Caribbean natives, they are still here, and they are still Stone Age, and in 1938 your government and my government gave them their own autonomous region. You might as well call it another country. Their own laws, they don't pay taxes, they do what they like. And what they like is to live in bamboo huts and paddle dugout canoes and swing in hammocks and collect herbs from the rainforest. For their own consumption, of course.'

Jones paused, swivelled on the heels of his loafers. They began pacing back towards the little airport with its green tower.

'They're into ecology, the environment. They own a

strip of the coast and all the islands. They see what has happened to the forest on the other side of the mountains. Gone. Not there any more. Basically, you want to do anything coast to coast, you can't avoid them. You knock on the door, you say, can we build a pipeline please, they slam the door. No, no.' Jones wagged a finger, tutted.

There was something comforting in Jones's paternal Latin ways. Rogers even prompted: 'So what do you do?' He liked this man, he couldn't help it, he liked this project, he liked the sound of these people and was already imagining how they too might benefit from it. It was good to help indigenous people, why not, let them come on board in some way. Wasn't this the way forward, the world fragmenting into tribes each with its own stake in the giant playground of the global market?

Jones paced carefully, each foot placed as if the shoe were made of glass. 'You have to go to the back door, which we did, you have to talk to somebody one on one, find out what they're interested in. Suppose there was one chief on your reservation who wanted, let us say, to build a new gas station. You need an excuse to get the right equipment in, and you also need the right contract.'

'How do you mean?'

'Like with some useful clauses. National interest, that kind of thing, things the lawyers can play with, interpret the right way once you're up and running and they try to close you down. So we found someone. Of course. Milagros, he knows somebody somewhere. Excuse me. Everywhere. A certain Cuna chief, a *sahila*, as they say, who is open to discussion. He wants to build a small marina for yachts. Then his people can sell ten times as many molas to tourists.' Jones chuckled. 'So this sahila, he told us he thinks he could get plans for his dock passed. So we come in with him, we help him out. That's enough, it's all we need to get the diggers in. But let him get wind of what we're really up to –' Jones spread out his hands, miming an explosion.

'These people, they can be a pain in the ass. They think they're special, everybody tells them so. Tourists pay to see them paddle their dugouts and wear their crazy clothes and dance their dances – the most boring dances you've ever seen, like stomp-stomp-stomp – and there are these German tourists and such, these do-gooders from Scandinavia and Canada, standing around paying for the privilege of using their video cameras, nodding and talking about the wisdom of tribal peoples, all that crap. I tell you, if they would let somebody come in with them, there's a fortune to be made. A nice big eco-resort, you could clean up. But they'll never get it together. The only way to help people like that is to do it without them knowing.'

He stopped smartly and turned to Rogers. 'Now the guy says he needs more time to persuade the elders, the council, or whatever they are. That's the problem. So we're going there to kill two birds with one stone. We need to pay a visit to our sahila, and we have to make sure the girl just took the money out of the wallet and threw everything else away. See? The last thing we need is for word to get out among all the Cunas.'

Rogers started walking again, frowning. 'Why didn't you tell me all this earlier?'

'It wasn't a problem earlier.'

'And why put it on paper anyway?'

'You read, you burn. It's the safest way. That's what we do here.'

Rogers felt the ground sway. He was thinking that if once a man found his path then strayed from it, all was lost. You paddled away from the shore and ended up anywhere.

'How many of these Cuna are there?' he asked, to ask something.

'Twenty thousand. It's a small place, a lot of small islands. But the depot will be offshore, three or four miles out. Once the pipe is in, they don't even know it's there.'

'Except the ships, the stations, the quays, the staff housing, and everything else.'

Jones shrugged. 'That's why we're going there now. We can't afford not to. If we're lucky the girl can't even read. First thing you've got to do is give her more cash. You OK for that?'

'The first thing we've got to do is find her,' Rogers observed, feeling suddenly depressed. 'How far are these damn islands?'

'No distance, twenty minutes. But there are three hundred of them, maybe fifty inhabited, and twenty airstrips.'

'So we charter and work our way down.'

Jones tutted and twitched his head. 'That's not the way here. You got to listen to me. Everything, you need the chief's permission. You go to the next island, you get the chief's permission. You eat a sandwich, you get the chief's permission. No private planes, only Cuna Air. Which is why we're here.'

Jones beckoned that way he had, inclining his head, hands in pockets. 'Come on,' he said. 'I have a plan.'

5

They had a beer in the bar on the airport roof even though it was only six thirty in the morning. Rogers' mood got lighter and lighter; he felt like celebrating; it was that good to be on the move, to be going somewhere new. Then they strapped themselves into tiny seats in a stuffy aeroplane and his mood swung the other way. It was awful that he was welcoming this side trip from a side trip, that his life had no centre, had had the heart ripped out of it. What in hell was he doing visiting hookers, then *chasing* hookers, of all ignominies, and getting caught up with coke-crazed businessmen? And what was he doing here, strapped into a midget-sized aeroplane seat made of tin foil?

The little plane scuttled to the end of the runway where the drone of its propellors turned to the sound of a fan. Rogers pulled open his collar, sodden already at the early hour. He felt an attack coming on. Strapped into his little seat, he was powerless to fend it off.

The meaning of his life had dissolved, clearly. That was the only reason he could be so interested in a hooker.

He had hoped to secure a deal down here that would bring in a quick forty or fifty right away, with much more to follow, and instead he was on a wild-goose chase, and something in him prevented him from simply getting out and going home. If there was any money at the end of it, it would be less, less, less. That was the way his life went: less instead of more. Less sex, less money, less love, less desire even. Sometimes he wanted nothing other than to want something. Or the big blank, of course. Sometimes he just waited and waited to be run over, drowned, dropped from the sky. But disaster shunned him, it wasn't interested in those who didn't care, only those who did. Buildings toppled, terrorists blazed, fires fell from heaven all over the earth, but always at a safe distance from him. Hell at work. It occurred to Rogers that perhaps on these torrid islands he might meet the devil. That would be something. To come face to face with his tormentor. And yes, he was suffering pointlessly. His misery was maybe chemical, maybe philosophical, but not practical, not realistic. It was inexcusable.

As the plane took off, the white office blocks of the Zona Banquera came loose from their moorings and drifted by. Beneath, a brown beach swung past, less a beach than a mud-flat. Rogers felt the pull in his head as the plane banked. He watched the filaments of thin breakers rolling slowly in across brown water on to brown mud. The sun winked at him from an oily bend in a river. Then they were already flying over the green and grey mountains, serious small oppressive mountains, and a moment later a great metal sheet was visible ahead, shining like brushed chrome. It was the Pacific. He could see vague black arms reaching into it and a dapple of cloud-shadows stretching away towards Darien.

Then he thought: The devil was you yourself. It was you who said there were no second chances. It was you who deprived yourself of the second chance with your myopia, your fixation on the one lost chance. For the man who lived in the now, who did not look back, there were endless chances.

He had a dizzy spell, leaned back in his seat and closed his eyes.

Christmas '92. He had bought Candlebury a set of earrings. Two jewels hanging from gold hooks. Simple, beautiful, expensive. She cried when she unwrapped them, and he choked up too. He was sure that without knowing it he had intended them as a pledge. Next time just the one: solo, solitaire, on its band of gold.

He was fortunate, he espoused the good, made his home in the positive and reaped the rewards. Every month the cheques grew larger. Top new broker of '92, clearing seven-fifty. A prince of finance at the prince of ages: thirty-three, the bloom of youth still on his cheeks and the sap of knowledge in his limbs. He had learnt a kind of inner patience too. Call it peace; why not? He loved sitting at home knowing Candlebury was next door doing her yoga, or chatting on the telephone. He learnt to love the smell of her incense, and opening a bottle of organic *vino nobile* while hearing the light bubble of brown rice cooking. He liked adding seaweed to their stir-fries and shopping in overpriced stores with wooden floors and sacks of grain and walls of vitamins. He began to love, he realised, health. Health itself. He quit smoking.

Candlebury left the Graham chorus line, stopped modelling and joined an avant-garde hula group who did cutting-edge movement therapy. They were not a big hit except on the workshop circuit. She bought a sequencer and composed music for them. Rogers would come home to the big place in the Heights to which they had moved to find it awash with her ethereal choruses, aglow with etheric light bouncing off the harbour. He'd see the cluster of spires on Wall Street across the slate-shiny water, and know their home floated halfway to heaven.

When the first fall of the nineties hit he welcomed it. He lost money and all his clients lost money and his commissions dropped from nine to six points, and on smaller sums, but he felt it was right. The world was being purged, all the bad stripped out. The pouring on of hyssop, the scouring of the Lord.

Candlebury called it these things. They passed monastic evenings on the floor of their big room with a tall church candle burning by the window, which threw back their reflections, and they considered that all they needed was dry ground to sit on and fire for light and warmth. As they saw themselves in the dark window so they really were. All they needed was right there hovering in the glass.

But the losses had unsettled him more than he realised, and twelve months later, it was all over, he had ruined everything. First he jumped an aerobic blonde – a spin, a tumble, someone who should never have occupied more than a few hours of sport, but whom instead he started seeing two or three times a week. Before he knew it Candlebury had found out, and she left for Hawaii, for a New Age camp hosting an inner-child seminar, where she said that she would think about what to do. He was scared, but guessed it meant she wouldn't leave him. And she didn't. But next thing he took a gamble and used information he shouldn't have. An unidentifiable recklessness had taken him over. He moved twenty per cent of his own portfolio into a company a client of his was preparing to take over. He shouldn't have done it, he did it without even wanting to. Though he was never definitively implicated, there was an investigation. He was yanked off the Asia desk and dumped on East Europe. They wanted him to get involved in debt-restructuring. They thought an ex-trader, which is what they made him, would be good in there, with special know-how. They sent him to London in February for six dismal weeks of training.

That was the real end. The ceiling came off the world. The tent came down. No more illusion, no more shelter. All the bland daylight that he and Candlebury had chased away with candles and romance had been gathering like a cold tide outside the door, waiting for a chance to flood back in. He didn't want to go to London, he didn't want to be involved in Eastern Europe or debt.

In London he started smoking again and spent long hours in the pubs attempting to resuscitate ossified friendships with bankers he'd known years ago. There was a queasiness to getting together with old friends you hadn't seen in years. Neither of you quite wanted to know what had happened to the other, in case it was too bad, or too good. In the swamp of beer and cigarettes and rain his new life crumbled. Everyone in London seemed to drink and smoke too much. One drunken night he slept with a woman in a navy suit and, it transpired, lacy underwear. Her mouth tasted like an ashtray. She lit up as soon as they finished. It depressed him no end.

The London rain washed the magic out of him. By the time he got back to New York he was sickened by himself, by his weakness and failure of faith. But equally he couldn't bear to hear how Candlebury's angels had guided her to the place where her inner spirit-child was to be born, on the shore of an island called Wowie or something similar. How did love run out on you like this? How did it run out like a clockwork toy? Did it have to? Did one make it? Or did it truly do it by itself?

And enter, into that state of terminal gloom, that whirling khamsin of doubt, Candlebury's sister Marieta, over from Europe with the Dutch Royal Ballet. She was both a dancer and a shiatsu foot specialist. She could do all kinds of things with feet. She massaged them, and massaged with them, probing the muscles of a back with her pliable toes. Rogers had first-hand experience of this, as it were. They'd met twice already. It was her party piece to discuss tension, then show how to release an overtaut Achilles tendon, trample miseries out of the spine. She was darker than Candlebury, and shorter, more ponderous. She liked to wear tights and a T-shirt around the house. One evening when Candlebury was away at a workshop, he cooked pasta with dried porcini, and the two of them lit a candle and sipped a Montepulciano. On the sofa she inevitably offered a foot massage, he as inevitably returned the favour. It couldn't have failed to happen: suddenly in his chest, a burning desire. He was foolish and reckless, they both were, they both knew already there was a flicker between them and instead of snuffing it they blew on it, fanned it in the hearth of his home. There she was, lying back with one leg bent and one foot in his hand, his fingers resting on the tight black weave. He had only to raise his eyes to see the same weave spreading over the whiteness of her underwear. In the back of the nose he caught, surely, a hint of her scent. When his fingers strayed to her ankle, then from ankle to calf, to crook of knee, when he said, 'You know, it really would be better if we could get directly to the skin,' and she unhesitatingly but unhurriedly peeled down those long black leggings, and once again lay back with her leg cocked, revealing now a gleam of white silk, and he could taste that scent on the air – they both knew what they were doing, they both knew the foolhardiness of it, yet carried on. He supposed, if he really thought about it, that he imagined there would be something purgative, cathartic, in these stray encounters, that somehow he would puncture a bubble of misdirection, find himself properly back where he belonged, in Candlebury's arms, longing to remain there. He hadn't considered what a special case a sister might be. When his hands strayed on to the silk she hummed appreciatively, let her leg fall aside.

It was a terrible wail that woke him two mornings later. He turned and found Candlebury's side of the bed empty. He lay still, waiting to see what would happen, then went into the kitchen. Candlebury was rocking on the floor, curled up like a child. Marieta was sitting at the table, staring into a cup of tea; she got up and walked out without glancing at him.

Candlebury decamped to Hawaii again. He unravelled further. He drank, he smoked, he guzzled espressos. Candlebury wouldn't take or return his calls. He sent flowers and letters and cards. He wasn't sure she even received them. The only address he had was an office on Maui called 'First Space–Sacred Space', which ran the workshop camp she was attending. Eventually he got a five-page letter from her written on lined notepaper explaining that although she had already forgiven him on a higher plain, on the earthly plain she never could and therefore their relationship could only hold her back in the divine work she had to do during her time on earth. Therefore, much as she continued to love his spirit, they must part and stay out of touch. It hurt her no end, she said. He didn't doubt that it did.

The long night followed. Weeks spiralled on weeks, eddying to the ground dead. Always you hoped to find in your hands once again the cable, the lifeline, but it wasn't there, it never was, you had to make your own way now. Error grew on error, mistake compounded mistake, and while you dreamt of redemption the satanic agents got busy erecting the bars to keep you just where you were, thirsting for deliverance. They liked you that way, craving change, forever deprived of it. You became a sleepwalker sleepwalking through a bereft world, clockworking through friendships, sex, work, everything.

When they moved him off the floor he had a flutter of anger which deepened and delivered him into the dark place through which he trudged. No one could join you there. When he came home from work to his small apartment in the West Village all he wanted was to sit at the counter by the kitchen window staring into the gulf of city night, nose pressed to glass, forehead cooled by the pane, eyes lost in the burning constellations. His girlfriend, if he happened to have one at the time, might touch his shoulder and he'd mumble something which meant: better not bother. Then came the Latin fiasco. At that point, of course, he ought to have done the noble thing and quit. Shown them there was only so much dishonour he would take. But a working life wasn't exactly a matter of honour. One had mouths to feed, for example, if only one's own. And soon they dumped him anyway. And he had had to scramble for a stool at an unknown bank called Sylvester's. And they too put him on their Latin desk.

He'd think of Candlebury, picture her married to some truck driver or didgeridooist in Hawaii, think of the moral integrity her life must have because it couldn't afford not to. He'd wish with a fresh intensity, as if it were a new discovery, that he had married her, that he'd opted for the life of the soul, not the bank. Every triumph in the bank, not to mention every failure, was another wound to the soul. Amazing that you could get so far down what had appeared to be the right road only to discover that you had lost the one thing worth keeping.

At eight or nine o'clock when the taxi clicked homeward over the jagged avenues of downtown, he would experience trouble, no other word for it. As the car bounced and rocked, his stream of thought tutted over submerged rocks, thumped over the boulder of a man having thrown away the best thing life had given him. The time when a life could go this way or that had passed. You might realise you had made wrong choices, but it was irrelevant to realise it now. Your only hope was to advance as rapidly as you could along the road ahead, however mistaken. And having seen one's choicelessness, having more or less accepted it, then to find the market shrinking and sinking, to find oneself shifted from the Far East to Eastern Europe to Latin America, watching younger hounds leap into one's place; to see that one had not only selected a course that with hindsight one would not have chosen, but that it was harder, slower and longer than one could ever have guessed; to find that instead of being rewarded for one's compromises and flexibility, one was effectively being punished, as obstacle piled on obstacle. What was the good of going on if the road was so mistaken? *A lost soul groping in the darkness of remembered ways.*

Well, come on, for Christ's sake, he would tell himself. This has a name, the name is depression. It depressed him no end to be depressed. Sometimes he thought he might die soon, and assumed it would be violent: a Colombian with a gun, a gang of teen warriors. Would he mind? Hardly. There was more, too. After two or three years of these thoughts, you had to admit they offered their own perverse solace. At first he had liked to believe that life could not possibly go on as it was. But hell's preference was for persistence. It liked an unpleasant track. It had found one in him and sought no cataclysm. The endless postponement of resolution: that was hell. But then he'd think: stop exaggerating. You've got a job, a roof, money in the bank, at least some money – you call that hell? And he would feel guilty, but chastened, fortified. He could put the madness aside and participate again. And then wake up at four in the morning knowing that he was not, unfortunately, exaggerating. The stakes were very high. They could not be higher. They were called *your life*. And his had gone down the tubes. Week after week, month after month: gone. He wondered if it might be better never to have been happy, not to know what one was missing.

As his fortunes dwindled, he had turned into a lackey. Or perhaps it worked the other way round: he had turned into a lackey, and therefore fortune had withdrawn her favour. But how had he become a lackey? What had toppled him off the pedestal? How did a prince of finance become a worm? Rotted from within.

Recently he had caught himself staring at a brown suit in a shop window. A brown suit. Uniform of the doomed, of the advisers and sub-brokers, attire that went with blue-carpeted offices out on the G and N lines, under a river or two on the R. Next he'd be having lunch down the block at the big Coffee Shop With A Difference, the Brown Derby, where the waiters wore bow ties and said, 'Can I offer you a preprandial cocktail, sir?' 'A what?' you were supposed to reply. To which they'd say: 'A little eye-wash before you attack the menu.' Or some such.

Then along comes Panama with its P, for pipeline, potential, prosperity. No wonder he jumped at the chance.

The little plane shuddered and began to descend. Rogers opened his eyes on a different world. A leopard-skin sea lay below, a silver sea dotted with cloud-shadows. Except they weren't shadows but islands, thousands of tiny islands. The engines whined, his ears creaked.

A circle of silver palms moved under the wing, followed by a congestion of thatch floating on the sea. In the middle of the thatch was an open space, a dirt yard. In it Rogers could see naked brown children staring up, each figure pegged to a line of shadow. He glimpsed the plane's crucifix blurring over a roof. Then it flickered over the sea, over sheets of aquamarine and mint green.

He felt a pang of jealousy. Why couldn't he live somewhere like this, in a straw hut in a warm sea, with nothing to worry about except the gathering of coconuts and the catching of lobsters?

A man with a gleaming belly of hairless springy flesh, wearing nothing but a dwindling pair of shorts, ferried Rogers and Jones in a small steel boat from the airstrip to the next island.

The water, blue like a pot of paint, ruffled by the breeze, slapped against the prow, sending up buckets of warm spray that landed neatly, tirelessly on Rogers' back. In no time his shirt was drenched. Jones grinned. Rogers smiled back. Jones raised his eyebrows, and just then a bucketful bypassed Rogers and slapped Jones full in the face. His brow furrowed and he allowed a pained smile into his glistening cheeks. Meanwhile, in the stern the pilot silently gazed ahead, planted firmly as a tree trunk in his seat, as if he had learnt over the years, over the generations, over the millennia, to make the sea his ground.

All around lay islands, some close, shimmering with silky palms, others further off, in receding shades of blue, grey, black, the furthest just charcoal dashes on the horizon, but all of them bathed in a Venetian haziness. Here and there Rogers could make out a gleam of thatch among the trees on some island, and two islands appeared to be nothing but bundles of thatch, like floating medieval compounds. Bright patches of white sail crossed the lagoon. Here and there a canoe made its way from place to place, a figure in the stern ducking and pausing, ducking and pausing as he paddled along. This was a neolithic Venice, a waterworld of canoes and floating homes, the people travelling by dugout among their water-borne houses and villages, the flotilla of multi-coloured islands. The iron mountains of the mainland closed off the rest of the world like a wall. Rogers felt, as he looked around, that this wasn't just another country. Countries were all much the same – straggling developments along the airport freeway, the high-rises of some kind of downtown, the villas of a suburb. But this was like arriving in another world, a world still in its original form, existing as it had first been built. Rogers couldn't exactly understand what he felt, except that it excited him. What was this watery suburb, who were these people in their dugout canoes? And why did the scene look so happy? Which it did. Somehow the sea and mountains and islands and dugout-paddlers all seemed to belong together.

II

6

'We gots big porpoyce out by the reef,' declared Señor Luis.

He was a fat old Indian in shorts and dirty baseball cap and thumped out each syllable of his tourist monologue. The owner of the Hotel Inadule, he lay slumped on a bench in the hotel's yard, one stumpy leg crossed over the other, entertaining his two new guests with his resonant voice.

Along the tin eaves of his hotel, palm fronds rustled listlessly, unable to decide whether to agree with the wind. The fronds had presumably been installed up there to add a native touch. The two plain wood buildings were all empty now because such guests as there were had left for the day. Without differentiating between his usual clientele and these *hommes d'affaires* who had come on a mission, Señor Luis was giving them his normal spiel.

'We gots three hunnerd sixty-fy islas. Yeah. One for every day,' he said.

They were sitting in the heart of the village, in the heart of the island of Inadule. Up above, a tall palm shivered in a breeze, its leaves glistening. Sweat ran down Jones's forehead. Rogers was still drenched from the boat but could already feel the suffocating heat. Neither of them could muster the determination to stop the old man wasting his breath.

'You say you want to get to Chichimen?' the old man finally asked.

Jones nodded and said, '*Sí, sí,*' without looking at the man. 'We need a boat, pronto.'

Señor Luis turned away and blinked in the sunshine.

Rogers was fascinated by another man who sat slumped in a kind of shack across the yard. He thought it must be a rudimentary shop. The man had long lustrous hair and appeared to be wearing rouge. When he caught Rogers looking at him he lifted his face from his crossed elbows and sent him a broad grin. Rogers looked away in embarrassment.

Two pretty little girls were playing cards in the dirt, in the shade of a bamboo wall. They slapped their cards down one after another. Now and then one would shriek, gather up a pile of cards and they'd begin again.

In a while Jones stood up. Señor Luis continued to sit with one chunky leg resting on the other and droned on, 'Yes, yes, no problem, I get you a boat. The señor doesn't want molas?'

Jones gave Rogers a look, then said rapidly: 'Sure, let's get some molas. Good idea.'

Señor Luis whistled through his teeth.

The long-haired man with the rouge lifted his head again, then slapped round from behind his shack in a pair of flip-flops. He wore a bright pink singlet and a towel wrapped round his waist. Without a word he sauntered across the yard, dragging the heels of his sandals, and down an alley between the bamboo houses, pausing to glance back over his shoulder with a tilt of the hips.

'Go with the mans,' Luis told them in his voice like emery paper.

As they got up Jones murmured, 'Can't come here without buying molas.'

'Why don't we just tell them why we're here?' Rogers asked in a whisper.

Jones tutted.

The houses, woven from rushes, with their high palm roofs, were like the longhouses in pictures of Amazonian villages. Inside, through the doorways, Rogers could see naked children playing on the earth floors with sticks, with empty Coke cans, deflated footballs, scampering around among dirty clothes and clay pots. Women swung in hammocks, talking softly as they worked at embroidery in their laps. The houses were all semi-permeable. Somewhere, it was hard to say where, a girl was singing in a thin, plaintive voice. Someone else was shaking a rattle. Rogers looked around trying to determine where the singer was, and stepped in a puddle of warm, brown water. He thought: this is a place to go barefoot.

The singer turned out to be a girl of ten or eleven with a long black ponytail, swinging violently back and forth in a hammock in an empty house, with a baby clutched to her chest. When Rogers appeared in her doorway the girl stared at him a moment without stopping. The baby sat mesmerised, eyes glazed in the dark, transported by the rhythmic singing voice and the centrifugal tide in its skull. In the semi-gloom of the hut the girl looked a little like Paulina. Perhaps she could even be her younger sister, Rogers thought.

Jones came alongside Rogers. The hut darkened. 'They sing all the time,' he said. 'If you can call it singing.'

Their guide came back and peered over Rogers' shoulder too. He called out in Cuna and the girl paused, laughed briefly, then carried on her singing.

The man touched Rogers' forearm, a warm, light touch. 'She's telling the baby when he grow up he'll be strong and catch a lot of fish and paddle a long way in his canoe. It's school. He has to learn.'

Rogers said, 'You start school young here.'

The man gave a little shudder and patted his cheek. 'Otherwise who knows what might happen.'

In a small yard several women sat on tree stumps, sewing. It seemed that whenever they had their hands free, the women got busy with their needles. One was hanging washing on a line. Rogers imagined that it would take for ever to dry in this damp, hot air. But his own shirt was beginning to stiffen already against his back, after its soaking on the boat. All the women wore gold nose-rings half showing at the nostrils, and on their ankles and wrists gypsy-like strings of beads.

The man said something which sounded like, 'Got two for.'

Immediately all the women left off what they were doing and ran silently into the doorways around the yard. One by one they emerged carrying wooden racks draped with squares of colourful cloth. Each woman's rack had a pole which she planted on the ground, holding it like a battle standard. '*Comprame, comprame,*' a chorus of whining voices rose up all around. '*Sólo fy dollars.*'

Fy dollars. Several others picked up the refrain. *Sólo cinco.*

Rogers was alarmed by the sudden bustle and backed off, bumping into the rack of a woman he hadn't seen behind him. She grinned over the top of her wares, seeming to take his bump as a sure sign of a sale, and sheepishly added her own note: *Sólo fy.*

Jones coolly plucked out his wallet and extracted some bills. The chorus amplified at the sight of them, but once Jones had pointed out the four molas he wished to buy, each hanging on a different woman's rack, the voices subsided.

Rogers followed his example and endeavoured to pull off a single note from the roll in his pocket. After an embarrassing flutter of several bills to the ground, he managed to get down to one, a fifty, then randomly pointed out several molas, losing count, unsure if he had ordered impolitely few and adding two extra. One of the women took his money and disappeared into a hut without being pursued or harassed by any of the others. When she came out again she gave him a ten-dollar bill as change.

Meanwhile, another woman took hold of his arm and before he realised why, she had wound a long strand of beads round his wrist. He was amazed at her dexterity. She snapped the end of the thread in among the beads. When she asked three dollars for it, he couldn't refuse. He wasn't even sure he could have got it off.

It was a hard day, a day of waiting. And hot. No wind reached them. Rogers envied the Cuna men who went about almost naked. His slacks clung to his legs, his shirt to his back.

He decided to go for a swim, and glided out between two little jetties, each of which had a peaked outhouse on the end, like something from a Chinese painting. A cloud of minnows drifted beneath him, glittering, a silver shadow. Even just a few yards out, a calm pervaded the world. The sea looked like silk, flat calm, and the hazy, milky air was filled with the soft sounds of the little village afloat in time, the sounds of humanity at peace with itself: children laughing, someone calling out for help with something, a knock-knock of wood on wood from someone at work.

Rogers felt at peace too. A moment of delirious happiness swept through him, he felt sure things would change for him, change in a good way, though he had no idea how. This world seemed instinct with hopefulness, as if the people carried hope in every muscle. It would infect him too.

Señor Luis, a stump of a man, a well-planted, stocky rolling-bean of a man, a man neither hurricane nor tidal wave could upset, was on his feet when Rogers returned to the hotel yard.

'Right, right,' Luis called. 'This man, he go take you, he know where to go.'

Another Indian, sullen, dressed in a singlet and an Esso baseball cap, sat on the back of a bench, elbows on knees, hands clasped in front. He glanced at Rogers, then turned away and spat.

Rogers had never understood the language of spitting. What did it mean? Did it mean anything at all?

'You haves to pay,' Luis added. 'He gonna take you.'

Jones drew himself up, loafers neatly together. 'He knows Chichimen?'

Señor Luis frowned. 'Yes, yes,' he said in a bored voice. 'He know all about it. Hundred dollars.'

'*Bueno,*' Jones said.

To Rogers it sounded like a lot of money. Perhaps it would be a long trip. Or else Jones didn't want to rock the boat. For all they knew, their business might already be suspected, they might already be watched men.

Their pilot climbed into a waiting canoe and fired up the outboard. Jones and Rogers clambered down into the boat. Rogers, alarmed at its pitching, felt increasingly encumbered by his urban clothes and shoulder bag. As they motored out, they saw all around the shore the canoes waiting on log rollers, their prows tipped clear of the water. They, their ranked savage prows, and the intermittent outhouses on stilts at the end of the little jetties, were the first and last thing you saw of the island-village. They gave it an exotic, menacing look from outside. Gradually the island shrank behind them, coalescing into a single impression of sunstruck straw topped by thin palms.

Many islands passed, some tiny, sustaining a single solitary palm tree like desert islands in a cartoon, others large, showing as distant ink stains on the horizon. Here and there among the glistening palms of the closer islands a golden roof caught the light. Otherwise, the islands formed blocks of watercolour, from iridescent green to faded blue, troubled grey to charcoal black, and as the boat forged through the open waters between them, they seemed to rearrange themselves constantly along the skyline, scuttling back and forth like beetles.

Rogers fell into reverie with the motion of the boat.

Fifteen minutes of fame are not as important as fifteen minutes of adventure, he was thinking. A beautiful woman and a beautiful home were not after all enough, if one possessed them for their beauty. Beautiful people were boring in the end. All the lanky young men with peroxide crewcuts, the skinny small-bottomed girls strutting the sidewalks of SoHo with their ballerina necks and dolls' faces – they amounted to a city's wallpaper, that was all. They prettified the environment. One day they'd be fat or bald or ugly or all three, and even then they still might believe nothing mattered more than those glorious years when they had had their day, when they had strutted the avenues in the gorgeous company of one another, and believed the city belonged to them. Now they had the real estate and it wasn't worth a fraction of what they'd had, they might think. But they would be wrong. Beauty was the wrong god.

He too had been duped. He was a fashion victim of a sort, had led a life, or tried to, effectively sheltered within the pages of the glossies. He had never touched anything real. It was inevitable if you made Wall Street your home. Clouds of perfume, veils of designer clothes, forests of mannequins had blocked his view of the real world for so long now perhaps it was better not to wake up to it.

Rogers got used to the intermittent drenching of the ride. Anyway, the water was warm. He wished he had a hat, though. The thrumming of the engine in his seat, the sparkles on the water that made one squint, the gentle heaving of the boat, all lulled him.

He remembered a time as a kid when he and the Jericho Street gang had dropped over the wall from Billy Thornton's, all four of them, into Mr Watson's garden. It was early autumn and Rogers was back from two weeks in Cornwall with his family. The gang, previously a loose consortium, had formalised in his absence.

They were looking for worms. Rogers was going to have to eat one. That was standard practice among gangs. Billy Thornton had found a garden fork and was raking through the soil, holding the large implement just above its tines, awkwardly scraping the lumps of soil behind the bean plants, then breaking through them with his fingers.

Eventually, inevitably, Billy found a worm. Until then Rogers had not worried or really even thought about the trial ahead. Whatever the others had done he could surely do too. And on the other hand it seemed unreal and improbable that it would really come to it. Now Billy had a worm dangling from a prong of the fork and he was excitedly saying, 'Come on, come on, take it.' With the result that all the others hissed at him to lower his voice. Which was unnecessary. Mr Watson's house was far away across an expanse of blue suburban lawn, beyond a hedge.

The worm was long, rosy, quite fat and hung limply, as if dead, until Billy waved the fork about, whereupon it writhed energetically, almost succeeding in freeing itself from its prison in the air. 'Come on,' Billy said.

The others were silent, watching. Rogers stepped closer. 'Put it down,' he said.

Billy Thornton tipped the fork over the flagstone path, making the worm drop in a self-contorting knot. The others moved closer. 'Ugh,' one of them said.

'Shut up,' Billy told him.

Rogers knelt in front of the creature, one knee on soil which quickly dampened and cooled his trouser, the other on the path. The worm was in a frenzy, desperate to find earth. Rogers put his hand towards it, thinking he might at least take the step of picking it up. It occurred to him then that if he was about to eat the worm he was also about to kill it, in which case the matter was between him and the worm, no one else. He didn't want to eat it any more than it wanted to be eaten. If neither he nor the worm wanted it to happen, then why proceed?

He tore a stalk of dry grass from the path and after several attempts which the worm was keen to resist managed to prod it beneath the animal's body, somewhere near the middle.

'With your hands,' Billy said.

'Bare hands,' someone agreed.

But Rogers simply flicked the worm away among the beans. 'You can keep your silly worm,' he told them. 'And your gang.'

Distantly a lawnmower droned, a car hissed by on the street. The others started calling him a sissy, a coward, none of which he minded. He had guessed by now that none of them had really eaten any worms. Except possibly Billy Thornton, he was just ill-tempered enough.

On Wall Street he had sometimes thought of that day as a key to his early success: listening to no one, making your own decisions. Now, in the boat, he saw the episode in a different light. There was a warmth to it that had escaped him, something tender. It no longer even seemed especially significant, just in some way nice. He had behaved gently, like a monk.

Of all the islands strung along the horizon, one began to expand from a charcoal smear into a breadth of vivid green. That was clearly the one they were heading for. It was like seeing your destiny emerge from vaporous suggestion into solid form. As they came off the bigger waves and on to the swells running into the island's lagoon, a sudden peace, and more than that, awe, swept over Rogers. The green, feathered water, the distant line of a reef beyond – the whole scene had something timeless, immemorial about it. It was like motoring into some picture, some fantasy world, the world of a visionary painter.

Four figures appeared on a steep beach by the shore of the green lagoon. It was late afternoon, the palms struck by sidelong light, enflamed by the last of the sun, tossing their heads like horses in a reef breeze. Rogers studied the figures, his heart in his throat, and couldn't make out if any of them was the girl.

He tripped as he dropped into the surf, soaking his trousers. The people on shore all laughed. When he waded up on to the dry sand they were still grinning. But there were only three people after all. Perhaps one had gone inside a hut, or perhaps there had only ever been three.

An old man with cropped white hair and a few stumps of broken teeth swayed about on a walking-stick wedged in the sand. Another man wearing a torn green polo shirt stood nearby with arms crossed like a totem pole, much the tallest Cuna Rogers had seen, wavy-haired, with an expressionless face like a tree trunk. The third figure was a woman with an ageless face, who chatted away, it wasn't clear to whom, undoing then tightening a wrap round her short sleek body and letting out a high-pitched giggle.

Just then, walking up the shore of a diminutive island lost in a corner of the Caribbean, Rogers could not believe that the pipeline was a real venture. Here they were, two men of finance stepping barefoot on to a desert island. This was not the way pipelines got built. Pipelines were surely a matter of boardroom tables, gala lunches, limousines meeting ministers at airports. Or maybe they did in fact begin like this. That was possible too, and the limos came later. Who knew the earliest origins of great schemes?

The woman stepped down the sand jerkily, with a limp, and seized Rogers' hand. Her grip was strong, yet soft, warm. Talking in the local language, she led him up to the small old man, still balancing on his wooden peg.

Perhaps he was in charge. The old man smiled, his eyes creasing up. 'Yeah, I'm Don Ramon,' he said. 'You come to Chichimen Isla.' He removed a knobbly hand from his stick and held it out for Rogers.

The man's eyes sparkled. The sight of that buried smile

made Rogers impatient. He had an inkling everything was going to take unnecessarily long. Where was the girl? They ought to just find her and be gone. And as soon as they had disembarked, the boat reversed off the beach and motored straight out of the lagoon. Rogers could see the little craft now, climbing the face of a wave, appearing in outline against the sky, then vanishing. Its gurgle was soon swallowed by the distant roar of the reef that showed as a white line a few hundred yards away, roaring like a waterfall.

Don Ramon dislodged his stick and shuffled up the beach, beckoning. '*Bienvenidos, Señor Albert,*' he said.

7

Inside the nearest hut a veil of smoke hung over what looked like a decades-old fire of smouldering coconut husks. A second old man sat in front of it, fanning the embers with a sheet of woven palm, producing a flurry of sparks and a crackle of fat, as a rack of grilling sardines dripped on to the fire. A line of smoke climbed towards the stained roof.

It seemed chilly inside the hut. Altogether, cold and dark and smoke-blackened and messy, strewn with odds and ends – a broken table with four label-less bottles, a pair of spread-eagled inside-out trousers, half a frisbee, sweet wrappers, broken coconut husks, two thin old hammocks, three lopsided palm stumps – the hut was not welcoming.

Don Ramon dropped on to one of the stumps and sat gazing out the door.

'May we?' Jones gestured at the other seats.

'Sit yourselves down,' he said neutrally.

The three sat in silence, listening to the lapping lagoon and intermittent cracks from the fire. Half a mile offshore that reef, which lay at the edge of Cuna territory, still roared like distant thunder, like an avalanche on the other side of a mountain, like a hum in the back of the mind. Beyond it was the open sea.

Rogers coughed and quietly asked Jones: 'Does he know why we're here?'

Jones seemed a big man now that they were squatting on the logs. He cleared his throat. 'Most pitifully and regretfully,' he began in his best Castilian, using a tone of almost ironic deference that Rogers had not heard before, 'it has been too long since I have been able to visit the land of Kuna Yala.' He pronounced the last two words emphatically, like a native in a Hollywood movie.

The old man hawked out the door and stared at Jones a moment, eyes sparkling.

'We're still here. We always have a hammock for you.'

'Thank you.'

'Yeah,' Don Ramon droned. 'Things trucking along down here *just* the *same* as ever.' He spoke in a sing-song, going high on the *same*.

Jones unzipped his holdall and pulled out a small black carrier bag with a gold 'V' on it. Rogers recognised it as a Valentino bag from some fashion boutique. Jones handed it to Don Ramon, who grinned and said, 'Yes, yes,' and put it on the ground between his feet. 'Anything you need, you let me know.'

Rogers glanced at Jones. 'You know these people?'

Jones shrugged.

'You've always been supremely helpful to us,' Jones said, reverting to his textbook Spanish. 'Just now we find ourselves in a quandary, this señor and I. A bit of a quandary.'

'Yeah man,' Don Ramon said, in a West Indian-sounding growl. 'So what's up?'

Jones frowned and smiled at once. 'We're looking for someone. This man, a trusted associate of mine, he wants to find a girl. Some girl he met. Wants to see her again. He's . . . well, he likes her.'

'She a Cuna girl?'

Jones nodded.

'Yeah, some of them real nice.'

'She's lovely, so he says,' Jones went on. 'Called Paulina. Met her in Panama City.'

The other old man who had been squatting in front of the fire now brought over three of the cooked fish. The fish arrived on a circle of white plastic with numbers round the edge, an old clock face. Where did that come from? Rogers wondered. It was as if someone had demolished a department store and these people had filched whatever scraps they found in the rubble. The real source, Rogers guessed, must be the sea, the tides, the great storehouse of the waves bringing in the flotsam of modern life. Don Ramon began to munch on a fish, eating it whole.

Rogers heard voices outside. It was the woman and the tall man. Rogers could make them out through the palm-frond wall. The woman giggled in a delighted squeal.

'Paulina you say?' Ramon asked, plucking up another fish by its tail. 'We'll find her. Ask around, like you say. Could take a few days.' He bit off the head.

Rogers had the feeling just then that to see the girl again would be to make himself doubly a fool.

Don Ramon continued to eat his meal. Rogers asked him where he had learnt his English.

'I work in the Zone ten year, then Pop die and I come home. Seventeen year I haven't left the island, not one day.' He nodded and hummed. 'We got four thousand palms here, twelve peoples.'

He looked like an old Chinese man, in his ragged, filthy slacks held up with rope. The lined face, the creased eyes – you could see he was of the original race that had crossed the Bering Straits from Asia twenty thousand years ago. His forebears had presumably wandered the continent, until one band, his, had pitched up on this island with their canoes and palm houses, and had been living here ever since. Home to four thousand palm trees and twelve human beings. Fourteen tonight.

'Paulina,' Don Ramon repeated, and wiped his hands on his trousers, as he was evidently used to doing, judging by the state of his clothes. He glanced at Rogers. 'So you like her.' He looked away. 'So what's she like? A *gordita*?'

'She's slim, quite tall.'

'A *flaquita* then. Works in Panama.' He said something to the other old man, who got up from his broken plastic chair by the fire and sauntered out the door. 'Yeah, we'll find her for you.'

'You know her?' Rogers asked.

'Yeah, yeah,' Don Ramon answered, in a voice suggesting nothing but apathy.

Jones pulled a cell phone from his trousers, snapped out the aerial and dialled a number, then walked outside. Don Ramon didn't show the kind of surprise Rogers would have expected at the appearance of a cell phone in the Stone Age. But from outside there came another long peal of laughter in the gathering dark of the lonely cay. The woman was still out there. Her voice rose in pitch and speed, until it sprinted off a cliff of a punch-line and she let out the biggest cackle yet. A deep thump of a laugh joined in, emanating from the chest of the tall man. It seemed that these two were not going to enter the hut, but carry on their own little get-together outside.

There was a moment of silence in which Jones could be heard saying, '*Sí sí sí, Colombia.*'

Colombia was not far. Perhaps Jones would be able to call there directly. Rogers wondered why he would want to.

There was a click, which Rogers guessed was Jones snapping shut the phone, then a lot of beeping and buzzing as he apparently tried dialling again.

Then a naked man walked into the hut. He strolled up to the broken table, drank from a plastic jug, leaning right back to tip it up, and let out a belch. A cotton wrap hung over his shoulder and he wore a tight singlet over his chubby torso, but otherwise, down below, he was stark naked, openly displaying his bald brown genitalia, the drooping shaft of which was the size of a small banana. He had the same long wave of hair the rouged man on Inadule had had. He unfurled his wrap and snapped it round his waist, then shuffled across the room, brushing past Rogers and Don Ramon, mincing out the door and on to the beach. He spoke rapidly to the woman, and the two of them then traipsed off down the sand. Rogers made out their retreating figures through the palm mesh.

What was it with these camp men? Was there one on every island? It was unusual enough to encounter such exaggerated effeminacy at home, but among these simple tribal types? Rogers began to feel uncomfortable. These people were weird, they had a screw loose. Not only that, but they were just going about their daily business, making no visible allowance for their visitors. Nothing was being done for them. Night was as good as fallen. Where were Jones and he supposed to sleep, for example? No one seemed to care. What were they going to eat? No one had added any more fish to that fire. Quite the reverse. The old man had pulled off the charred glistening bodies of the sardines and laid them in a cracked frisbee, then broken up the fire. And how on earth would they find the girl among all these islands?

When Jones came back in, Rogers asked him, 'Get through?' As he spoke, he felt like the unpopular boy at college asking yet another dreary question. What did he care if Jones had got through to anyone? Jones shrugged and sat down.

Rogers began to panic. It alarmed him to be facing a night of discomfort. He came under threat of another attack, a harsh one, he felt himself turn sour inside at the thought of being bitten alive by mosquitoes, of freezing on damp sand, of going to bed, whatever bed was, on an empty stomach. Years ago he had backpacked and roughed it, and on tour with Candlebury he had spent the odd makeshift night curled on the mats of dance studios after late rehearsals. Once he had slept in the aisle of the dance company bus, driving between Cincinnati and St Louis. He had slept on the carpeted floors of crowded motel rooms too, letting her share the bed with her female colleagues. And these in retrospect had been some of the most enjoyable nights. But that was all years ago. Now comfort was necessary to him. It sickened him to realise it, because he knew that really he didn't believe in comfort, never had, yet it was too late to stop living as if he did. Why? Because everyone else did. Because why else work in a bank for fifteen years? Because how was he, one solitary individual, supposed to succeed in living a life that actually made sense, when no one else did? Though comfort had made his spirit no less restless than ever. That his career had bellied out, to put it politely, that he no longer enjoyed any of the flights of luck, of intuition, that he used to, that he never got on a roll and let himself go, creaming thousands in minutes, blowing them on limousines and dinners – that that kind of life was over didn't exactly bother him. He was approaching forty, after all. You couldn't keep living like that for ever, perhaps. But one way or another he had grown accustomed to comfort. And not just accustomed but attached. Comfort assuaged the soul. Why was the soul tormented, though? Because that was life for you. You neared forty and maybe you had done all right, had done the things you planned, but most likely you hadn't, most likely you had turned off the right path a long time ago only you hadn't noticed, or had chosen not to notice, until pretty soon you couldn't fail to notice, and by then you had lost loves, brides, mortgages, portfolios, and it was too late to do anything but shrug and say: so I have disappointed myself, life goes on. And it was easier to maintain that kind of attitude in *comfort*. That was the point. A man of a certain age and predicament needed his dinner, his armchair, his cognac, his firm bed. He needed mollycoddling, whether as reward or solace. Why? Because he felt like a fool without it.

He thought of Candlebury again. She was remoter than ever, a silhouette, a permanent profile in his mind.

But it wasn't just the prospect of a chilly, sweaty, itchy night that bothered him. It was also the constant din of the reef offshore, thundering faintly like a half-forgotten memory – like the ruler-line at the margin of the page, the dark beyond the edge of consciousness.

Jones picked up a stick and doodled in the sand between his bare feet.

Rogers felt something nip his ankle. He brushed the skin with his hand then decided to put on his socks and shoes. He picked them up and went out and sat on one of the logs they used for rolling the canoes up the sand, and spent a long time dusting off his feet. Someone lit a lamp inside the hut. The whole building lit up like a lantern, striped with light, a tiger-skin dwelling. The water of the lagoon was black except for fringes of white on wavelets slapping the beach.

Rogers calmed down. Whatever problems he had, they were not physically present right now. If his life was a mess then he must tidy it up. It was possible to do so. But that idea produced another plunge, for it was equally possible to mess up one's life to a degree where it was beyond tidying.

He got himself under control again. All he really needed, he thought, was a break from worry. A streak of phosphorescence shot through the lagoon nearby like a shooting star, and he decided to take it as some kind of auspicious augury.

8

The long-haired man who dressed like a woman said, 'I'm Jorge.' He gave a little shrug as if to prove it, then led them to the hut where they were to sleep.

It had only one wall. Dry fronds hung down from its roof. The boom of the reef ran right through it, and you could hear the waves breaking on the beach, coming in larger here than on the lagoon side.

Jones brushed a hand through his hair. 'This is an old house.'

Jorge span around. '*Qué?*' he said, resting one foot on the other, arms crossed in front.

Jones hesitated, then said softly, 'When was the house built?'

'This house?' Jorge limp-wristedly batted his mouth, shrugged his shoulders, then held a hand out, palm downwards. 'Since I was that high.'

The man was not just outrageously camp, but camp in just the way you might find in the West Village. Same gestures, same persona. It was uncanny.

There were two hammocks. Rogers tested his weight on one. It was thin, thin in every sense: the fabric threadbare, barely stronger than an old tea towel, and barely the width of Rogers' shoulders, not wide enough to contain him. Without even trying to raise his legs into it he could see that it wasn't going to be long enough.

Oh well. Perhaps he'd sleep on the beach. Perhaps he'd figure out how to untie the hammock – though that looked unlikely, judging by the huge knots at either end – and simply spread it on the ground. Perhaps he'd just be up all night. There might be a certain pleasure to that: a vigil on a lonely little island in the furthest corner of the Caribbean, in a total backwater, a real desert island.

Rogers said: 'You'd think the hurricanes would have pulled this place down by now.'

Jorge answered with sudden animation: 'The hurricanes never come here.' He shook his hair away from his face. 'When they try to come we all go on to the beach with pots and pans and bang them, we make as much noise as we can. The hurricane hears us and goes away.' He gave a lame smile and let a kind of shiver run through him.

Rogers cleared his throat. 'You scare it away?' He was rather appalled by the man.

Jorge let out a high giggle that cascaded into an emphatic: 'No, no, no! We tell him where we are. A hurricane is a bad pilot. He's got lost. When he hears us he knows where he is and goes away. He's just trying to find his way.'

Rogers shook his head and glanced at Jones. But Jones was already rocking in his hammock, facing the other way, hands clasped behind his neck.

Suddenly Jorge let out a falsetto whoop and doubled up with laughter. 'I forgot,' he exclaimed, like it was the funniest thing imaginable. 'Do you two *caballeros* want to eat some fish?'

Supper – four small grilled fish and a lump of yucca – arrived on a cracked, worn frisbee. The woman brought it over, and gabbled away in rapid Cuna as she set the meal on an old crate. From inside her clothes she produced a bottle of Maggi tomato sauce. She cocked her head, spreading her hands, then stomped out of the house with her brisk limp. Rogers felt a spasm of gratitude.

They ate with their fingers. The fish was delicious, tasting faintly of coconut, and even the yucca was sweet and creamy, like a giant sweet potato, and had been cooked to the perfect consistency so you could break off chunks that melted in the mouth. He had not realised how hungry he was. 'All we need now is a beer,' he said.

Jones passed over a handkerchief for Rogers to wipe his hands on. 'I've got a cigar,' he intoned like a question, reaching for his bag. He unzipped a side pocket and fumbled inside. He lifted out a little cardboard box not much bigger than a matchbox, which rattled as he passed it to his other hand, then returned it, with another chortle of its contents, to the pocket. Then he extracted two slender cigars from the bag.

Was that a box of nails? Rogers wondered. Screws? Staples? But why bring them here?

The conditions didn't bother Jones. That was the difference between Third World man and First: in the Third World even the wealthy had had some experience of discomfort. They still possessed some sinew of endurance lost to civilised man. You noticed it only when circumstances called it forth. Jones now acted as calmly and stoically as a man who had known innumerable sleepless bus journeys, who was used to eating watery soup off market benches beneath which he would later sleep. He rummaged in his bag, unbuttoned his shirt, hung it from a nail on the house pillar, a nail which he found as readily as if he had known where to look, and pulled on a Yale sweatshirt. The more at ease Jones appeared the lonelier Rogers felt.

The sweatshirt seemed like a good idea. Rogers pulled out a bundled-up windbreaker from his bag and the two men rested in their hammocks, not talking, puffing on their panatellas while the thunder of the reef grew, invading the shelter like an advancing storm.

At a certain point – an hour or two later – Rogers realised that this was night already, night had arrived and they had gone to bed. They were simply going to half sit, half lie in their diminutive hammocks all night long. His cigar had long since gone out, and he didn't want to disturb Jones for a light.

A storm did in fact arrive in the night. It announced itself with a soft flicker like a striplight trying to turn itself on. Then it murmured from far away, detaching its voice from the low roar of the sea. A series of explosions clattered forth, falling down the sky like fireworks, and an angry flashing began: a sharp crackle of a retort, followed by a gurgle like the sound of someone clearing their throat, but heard through a stethoscope.

'Jesus,' Rogers said quietly, wondering if Jones was awake.

Silence. Then Jones's voice, low and clear. 'Beautiful, no? They have the best storms here. Won't be long.'

Rogers didn't know if that meant long in coming, or in staying. He got up and walked out through the palms to the strip of beach. The darkness fell open, revealing a cloudscape of enormous thunderheads. They looked like a painting. Scared, Rogers returned to the shelter. And just in time, for the wind had died down completely, replaced by a cloying stillness, an unnatural warmth, out of which exploded a hissing roar.

Rain fell hard for a quarter of an hour, a deafening surf-crash that eased suddenly. Then a tap-tap of drops from the roof found Rogers' cheek. When he rolled his head out of the way he could feel the drops drumming on the taut cloth of his hammock, gradually drenching it. Half the night he couldn't tell if he was asleep or awake.

Morning. Outside, the palms made a kind of forecourt as in some ruined hotel, littered with pebbles and old coconuts, as if the servants had long neglected to sweep. The air was milky, sunless. A curtain of oyster-shell clouds hung around the horizon. The place seemed oddly familiar, ordinary, reminding Rogers of an abandoned construction site, as if nature and industry came up with the same moods when left to their own devices. The sound of the reef brought back the night, disturbing the morning with its troubled note.

There was no sign of Jones.

Rogers' limbs were stiff in a way that seemed to suit the cloudy morning. He stripped off and swam in a channel right off the beach. The water had no morning chill. He looked at his pale brown shoulders, the colour of milky coffee in the turquoise water, and thought he'd like to see them go nutty brown, become the shoulders of a lean man living in a lean-to on a coconut island. What a thought. And what was there that really would prevent it?

Rogers spotted a white sail against a distant island. Just then he heard a creak, and turned round in time to see a canoe, fully rigged with mast and patchwork sail, scuttling down the channel towards him, not twenty yards away. He paddled back and stumbled up the beach.

Four people filled the craft, a woman, two children, and a man in the stern holding a paddle vertically in the water. They all stared at Rogers as they passed. No one said anything. The man joggled his paddle. Rogers heard the wind scuffle with the sail. The apparition was gone as quickly as it had come.

He walked round to the lagoon, where Don Ramon's

hut was. There was no sign of anyone, except for one small figure sitting motionless in a canoe far out on the water. Whoever it was must have been fishing.

Back in the hut Jones was swaying in his hammock. Rogers asked to borrow his cell phone.

'Battery's dead.'

'How long are we going to be here? I've got to call New York. I haven't spoken since the day before yesterday.'

Jones didn't reply. A distance seemed to have grown up between them since they arrived on the islands. Jones had turned into a tough man of few words. He even looked different. His snowy hair matched his leathery face in a new way, and his tan no longer seemed a salon product but the result of a tough life. He had shed his boardroom manners as easily as his suit. Faint dimples had appeared in his face too, making it look weathered. It reminded Rogers of a drunk Colombian he had once met in a bar in Barranquilla. He began to wonder if things had got out of hand. It was all very well to have a bit of fun and lose the suit for a couple of days, but here he was stuck on an island in the middle of nowhere with no means of transport, with a man he hardly knew.

Jones sat up in his hammock, rocking himself gently back and forth with his feet. He looked at Rogers. 'Nice place, no?'

'I guess,' Rogers said.

'A man could build himself a nice villa here, a dream house. Retire. You think about retiring?'

Rogers thought about it, and no, he didn't think about retiring.

'I guess that's for later,' Jones went on. 'All I really want for now is to get myself totally legit. I'm through with the war.'

'The war?'

'This is Panama, man. No one's legit until they're rich enough to be, then they get out of the battle zone. Don't play naive. Where do you think people put their money down here? In banks? No, you go buy a stake in a transit operation, five times out of six something goes wrong, but you only need it to go right once in six. Russian roulette, man. Blam, when that baby hits, it hits big. A thousand per cent easy. You give me ten thousand dollars, it may take me a year and a few tries, but I'm going to give you back a hundred grand. And that's allowing for the fuck-ups. Everybody does it, everyone's in a consortium. Only thing is, the more you put in, the more control you want. It's only natural. But you get too close, it gets hairy. We're not talking guns down here. More like subs, torpedoes, rockets, the whole deal. This is a war, that's why they call it a war.'

Rogers didn't know what to say. The man was obviously talking about drugs. But that drug-runners had submarines?

'Yeah, everyone's in on it, even the fucking Russians. Used to help out M-19, the Marxist guerrillas in Colombia. They made a lot of contacts there. Half the cocaine that got into the US used to come in Russian subs, at least part of the way. Undermining the enemy. Anyway, I'm through with it. I want my returns another way. That's why Carreras brought me in. I know the scene.

I know the players, how to deal with them. This island, for example. Why you think we're here?'

'I thought we were looking for the girl.'

'I know these people. They used to put me up from time to time when I was waiting for a drop or whatever. This is a nice, quiet place, well out of the way. If anybody's going to help us, Don Ramon will. He knows everyone. They all know each other down here.'

Rogers frowned, feeling even more alarmed. 'Why should he help us?'

'Why not? He always gets something from me. He and Jorge. He hates to leave the island, so he says, but there are things he misses. Marlboros and whisky and steak. I used to keep him stocked up. Other things too, not for him but his *friend*.'

Jones put an enigmatic emphasis on the word.

'Friend?' Rogers had to ask.

'Jorge and Don Ramon –' Jones flicked up his eyebrows. 'Jorge likes things, magazines, cosmetics, make-up, that crap. All the fashion stuff. And clothes. I used to bring a load of Dior and Lancôme every time I came. Keep him sweet for Don Ramon.'

'You're kidding me.'

'No way, man. That's what they do down here. They have two kinds of women, it's a traditional thing.'

Rogers exhaled slowly. This was all more information than he needed. He had had his suspicions about Jones, it was only natural when you dealt in this part of the world. But that the man should be so open about it – he didn't want to hear it. And that Jones was in cahoots with these odd people only made Rogers more desolate.

'Anyway.' Jones tipped himself out of his hammock on to his feet. 'Time to check in with Don Ramon. See if they've figured out who she is.'

Which they had.

'Yeah,' Don Ramon said, when they had settled on the tree stumps in his hut. 'The girl you're looking for, we calls her Nikiri. Nikiri is a turtle.'

The old man glanced at Rogers. 'She a bad girls. You catch a turtle, leave it one minute it's gone. Look slow but man they fast. Only way to keep a turtle once you got him you got to turn him on his back. That's why we call she Turtle.'

'You know where she is?' Jones asked.

Don Ramon glanced at him. 'Maybe. We go find her. Got to get a boat ready. Go looking.'

Rogers wondered what it would be like to see the girl in the flesh, to be face to face with her again. She could hardly be happy to see him. But what about him? Why wasn't he angrier with her? She had defrauded and robbed him, yet he felt in a vague way that he owed her something, as if her actions had been justified and his hadn't.

'Reckon she's a long way down Kuna Yala. On Rio Tigre,' Ramon went on.

'Where's that?'

'One of the last islands, man,' Jones explained. 'Practically Colombia.'

* * *

The rest of the morning passed slowly, as they attempted to organise a boat. There wasn't much Rogers could do to help. His watch, normally reliable, stopped at ten to eight. He walked round the island. The side that faced the mainland was warmer and scruffier. In the distance rose a dark-grey bank, the forested Isthmus of Darien. Old coconuts littered the beach, along with a waterlogged dugout and cracked sheets of fibreglass from some old launch. Dried weeds that looked like pine needles had been brushed by the waves into little arcs, like hundreds of disembodied eyebrows.

He felt oddly excited, like a kid on summer holiday. They had figured out where the girl was, now all they had to do was get there. Meanwhile, he could explore the island. *Explore the island*: were there any more exciting words? He couldn't think when he had last been on an island. And he looked forward to seeing the girl again. Who knew what might happen? He could even decide to drop out and marry an island girl. What a way to do it, here in the aboriginal Caribbean. It wouldn't be like opening up some Rum Runners' bar in Antigua with burgers and Bud on tap and a steel band on Friday nights. This was the real thing, more Crusoe than Crusoe, a whole society living like Crusoe except they had been doing it for thousands of years. They had none of Crusoe's cupidity, all his ingenuity. How could a man get rich here, even if he wanted to? He might hoard coconuts and dried fish, presumably, but why bother, when they were in limitless supply anyway? In fact, he couldn't imagine anyone wanting to grow rich here. There was just no need. Their husbandry was subtle and secure. They didn't hoard because they didn't need to.

There was a second homestead round the other side, three or four huts just like Don Ramon's, with a rudimentary bamboo table beside a blackened outdoor fire-pit.

As Rogers passed it a man in black satin shorts appeared in the doorway of one of the huts. He glared at Rogers. Rogers waved but the man didn't respond, and after a moment he went back inside.

Then a little boy came out chewing on a wooden doll. He smiled at Rogers. He couldn't have been older than two or three. The same man scooped him up from behind with a skinny brown arm, and pulled him back in the hut. Then the man reappeared alone.

'Who you looking for?' he asked.

Rogers was taken aback, and literally stepped backwards, catching his breath. He was about to answer, no one, when it occurred to him that it might be worth a try, and said, 'Paulina. I think they call her Nikiri here.'

'Nikiri? She ain't on the island here. She over there.' The man nodded towards the east, either at the next island or down the chain of islands.

'You know her?'

'Sure. She with her father. He works for Don Ramon with the palms there. They got ten thousand trees on the island. Lot a work.'

'You know where she is?'

The man looked at him. 'Sure. She just there. Next island. She come a couple days back. You find her there. Achutupu, Pelican Isla.'

Rogers didn't know what to make of this information, and decided to ask Jones about it later. He wandered on round the island.

Jones had changed into a pair of shorts and a red T-shirt. He stooped under his hammock and reached for his bag just as Rogers shuffled into the hut. He zipped up the top of the bag, but halfway along he had to stop to push a small tube out of the way. Rogers saw it. Perhaps it was some kind of pen, or some kind of scuba gear, or even the tip of a collapsible coat-hanger, he thought. Except he knew exactly what it was: the barrel of a gun, an old-fashioned Luger-like handgun. And Jones had tried to hide it. Why? Rogers knew people in New York who carried guns. He wouldn't be surprised to learn it was customary in Panama City. Briefcase, wallet, handgun. Spectacles, testicles, wallet and Walther. Why hide it?

On the other hand, Jones had packed his bag. That could only be a good sign. Rogers imagined leaving the island right away, and thought that already he would feel a certain nostalgia for it. 'We off?' he asked.

'Sure are. They've got the boat together. Let's go. Pack your stuff.'

Rogers was about to tell him what he had heard from the man on the other side of the island, but decided to keep quiet for the moment. If Don Ramon had a reason for not letting on where she really was and instead sending them down to the far end of the archipelago, it might be better to wait until they had left his island before mentioning it.

They sat on log rollers by the lagoon. Rogers felt like a lad on holiday idling time away. After a while Carmelita the woman and Jorge the effeminate one came out on to the beach and stopped in their tracks. They whooped and waved, then disappeared into the furthest hut.

A faint buzzing, the buzz of a fly, detached itself from the thunder of the reef. A small boat appeared in the mouth of the lagoon, a canoe without a mast, its prow riding high. When it was a few yards offshore Rogers saw what a strange-looking man the boatman was: white, not as in Anglo, but utterly white, with skin like paper and bloodshot eyes.

Don Ramon emerged from his hut, a derby hat perched on the back of his head. Rogers asked, 'Is he all right?'

'They calls that a moon boy,' Don Ramon said. 'Shouldn't be out in that boat, they don't likes the sun and the sun don't like them. They got a short life, those people.'

The man was wearing a red baseball cap that exaggerated his unearthly complexion. He brought his boat into the beach just hard enough to lodge it on the sand. The stern began to drift as Jones, without a word or a wave, waded straight out into the water, shoes and all, and clambered aboard. Rogers followed him, slinging his bag into the trough of the boat. The boatman withdrew the prow with a rev of the motor, then let it idle a moment as he changed out of reverse gear, and they began to move towards the mouth of the lagoon.

Once the boatman had ridden them out of the lagoon and into the calm waters of the island chain, where the green water gave way to blue, Rogers turned round from his place at the canoe's prow and said to Jones, 'I don't know if I believe Don Ramon.'

Jones smiled a little patronisingly and shrugged. 'What does it matter?'

'I mean about the girl.' He told Jones what the other islander had told him.

Jones squinted across the waves. 'Which island?'

'Somewhere called Pelican Island.'

They had been travelling only ten minutes but already Rogers was disoriented. It took him a moment even to figure out which green oblong was the island they had just left. It had a blue half to it, presumably further away than the rest, that confused him. There were three or four islands that could have been the one the man had meant, each a dash of grey-green, smoky in the morning sun. As he stared at them, the sparkle on the early sea dazzled him and became too bright.

Jones tapped the boatman's shoulder and waved his hand down. The man eased up on the throttle, which made the small engine sputter, falter and die, and the dugout glided silently through the wavelets.

Jones was sitting in the middle of the tiny boat with his elbows resting on his bare knees. Silver hairs covered his legs. Rogers stared at them and wondered if he had totally misjudged this man's age. He had assumed he was only a little older than himself. 'So what's all this about?' Jones asked.

The boatman meanwhile was busy at the outboard with the cowling off, wrapping the cord of rope round the spindle. He gave it a sharp tug and the engine coughed.

'Well, that other guy, like I said, told me she was staying just on the next island, with her dad.'

'How did he know?'

Rogers could only shrug and add, 'He seemed to know exactly who I meant.'

Jones frowned. 'Rio Tigre is like the last island in the chain. It could take us most of the day to get there. Especially at this rate.'

The albino boatman had failed again to get the motor started. Now he removed its metal manifold and adjusted a nut with his fingers. The boat pitched as he tugged the cord again. It started at the next try, and he kept it revving high in neutral, pouring a stream of blue, fragrant smoke and spitting gobbets of water. The man's pale hands shone under a film of wetness.

Jones spoke to him in rapid guttural Spanish. Then he turned back to Rogers. 'We better try. Don't want to waste the day.' He frowned again. 'But I don't get it. What's up with Ramon, if it's true?'

The boat began to move again, and the boatman swung the prow till it pointed at one of the low smudges of green lying on the horizon.

This is bloody heaven: the thought surprised Rogers. A wave of elation ran through him. He didn't know people lived anywhere like this. Scuttling between the palm islands across a sea they knew as well as the backs of their hands, in tree trunks that grew for free in the woods, powered, many of them, by wind that blew for free. But it wasn't the freeness that got to him. It was just this happy world, all the islands strung across the warm sea, and the people able to scurry to and fro in their canoes: it all seemed so perfect, so well designed, so ideally thought out. They'd hang out on the beach, in their huts, then take a little trip across the blue water under the sun, and be back in time for sundown. And they had all they needed.

It stirred a vague memory in Rogers, perhaps of childhood holidays on the beach. It was as if he had once known that life could be this good, this happy. Sun, sea, beach, palms, boats, fish, hammocks, thatch roofs: why did these seem to be the ideal and always-intended ingredients of life? It wasn't so much that life here seemed happy, or that the people did, but that he himself did.

When he thought of the girl, his stomach collapsed in excited dread. He sensed that in some way all his good feelings were connected to her. He was looking forward to seeing her badly enough that he could hardly bear to think about it, felt sick when he did.

Which made no sense. She had ripped off his wallet, screwed him two ways for money. Talk about sentimental: to fall for a hooker who robbed you. It was lamentable. But then again, he hadn't exactly fallen for her. He reminded himself of that and felt better.

The island they were aiming for grew until Rogers could make out the individual trunks of its palms, gleaming like stalks of straw. But the engine kept faltering, gurgling and threatening to die, then finding a new spurt of power for a while before again faltering. It took a long time to cover the last half mile. As they approached the shore, another dugout with a triangle of dirty white sail crept along the beach, coming closer and closer to where they seemed likely to hit land. Finally the boatman drove their canoe hard up on to the beach. It glided for a moment over the sand with a deep shush, then abruptly stopped. Rogers pitched forwards and stumbled on to the beach just as, a few yards offshore, the sailing dugout went scudding by, carried along by the slight breeze at a pace that seemed if anything faster than their own motorised transport had managed. Rogers could hear the wind in its sail.

A man was standing in the stern, holding a paddle as a rudder, and wearing a pair of glasses with thick black rims and a dark office suit, but no shirt. Rogers watched as the boat slipped past, and the man called out in a hoarse voice and skipped up to the mast of his vessel and plucked it out of its socket, folding it down sail and all among his passengers.

A few yards on, the boat slowed. The man with the suit and glasses jumped out, up to his chest in water, and steered the craft in, giving it a shove to drive its keel on to the beach. It hung there, the length of it drifting round towards the shore.

'Yes sir.' The man lifted an arm to hail Rogers. 'You're looking at Henry Rawlinson.'

In spite of the Anglo name, in spite of the unexpected attire, with his mop of black hair and sleek features the man was visibly a local.

'You sirs need a guide, I am at your service. I expert in Cuna culture and territory. I born here,' the man explained, 'and I work in the Zone fourteen year and now I back making my researches into Cuna culture and history. What can I do you for?'

Jones already stood on the beach brushing down his shorts and was ready with the obvious reply: 'We're looking for a girl called Nikiri.'

'Yes, you come to the right place, man. She just across the lagoon, I go fetch her, meet you round the other side.'

'The other side?' Jones asked.

'Where the village is. You go see.'

With that, the man heaved his canoe off again, with its three passengers, and scrambled among them to hoist the mast. The makeshift sail flapped until he hauled on a line and it filled.

Jones and Rogers arranged with their boatman to meet them at the other side of the island and walked off, leaving him fiddling with the engine.

The village turned out to be four palm shacks, with only one person around, a tall Cuna with a dark smooth face like polished walnut. He introduced himself as Achu, then bent down to resume his work untangling a small blue net. 'That a bait net,' he informed them, in case they wanted to know.

Rogers and Jones sat on the sand to wait. 'Looking good, no?' Rogers said.

'Maybe,' Jones muttered. 'What the hell is up with Ramon, sending us off to Tigre?' He spat neatly, landing the gob in the froth where the ripples dissolved into the sand. 'When she gets here, I'm going to leave you to sort things out. I've got business with our sahila. Then I'll come back and get you.' He rubbed his face. 'I've got a good feeling about this trip, you know. There's nothing like being on the ground, in the field. We could tie it all up once and for all.'

The prospect of being left alone here alarmed Rogers; then he thought with anticipation of being alone with the girl on this atoll. Except who knew how she'd feel about seeing him.

'I don't need to tell you you've got to give her more,' Jones said. 'First thing you do. Make sure she knows she's OK with you.'

Rogers took a stroll up and down the beach. This island was if anything closer to the roaring reef that bounded the Cuna territory.

9

It must have been close to noon when the dugout arrived under sail. It glided into the lagoon slow as a galleon, deep-bosomed in the water even though it was so tiny. Then, once close, it seemed to skitter into the beach like a toy. Only when the strange office man steering it scrambled up the length of the craft to whip the mast out of its socket, letting the sail collapse any old how, and jumped off to guide it up against the sand, and the other passenger, who sat smiling ahead all the while, stood and turned round, revealing a fine rump clad in a pair of tight black cycling shorts – only then did Rogers realise that it was really her, and as in a dream discovered that he was about to step into the kind of experience he would no longer have believed could come his way. She had arrived. She had come laden with smiles and bicycle shorts and a little red knapsack containing a bikini and a bottle of almond oil.

Rogers knew by her first smile that she was happy to see him. She was a Cuna, an Indian, this was her homeland, she was answerable to none.

Rogers imagined Henry Rawlinson's and Achu's eyes to be on him when he embraced her. Perhaps this was like El Salvador or Cuba, or pretty well anywhere Latin, where there was no better catch for a girl than a gringo passport. Except he doubted that.

She seemed to have accepted her summons without question, wherever she had come from. It was hard to understand. But then these people were hard to understand. They seemed both childlike and more mature than westerners. When Rogers later struggled with a canoe paddle, he felt like a little boy who ought to know how to use one by now, at his age. When his feet pricked on washed-up flotsam, he felt that he had the tender soles of an infant. And when that night the girl began to teach him things about a hammock he would never have imagined, he felt like he and everyone he knew lived up a side track off evolution's main highway.

Paulina led Rogers to the last of the huts, a little way from the rest, and screened from them by a stand of almond and seagrape trees. The first thing Rogers did was pull out two hundreds and fold them into her hand.

'I owe you this,' he said.

She sent him a heart-warming smile, thanked him, and put the money in her little knapsack.

They sat in the sand outside the hut. She lit herself a cigarette and ran the match through the sand in front of her, drawing a star. 'I shouldn't have done what I did,' she said.

Rogers couldn't take his eyes off her neat, dark eyebrows; the complexion around them was so smooth and edible-looking. He wanted to tell her that of course she should have.

'There was a reason,' she went on. 'You know I had only just started that work. I need money for my father. I'll have to go back soon. It's complicated.'

'Is he unwell?' Rogers tried, surprised by a warm concern.

She tutted, drew on her cigarette. 'It's nothing like that.'

After a moment Rogers asked: 'Do you still have the wallet?'

'Of course.' She smiled. 'I forgot.' She reached for the knapsack.

He felt an instant of relief just to see the wallet again. That was a number of hassles deleted in one go. He glanced inside, saw that Jones's paper was still there.

'Hombre, I just took the money. I have it here still. I'm sorry. I was in a hurry, I was desperate.' She shook her head and looked to the horizon. 'I have to get a thousand dollars for my father.'

Rogers nodded. She already had the three hundred-odd that had been in his wallet, plus the two he had just given her. He himself had a further eight still in his pocket.

'Twenty years my father has been working for Don Ramon. Can you believe it? And now it's his turn to be the sahila of our island. I don't want Ramon to stop him. But he has to be paid off.'

'Is this the Don Ramon I know? From Chichimen?'

'Hombre,' she said quietly.

'So all that's left is another five hundred dollars?'

'Why do you think I went to Panama? They told me I could make that in two weeks.'

Without a second thought Rogers reached into his shorts and counted out the bills. 'Here.'

She took the money thoughtfully, folded it and clasped it in her hand awhile. Then leaned over and kissed him on the cheek.

'It's nothing,' he said, though she hadn't expressly thanked him.

They sat in silence a moment. Then Rogers asked, 'So you didn't mind how you got the cash together? You didn't mind that work?'

'It's easy. We're not like you people. We get older lovers when we're young. We have to, or we can't get married.' She shrugged. 'And I met you.' She kissed him again, on the lips. Rogers felt that his heart was not in his throat but his skull. He could feel it throbbing against the bone cavity, and his brain seemed to be melting.

In their three days together they never again mentioned the wallet. These people didn't care the way others did.

He had the feeling that whatever he asked her, she would smile and say yes, why not. It wasn't that she didn't understand. Perhaps it was him, and the island had lulled him into a rhythmic sea-dream into which she slipped as easily as someone joining him in a hot tub. Life here was a dreamy dreaminess, a lullaby of sea and waves and palms. The islands rocked in the cradle of the sea. Here no one thought too hard but lived by perfect intuition.

Yes, yes, yes: all uttered with that ironic smile. How did she get away with it? By being a beauty, by being an island girl, by living a life where all that mattered was getting the next plate of fish, of which one was assured as long as the seas stayed clean.

She had glided into shore smiling, head erect, and jumped into the water as soon as the canoe's prow dug itself into the beach. She had performed the leap gracefully, allowing the momentum of the boat to propel her, and everything she did followed with the same grace.

That first night they lay side by side in their hammocks. She held his hand and gently pulled, causing the two of them to swing in unison. Now and then they would get out of sync, and collide with a soft tingle-producing thud of rump on rump. She had brought a candle with her, which guttered on a stump by the back wall. Giant shadows flickered and flapped across the thatch roof.

He said, 'I really wanted to see you again.' The words flowed easily from his lips. He was lulled by their lovemaking, and more than that by an irrefutable feeling of love. He longed for her and at the same time felt the thrill of a longing fulfilled. He was happy. He would have liked to rest his brow on her breast and listen to the thump of her heartbeat, have it carry off his worries, drum them out of his bloodstream – give himself a transfusion of her clear, calm blood. She was young, unspoiled. He lay his cheek against the taut cloth of the hammock and looked at her – those immaculate sleek cheeks, the fine mouth, and that faint smile that always seemed to show in her eyes. As if he slightly amused her, and as a result caused a reservoir of affection to be tapped. As if he could already sense the kind of love she might have for him, a caring, amused one, with a tenderness at the core that could be fanned into passion.

They took care of the dilapidated shelter. He tied up a driftwood board for a shelf, rolled a useless but beautifully smooth branch a hundred yards along the beach, letting it stand as a sculpture outside the hut.

In the morning she came out blinking into the palm-dappled sunshine with a black and white Valentino scarf tied round her waist. It looked good against her brown limbs. She watched him with hands on hips as he attempted to sweep up the grove between the hut and the beach using a palm branch. She tutted, shook her head, set a knife between her teeth.

In a matter of seconds she had shimmied up into the head of a palm, where she sawed away until a frond cracked, shushed to the ground. As he watched her up there, crouched among the fronds, nimble as a monkey, he realised he could not remember the last time he looked at a slender female thigh from such an angle and saw nothing sexual in it, rather just the limb of an agile creature, skilled and lithe.

Back on the ground she stripped the backs off the leaves, pulling a sinew that came away in thongs. Five minutes of squatting, tugging, cutting, holding things with her teeth, and she had made a new coconut broom.

She seemed small, standing there at the foot of the tree, yet a decisive presence. He felt awkward and self-conscious as he gave her a hug by way of thanks. But she received it, along with his awkwardness, with her usual placid smile. It was impossible to upset her.

This was the house they shared for now; he would sweep it clean.

Rogers had no way of contacting Jones; he could do nothing but wait for him to return from his business with the sahila. Then presumably they'd return to Panama City and press ahead with the negotiations, knowing they were good to go on the ground. But it was strange how staying here on this little island, all lust slaked by Paulina, and a glow of love kindling in his belly, he couldn't muster any feeling about the deal: if it came off, well and good, but if not, so be it. It hardly seemed to matter, a small and remote affair.

He let himself drift along with the life of the little community. Paulina's father was Achu, the tall Cuna with the smooth, dark face. He took Rogers fishing.

Achu's boat was a hefty bole with a chunk missing from the stern. He spoke some Spanish and Rogers tried to make a joke about whether a *tiburón* had chewed the canoe. Achu told him he needn't be afraid of sharks.

They rolled the boat down on its roller until the log was all the way up at the prow, whereupon they had to drag the boat the last few feet, cutting a deep groove in the sand. Rogers was relieved to see the craft had some kind of keel. But it wasn't much of one. Every move he or Achu made set his heart thumping.

'Yes man,' Achu began when they were bobbing out on the clear green water. 'Nikiri been working her butt off for me in Panama. She a good girl, man.'

It struck Rogers as an unfortunate expression: but then he asked himself why. Even if the man had meant it literally, which wasn't implausible here, there was no shame attached to sex in this community. You couldn't change what the human body wanted, all you could do was take care to provide it.

The big Indian nimbly walked up the boat, stepping right over Rogers with hardly a pause, and picked up a lump of grey rock in the bow, heaved it over. The water swelled around it and the yellow rope attached to it thrummed rhythmically as it fed over the side, then went still.

First Achu uncoiled a line, fed the hook through the eye socket of a minnow, then tied on a rusty bolt. He knotted the line round his big toe, cocked for the trigger tremble, then set up another line for the other foot.

Rogers used fingers rather than toes. He'd feel the tremblings on the line, soft, electric tingles, and whip it up hand over hand only to find the bait fish gone or half gone, and sometimes only its head remaining on the hook. Then one time as he started hauling in he couldn't believe how heavy the line was. He could barely pull it in, especially with his fingers being wet. He thought the line must have got trapped under a stone, and tugged it hard a couple of times, let it go, pulled again, and the weight was still there only this time he felt a livid tugging. He hauled harder, faster, the line slipping in the creases of his knuckles. He had been trying to keep the line tidy but now, in his panic, created bundles of knots on the bottom of the boat.

A glitter in the dark water, then he saw the fish itself just a few feet beneath the surface like a silver leaf. He lifted it clear, wriggling, and dropped it in the hold. It was beautiful, silver tinged with orange, and not more than six inches long. Its spiky dorsal fin rose and fell like a fan opening and closing as it gasped for breath. Then as the boat tipped the fish found itself swimming in a puddle that Rogers had failed to bail. It flinched, recomposed itself and twitched about the boat. Then once again, as the water sloshed to the other end, it found itself high and dry on its side, and fluttered furiously.

Rogers was delighted and horrified at once. It was a long time since he had deliberately killed anything except a mosquito. One forgot what it was like.

Achu said, 'That one stings, be careful of the spines.'

How could he be careful? He had to dislodge a barbed hook from inside the fish's skull. There was a crunch as he tugged it out.

Achu brought in a chubby parrot-fish a foot long,

sweeping in the line in long loops that sailed neatly to the floor of the canoe as he discarded them. In a second he had the hook removed, rebaited and lobbed out again, while Rogers was still recovering from his first triumph.

At night Paulina sang to him. She rehung the hammocks side by side and taught him the many and various Cuna love lore that took advantage of the slings.

In his few days he began to learn the island ways – how they erected a new house, knocking up a lashed bamboo frame then simply heaving up the already woven walls of palm; how they scampered up trees to cut coconuts and tied them by their stems into bunches of four; how in the corners of the huts they stored piles of green plantain and yucca from the slashed fields of the mainland, which they'd swapped for coconuts with the Cuna who brought them over, piled high in the bottoms of canoes; how they grated the fresh copra to make coconut milk, and boiled the milk to make oil. He counted the uses of the coconut tree and reached twenty. When he asked Paulina about it she shrugged and said, 'Hombre, who knows? One hundred uses? One thousand?' One way or another, it was food, shelter, heat and even light to them. They made wicks out of the husk hairs, floated them in bowls of coconut oil.

But that wasn't what mattered. What mattered was how it felt to live on a beach. To be ten miles from land, to be so roundly accepted into the world of sand and sea, to see your shoulders turn coffee-brown and to feel the vigour of the sea unfurl within you from some hidden place where it had been stowed all along: that was to come alive.

It wouldn't occur to these people, he thought, that food could be anything other than fresh. Nothing remarkable for them in a meal that had been growing on a tree or flickering over a reef two hours before.

The only thing Rogers found hard was going to the lavatory. He didn't like to squat in the lukewarm sea to excrete, nor to see his dung bob up beside him. But the alternative was to go inland among the palms, where quite apart from the harassment of the insects there was always the risk of being discovered by one of the inhabitants. And there was something particularly unpleasant about the smell in that dark tropical warmth. Almost as if the smell was welcome there and suited the environment, which only made it worse.

Rogers got the story of the little villages here and on Chichimen piecemeal from Paulina. She knew Don Ramon and his entourage well. In fact she regarded Don Ramon as an enemy.

'Twenty years he has kept my father here,' she repeated. 'He has to look after all the coconut trees here. They are Don Ramon's.'

It was hard to think of the scruffy old Don Ramon eating off broken frisbees as the cruel latifundista, but Paulina did. Apparently many years ago Achu, her father, had fallen in love with Paulina's mother, now dead, a woman who had been betrothed to Don Ramon. Ramon had invoked an ancient custom whereby on her death Achu had been obliged to make up the theft, as they saw it, of the bride. Meanwhile, Don Ramon had himself anyway grown estranged from his own wife, who lived on another island, and had taken up with Jorge, the excitable homosexual on Chichimen.

It was like a light opera, Rogers thought, or perhaps a soap opera; a folkloric drama of the kind that might have amused an Enlightenment court. Delightful because the protagonists lived in concord with their environment, were made of the very same fabric as their world, constituted of salt water, coconut juice and fishbone. When he was fishing in the canoe with the blood and scales scattered about him, the smell of fish oil on his fingers, the odour of death and the sea in his nostrils, Rogers would feel that he too was entering the embrace of this world.

Every evening Achu would saunter over to their hut with a frayed tea towel over his shoulder and stand just outside the eaves in the last of the light conducting a stilted, formal and somehow necessary chat. Then he'd make his way to the well under the trees and in the grey light strip his long, sinewy body and wash it with fresh water scooped from a bucket.

Around the same time, when the sun had retreated and the water was thick as paint, Rogers would go for a swim, marvelling at his shoulders being dark already as wood against the green water. Every evening they seemed darker, a wonderful deepening colour, as if he were a creature of sand, made of sand for sand.

'Why don't you come to America?' he asked her one night. Surely everyone wanted to come to America. He himself had longed to, and been glad that he did.

'America,' she said, turning her head slowly, and looking out the door as if to catch a glimpse of the continent.

She could come and live with him, why not? And if there were visa problems, well, they could just go ahead and marry. He didn't see why not. He could handle it, he wouldn't ask too much of it. Was this all that he had been missing, the company of a calm woman?

She pulled his hammock close and kissed him.

He liked the island best at noon when the palms stopped shivering. The sea became the optical equivalent of a tree full of singing cicadas – a dazzling light that deafened the eye. Nothing moved. The stillness would crawl up him like warm water.

He looked out from their shelter at the sea of ancient masts, of ships and tenders, dugouts and yawls, the pirate's silver anvil, the merchant's bowl, and reflected that there was nothing to date the scene, not even he himself. Three nearby islands hovered on the horizon, blue, black, grey, hanging there like dreams you couldn't quite remember, or quite forget, like dreams waiting to be dreamt.

Now and then a coconut would thud to the ground. Half a mile offshore the reef roared: the thunder at the edge of the world. The girl might sing a song. If he asked her what it was about, she would laugh and say it was a song for wind – if the seawind blew then the mosquitoes wouldn't get out of their beds – or a song for fish so they would not go hungry. Once she told him a story about her uncle who became a shark. She would swim out to meet him when she died.

Several times at night immaculate thunderstorms arrived. They'd sit on driftwood logs while fantastic cloudscapes erupted from the night, hovering and flickering overhead. He would consider: this is a good place to be, under palm thatch on a sandy island, as explosions pealed from the sky like gunfire, like flak. When the rain came they'd retire to the hammock and make love to the water-chime of droplets streaming from their roof. She was an expert, a maestra of love in a sling, hooking it behind the knee, beneath the thigh, for expansion, contraction, rhythm and tension. When finally they slept the night would be warm and still, and he'd hear the reef thundering in the back of his mind like a memory of safety.

He woke one morning and discovered that he didn't know what day it was. He was alarmed, then delighted. He couldn't remember ever feeling that before – the day of the week simply made no difference.

He began to imagine how easily the island could feel like home. This was a world that in its very fabric wanted to hold and nourish you. The plainness of its mornings, the chalky dawns, the need to get up and swim and go fishing, the somnolence of the afternoons when it was best to lie still and listen to the slapping and running of the sea and hope the wind was coming off the sea not the land, to keep down the biting insects – all this felt like home, like a world he had been built for.

10

One morning a speedboat appeared in the lagoon. Rogers couldn't quite believe it was really there. The gurgling, smoking vessel of white plastic didn't belong in this world of sand and wood. Its presence seemed to defy the laws of physics. It came like an apparition, smelling strongly of exhaust, a sweet, exhilarating smell.

He stood staring at it, rooted to the spot. Only when it turned and began its approach towards the beach did Rogers realise that it could mean only one thing: Jones was back.

Dread opened up in him. He didn't know what to do, but felt a pressing need to do something. In his dazed, island-lulled condition, and with the quiet roar of the reef as if permanently implanted in his ear, he couldn't figure out what it was.

He turned and ran back towards the hut. He met Paulina coming down the track through the wood.

'Jones is here,' he told her. 'You've got to listen to me. He's going to want to take me to a council meeting. Is your father a sahila yet – now that you have the money –'

'As soon as he pays Don Ramon.'

'Did you give him the money?'

'Of course.'

'So he and I will go over to Don Ramon's so he can pay it. You stay here. I have to sort some things out. But hide. Don't let Jones see you.'

She smiled and shrugged.

'Go into the interior of the island. He's crazy. I don't know what he might do.'

'This is Kuna Yala, I don't need to hide.'

'You do. Please.'

She smiled and cocked her head like it was a game and she would humour him, why not. She shrugged and kissed him on the cheek and sauntered away.

Rogers ran back to the beach.

Albert Jones called out to him from the boat. He beckoned from his seat, one hand on the gleaming chrome steering wheel as the boat's stern drifted towards the sand, spitting from two exhaust pipes. 'Get your stuff, let's go.'

For a moment Rogers couldn't think how he knew this man. The silver bouffant and white shorts and clean brown body sprinkled with curly silver hairs seemed to be part of the boat. He, Rogers, had been living in his sea-dream; now the land had come to wake him and he didn't recognise it. His chest tightened and he became aware of the blood in his veins – especially once Jones tossed him a can of beer. When he levered the top with his big-nailed finger and heard the explosive gasp of aluminium and smelled the smell of beer the dread came back. He shouldn't be leaving, it wouldn't be as easy as he thought to get back. And that wasn't all.

Rogers left the beer on the beach and ran into the first hut, where Achu was just getting ready to light a fire. 'You have to come with me. We'll go to Don Ramon first. I'll explain. You're a sahila now, I need you to talk to the other sahilas. I'll tell you everything on the way. Hurry please.'

Achu stood to his full height and walked out. 'I did hear the boat,' was all he said, and Rogers wondered that a man could go on a journey with nothing but the shorts he stood in. No bag, no briefcase, no wallet even. Just his bones and flesh and skin.

As they climbed into the boat, Rogers told Jones: 'This is Don Achu. He's a sahila and friend. We need him. And I left something on Chichimen, I need to swing there first.'

Jones looked at Rogers and was about to say something. Then he lifted his shoulders and said, 'OK, we've got time.' He reached back and shook Achu's hand. 'Achu?'

'Don Carlos,' he said. 'They call me Achu.'

Jones raised his eyebrows, then in English said to Rogers: 'Achu's not much of a name round here. It means dog.'

As the boat roared out of the lagoon, squirming on its trajectory then settling into a true course, Rogers stared back, transfixed by the V of its wake, by the flattened hood of bubbles at its apex. The shape was so like something he knew. When he realised what it was, saw the watery shape take the girl's intimate form, he looked away embarrassed, then kept sneaking glances at it. It was mesmerising.

The first swig of beer reminded Rogers where he was now: back in the brassy world. He looked at Jones's back. A plastic man who belonged in his plastic boat.

Rogers wanted to jump off, anything to get back to the island. He imagined how he'd swirl about in the bubbles then swim to the nearest island. He'd make it. He could wait till they were passing some islet. The dreaminess was still there, and as long as he could stay in touch with that it would carry him to safety.

'Here's the deal,' Jones shouted over the engine. 'The chiefs want to meet you. They're holding the council meeting tonight, on Rio Tigre. We're building a dock for them. We get that through and we're OK. We've got the contracts drawn up and ready to sign.'

Rogers listened to the voice but his mind was still hearing the boom of the reef, still floating in the little island's lull.

At Chichimen they found Don Ramon sitting outside his hut on a log roller. 'Yes sir,' Ramon called as they climbed from the boat. Without a word Achu went up to him and handed him a folded wad of notes. Don Ramon took it and looked up at the man, then got up and walked into his hut. Jones followed him, and emerged a minute later.

When they were back in the boat, roaring along with the great barrier of mountains always to their right, Jones beckoned Rogers up to the cockpit.

'Who is this guy?'

'The girl's dad.'

'Why is he here?'

'He's a sahila. He's on our side.'

Jones frowned. 'Ramon says we shouldn't trust him. I don't like it. He should take a hike. We don't need anything rocking the boat right now. We're good as we are.'

'He won't rock the boat.'

Jones cut the throttle right back and said, 'Something up with the propeller. Hey,' he called back to Achu. 'Can you see anything back there?'

Achu peered over the stern. Just as he bent low, Jones slammed the throttle forwards, and the boat surged, tipping Achu neatly into the water.

As they gathered speed Rogers hesitated a moment, in the grip of unknowables, and seeing that he could not know just then what was best, but aware that Jones still needed him, he had the American angle to bring to the table, he stepped up on to the side and jumped off too.

A shiny, dark surface hit him in the face, and he was paddling in seething white, and the sound of the boat had gone, replaced by a tremendous hiss. He turned. Achu was already calmly swimming towards a bright green island close enough for the mesh of its palm trunks to be distinguishable. Rogers paused, searching for the boat. It was far away, a little white box moving above a little jet of wake. Its shape changed as he watched, elongating. It was veering to the right. Then it diminished again, and a star settled right in the middle of it, on what must have been the point of the prow. He couldn't hear it at all. He kept swimming.

When the boat was getting close Rogers tipped himself up and sank head first. He swam slowly in order not to waste his breath, and guessed Achu would be doing the same. The boat sounded like a little toy now, a tinny drilling passing overhead. He saw the white fork travel over him like a zipper, blurred. Water got in his nostrils and he looked down again. Underwater, he carried on swimming in the direction of the island. Five strokes, six. When his lungs were aching and gagging he let himself come up. The boat was all but inaudible now, a faint ringing in the ears. He exhaled before he broke the surface, came up into the brilliant day long enough to inhale, sank under again, hanging just below the surface so he could rise to take another breath, and another. After the third, during which he glimpsed Achu's small head sinking under the surface ahead, he resumed his slow submarine progress towards that nearest island.

Jones in his speedboat skated over the surface in figures of eight, loops and curves, a shiny little chunk of Panama City searching, searching, not knowing where to go, winking in the sunlight on the broad blue sea.

Rogers rolled in the shallows of an empty beach, raising his head to breathe, lowering it again into the green water. When he looked again, he could just make out the speedboat, glinting far away.

Achu was already standing among the palms at the edge of the beach. Rogers got up and joined him.

'What do we do now? We need to get to Rio Tigre.'

Achu didn't answer, but set about gathering sticks and dried sea-moss that lay scattered on the sand. When he had enough of a pile, he set to with two sticks, drilling one against the other with his palms. Rogers had always believed that method of starting a fire to be near-impossible except in archaeology textbooks, but in a little while, smoke drifted from where the sticks met, and quickly Achu fed moss to it, blowing hard, in fast, deep breaths. The moss kindled and sparked, and a smoking line travelled across the bunch. Achu piled more on, kept blowing, and soon Rogers heard a crackle and saw a small pale flame lick across the parched web.

He gathered more twigs to feed it.

It was late morning by the sun, perhaps a couple of hours later, when a sailing dugout came scudding along the beach.

'I see the smoke,' its pilot, a man in glasses, called out.

It was Henry Rawlinson again. 'Yes, I see the smoke on Delfina Island, I thinking, nobody live there. What's up? You gentlemen step aboard.'

'Rio Tigre, fast as you can,' Rogers said, adding: 'If you possibly can.'

Henry was happy to pass the day helpfully, it seemed.

Rogers reckoned that in a good wind the sailing canoe might average five knots. He knew Rio Tigre was the last island, but the whole chain was only a hundred miles long, and they were already some way down it, so it couldn't have been much more than ten hours away. If the wind kept up they'd surely make it in time for the night's council session. And anyway, surely if new information arrived, the council of sahilas could reconsider a decision.

But it seemed not.

'It's a matter of principle,' Achu explained. 'There are seventeen sahilas. If they put their name to it, they can't go back.'

Jones would have them signing tonight if he could.

As they rustled along the coastline, past the many islets, Rogers told Achu: 'You'll have to use your vote tonight. And your voice.'

They passed dugouts with sails, dugouts being paddled, and island after island. Sometimes grinning families sailed past them. Rogers began to enjoy the ride, the sunshine, the silence of the boat. What a week, he thought. He had possibly fallen in love, he had lived a neolithic life, learnt to live on a desert island. And now he was gliding along the coast of Darien in a Stone Age canoe.

He soon dried off in the hot breeze. His shorts and shirt felt stiff as canvas.

In the late afternoon, when the light was beginning to grow rich, and the sun laid a glittering highway across the dark sea, they reached a far-flung island all on its own. Judging by how far they had come, they must have been close to the Colombian border. All the island's ranked canoe prows bristled from the shore. It was a thatch fort, a Viking camp.

Somewhere on the south side a concrete wharf had been half built. Tied to it, a beaten-up barge sagged in the water under the weight of piles and piles of supplies, heaps of orange sacks and onion sacks, stacks of boxes. Among all the produce on deck unshaven men dozed in hammocks. Sailors. A small army of sailors. In the prow of the boat a mountain of green coconuts bleached in the sun.

The men shocked Rogers. They were fat and their facial hair was a surprise (he hadn't looked at himself in a mirror for some time) and they were altogether big. Big and coarse. With a sudden discomfort he realised they were his people, westerners.

'They come from Cartagena to buy coconuts,' Henry

Rawlinson informed him. 'They buy them green. The people here buy clothes and shoes and pots from them.'

Big people, ugly, fat, without any grace at all, completely lacking the Cunas' lightness of touch and build. Rogers stood in the sunshine in the middle of a concrete plaza beside the quay, shocked to realise that it was these men he had been planning to help. His job was to get behind Jones and help him open up this paradise to fat, ugly men who had no idea how to treat themselves, much less a desert island, who could only come up with roaring engines and beer and plastic trinkets to sell for green vouchers exchangeable for more beer and motorboats. This, right here, was the very point of civilisation's drill; here, where the men of finance were preparing the way for the men with hard hats and survey sticks; here, where Balboa first saw the Pacific and knew he had found not the East Indies but an unknown continent, and gave birth to the Atlantic market of iron, of chains and cauldrons and human bone. The jigsaw towers of Manhattan, Milwaukee, Cincinnati, all the concreted prairies and drained swamps sold over and over, owed their beginning to this very meeting of Colombian and Cuna. And what had it all achieved? A wake of ruin, of bereft children, miserable mothers.

They idled away what was left of the day in a long-house with just three scrawny hammocks in its cavernous dark. Tall wooden drums and giant panpipes leaned against either wall, waiting for some ceremony to call them forth. Rogers wondered when the people used them. He had heard little of Cuna music. Now and then a child would peer in from the street, stare at the strange men and go away. It was more like a warehouse than a home, an abandoned place with a few relics left in it.

In the evening they moved through the hurricane-lit village to another longhouse. This one was filled with a haze of tobacco smoke hanging above rows of benches, on which sat a crowd of Cuna men, all of them smoking pipes or cigarettes, and chatting away, raising a thick murmur of sound. At the front three elders swung in white hammocks chanting to one another in high-pitched voices. The mumbling and chanting together made a kind of music.

As soon as they walked in, Jones was at Rogers' side. 'What happened to you, man? What's up with you?' He stared at Rogers, his eyes gleaming in the dark. 'Anyway, you're here. This is our chance. Don't fuck with it.' Jones led him to a bench.

An old man in a chair at the front pulled his pipe from his mouth and began talking in a muffled voice, addressing the floor a few feet in front of him, and gradually everyone fell silent. Then they all laughed. The old man had apparently cracked a joke. He stood up, as if getting into his stride, and began to find a rhythm in his speech. His voice was a masterpiece of rhetoric, even if you couldn't understand a word of it. It climbed imaginary staircases, sprinted over cliff edges, plummeted to valley floors, climbed all over again. Here and there, in pauses, you could hear the soft bubble of men sucking on their pipes as they waited for the next punchline, and the hiss of the one hurricane lamp hanging on its nail at the front, casting a sharp glow through the room.

Eventually the old man sat down. Then one of the three elders in hammocks, a toothless man who could have been cousin to Don Ramon, without getting up, without even lifting his head from the pale strings of his hammock, began to chant again. He finished with a curious singing coda, a series of rising curlicues of falsetto, then carried on swinging as calmly as if he had been silently listening all along.

Jones sat beside Rogers on the bench with his arms folded across his chest, immovable. Rogers could feel Jones's bony knuckles digging into his side. Finally Jones prodded him and murmured in his ear: 'Tell them you're happy to be working together with the Cunas. It's a big honour for an American company to bring its expertise. Big honour.' Then he prodded him again and told him to stand up.

As he stood, Rogers realised it hadn't been Jones's knuckle he had been feeling in his side, but something smaller, rounder and harder. In the shock of realising what it had been, he found himself repeating Jones's words. Then he sat down again. A man with a dark shiny face gave him a cigarette, and someone rang a bell at the back of the hall.

Rogers had been in a daze, numb and automaton-like. But at the sound of the bell an acute sadness welled up in him. He thought of Paulina, a beautiful woman forced to bring herself to the ugly city, and of the awkward advantage he had taken of her, and of how he felt towards her now; and a boiling, angry, active sadness drove him out of his seat towards the chiefs in their hammocks. He stood before them and spoke his mind. They lay there swinging as he talked, giving no sign that they heard anything he said. He told them that neither he nor Jones were to be trusted, that their plan was to deceive the Cunas and profit from them.

When he finished still no one said anything. One of the elders glanced up at him with a lively, animal eye sparkling in leathery folds of skin, and struck a stick on the floor. There was a murmur among the benches. Rogers looked round just as Jones arrived at his side. Again he felt the barrel tip in his ribs.

'You come with me.' Jones grabbed his arm and pulled him to the back of the hall, then outside. As he left he glimpsed Achu rising to his feet to address the assembly.

Rogers wanted to explain to Jones, convey why their plan was a bad one and must be abandoned. This place could not possibly survive having a pipeline stabbed through it. It was a delicate world. He started speaking, but Jones only jabbed the gun harder into him, making him wince.

He walked Rogers down an alley to a strip of shingle among the houses, where a dugout was waiting, with the albino man in the stern. They climbed in and the albino began to power the canoe out with choppy heavy strokes of a paddle. In a while a pale hull suddenly loomed out of the darkness pushing a plume of white water in front of it. It sank and settled into the black water just ahead of them. Jones reached up for the boat's gunwale and scrambled on board, followed by the albino, who as he climbed up pushed the canoe away with his bare foot.

'No, no,' Jones snapped. 'Don't let it go. He's coming too.'

Rogers threw up the dugout's painter, still vaguely hoping he might win Jones round. Someone up on the boat wearing a black commando hat caught the rope. Rogers recognised now that this wasn't the same speedboat Jones had had earlier, but something bigger.

Jones told the man to tie up the canoe, then shouted down to Rogers: 'You shouldn't mess with what you don't know.' He held out the gun. 'This is fucking real,' he cried over the boat's gurgling engine. 'Do you realise how big this deal is? Do you have any idea of the kind of money involved? This is the kind of thing that changes the world, amigo, changes it for ever, makes it a better place for all of us. You really think we can't find other investors? Someone like you should fuck off from where you don't belong. You could have had a piece, my friend. You should learn to keep your fucking nose clean.'

The big launch began to roar, pulling the dugout after it.

Rogers, who hadn't eaten all day and was still dazed by the long hours of sun and by all that had happened, sat in the bottom of the dugout gripping either side of his wooden torpedo, which slid and slithered and tipped and sprayed him from its snub end as it shot through the water.

Finally they cut him loose and roared off with a parting shout he couldn't make out.

Rogers knew that all he had to do was determine

which way was south and go that way, towards land. They hadn't come far. He would soon reach shore. He had a paddle. And he was in the safest place in the world, on the warm black sea under the blanket of night, within the encircling reef.

The buzzing of the big launch had already taken itself into silence. Quiet. Black sea. The sound of surf pounding somewhere, noisily drawing breath. He would go towards it.

He paddled through darkness. The sea rippled under him, carving long easy swells, tremendously long gentle slopes that went up for a hundred yards, then down, so gentle you could miss them in the dark.

Suddenly the surf was louder. He had been dreaming. And the paddle, as he dug with it, struck something under the water and flew out of his hand. He turned round and the canoe wobbled and already the paddle was moving away, out of reach, and was nothing more than a pale gleam in the water. He could see it but only just. He got to his knees to dive in after it but thought: What about the canoe? Supposing it drifted too far for him to see it in the dark? It seemed pre-eminently unwise to leave his vessel. So he decided to dive while holding what was left of the boat's painter. He wrapped the cord round his hand and leapt. Time was everything, the paddle was moving away, already he had lost sight of it and as he dived he wondered if the rope was long enough, wondered how short they had cut it, and the next thing he knew a flash bulb had exploded in his shoulder. Then something was running over his back, something long with coarse skin.

He span round. It was just the canoe. But his shoulder had gone ice-cold now and he had lost all sense of direction, had no idea which way the paddle had gone.

The rope was still attached to his hand, though. He tugged on it and the dugout turned and came smoothly towards him, as if gliding on runners, so that he had to dodge it.

He had never known it be so hard to climb on board. With one arm out of action, he had to lodge his elbow over the prow and try to kick his leg over the side, all without capsizing the trunk. It didn't work. He tried innumerable times then hung still, getting his breath back. His chest felt heavy, and stung badly. Perhaps he had grazed it against the wooden side. He passed himself hand over hand to the stern. It wasn't easy there either. There was nothing to get a foot or knee on, being right at the end, and the only way was to drag himself, heave by heave, right over the wood, which made his chest rage and burn even more. But he managed it.

He rolled on to his back and lay still in the bottom of the boat. Ripples lapped against the hull in a way that at first he found irritating, then soothing. But still, to be floating in a dugout without a paddle – it was unbelievable, and all night long too. At least it was warm and he would soon dry off.

Meanwhile, his chest was gently bleeding. He looked down and ran his hand over it. It was covered with little slits. Soon they coalesced into a single dark patch. The side of the boat must have done it as he dragged himself over. There was nothing he could do except lie still and hope the cuts congealed quickly. He didn't want to inspect them. Better not to know. One leg ached, his shoulder was still completely numb and his chest stung. But that might be a good sign, a sign of shallow wounds and things on the mend already. Just cuts.

The worst thing by far was that the boat leaked. Perhaps it had struck a rock while he was out of it, loosening a tin patch that had been nailed in. He lay in a cold gutter of water. By heaving himself into the bow he was able to keep most of a gash in the stern clear of the surface, but he could see the crack gently seeping. Sooner or later he would have to figure out something to bail with, if he could manage to move. But he was drifting off, finding it hard to remember where he was. Thank God he liked sushi. Later, when it got light, he could try to fish. Though how he'd gut a fish without a knife, or catch one without a hook, he didn't stop to think.

The water stirred, the canoe shifted. The thunder of the reef had abated. His heartbeat steadied. When it grew light and he could see where he was, he would paddle for shore. For now, he folded his hands high on his chest, above the wounds, and waited for dawn.

He woke up in his apartment on West Thirteenth. It seemed a lovely place, small, just the right size for him. How lucky it was that he had no children yet, that there was time still for all that if he wanted it, that his and Candlebury's had been a clean break. In a sense he had even yet to begin his real life, there was still time, he could start all over again, for real, he could leave Wall

Street, move into some entirely different field, and concentrate on things that mattered. He longed to sit again in his black leather armchair and watch a soccer match with his Colombian neighbour. That man had short hair. A number two, he guessed. He could see the lovely strip of dust-rich sunlight that lay across the dark kitchen counter at a certain hour of the morning. He would look at it and imagine he could almost hear it, it was that peaceful a sight.

It was the hardest thing, to admit a mistake. He had made a mistake. He had lost Candlebury. He had allowed them to lose each other; he had lost her because he had lost himself. And he hadn't been able to admit it, neither part of it. To accept that he had steered his life up the wrong creek was to say he should still be with her; which he hadn't the heart to say. Equally, to admit he had erred in losing her could only mean that the new life he had sought after her was also mistaken; which he could not bear to consider. But it was the truth. And although there was no chance now of winning her back, he could own up to the loss, and mourn it finally. He could do it within the embrace of the small life he had inadvertently created for himself. He could really be all right. Which meant happy. He was astonished by the realisation, and felt a buzz in his limbs.

It was all because of the girl. She was right for him. How she came to be so, a girl from such a different world, he couldn't say, but she was. He missed her, but more than that he was happy to have found her.

Why wasn't he worried? Despite the aches in his flesh, he felt flushed through with achievement. Then it occurred to him that feeling this good might mean he was about to die. Even that didn't dent his mood. If he was on his way to the end so be it. He could enjoy that too.

It was hard to believe he really was where he was, adrift in a boat hardly bigger than his own body. It was hard too to know how bad the situation was. Many islands lay nearby, and plenty of dugout traffic moved between them by day. Someone would surely see him in the morning, and anyway he was floating, thank God, within the reef. At some point if the worst came to the worst he could simply swim to the nearest island.

He thought of Paulina with a twist of longing. He knew she would be all right. She was that kind of woman: strong, and she knew her world well. He would have to find her right away, as soon as he could. Would she want to come to New York? It was a possibility. And what if not? Perhaps he'd set up some kind of business down in Panama. Or perhaps she would just end up being a beautiful episode, his rescue.

The matter in hand now was to get to shore, any shore. It was lucky the lagoon was calm. There was nothing for it but to sit up and paddle with his hands, he supposed. He began to do so. What did it matter which way? You couldn't go wrong here.

The only sound was the light, rapid slapping of wavelets under the trunk. It was a dark night. A firmament of stars, fierce and crackling, and no moon. He thought he could see the mainland because it ate a chunk out of the stars, a great black bite. But you couldn't really see it. And later the stars overhead had been eaten up too.

The water felt warm in his cupped fingers as he paddled. He sat with his knees pressed against either side to help steady him. More than anything, just then, he was relieved to be by himself, out of the vortex that trailed behind Jones and whoever his cohorts were. It was clear that they would bother with him no more, because they didn't need to. He was nothing, a Walter Mitty in the wrong place. And the wrong place had spat him out. It was a huge relief to be in the right place once more, where there was less money, much less, and less excitement and madness and drugs, but where he belonged.

A shooting star frothed past beneath his left hand. He stopped paddling. What was it? Probably a bonito, he thought. But it unnerved him. And he was tired. His shoulders ached as if he had been lifting weights. They felt abominably stiff. He would rest for a while. He lay back in the boat and waited, he wasn't sure what for. That didn't work, so he sat up and resumed paddling, keeping a lookout for any more water-borne shooting stars. The ache in his right shoulder got worse. He must have hurt it in the scuffle with the shark. What shark? What scuffle? he wondered. He couldn't keep up the paddling. Every stroke made the hurt worse. A colossal sleepiness overcame him. He lay on his back and shut out the stars, hung in universal blackness.

Dreams thundered in his skull.

He awoke to universal ache. His body was so stiff he couldn't even lift his head. The whole world was grey. Grey and drab-looking like an English afternoon in

February. He decided he'd lie still and wait for the sun to warm him. Luckily the boat had filled with only two or three inches of water. His back, and the backs of his legs, lay in the water, but the rest of him was dry. In the night he had lodged his head on what was left of the rope. He thought he could feel it still there.

The happy feeling quickly woke up too and flooded him so thoroughly that he couldn't move at all now. Why so happy? He remembered, and felt doubly happy that he did remember. He was somewhere he loved. And the girl. Paulina. Nikiri. He loved her. It hardly mattered if he saw her now; it was good just to feel this love. How did he know he loved her? Who knew? Who cared? The world was simple. It consisted of palm trees and islands and salty water in between, and a big mountainous mainland nearby where big trees grew and there were people on the islands who kept them clean. The people travelled between the islands in boats made of tree trunks that grew on the mainland and intended to love their islands and one another. Nikiri loved him and he her. He didn't have to think of her, her brown eyes and bronze face and tobacco limbs, because she was already quietly living in him. Once he lay still and the ache quieted he could feel her all through him.

Daybreak was pleasant. Gentle light, gentle sea, gentle islands like smudges of paint. The mainland was invisible today, lost in cloud. He would see these things as the canoe rose and fell. Everything had gone quiet: other than the tinkling of the ripples against the hull there wasn't a sound in the world. The whole of Darien had gone quiet.

Quiet as a picture. Even he too had become silent. What was this sensation? It was like turning down the sound on the TV. Except here it happened to you too. When a little wave slapped, it slapped inside him.

The sun dislodged itself from the cement horizon, rising like a great old bloom. But quickly it shed its old petals and became too bright to look at. Rogers could move now. He propped his head on the side of the boat to get a look at what was going on.

Throughout the day the sun embraced you, kissing you right on the forehead. It heated up your flesh and warmed your wounds. He found he could rock from side to side. He thought he would need to move in order to bail and fish, but the leak seemed to have stopped itself, and he wasn't hungry. He'd fish once he was hungry. The fresher the better, if they were to be eaten raw. And anyway, he'd be picked up soon.

The sun was a hole and it drilled a hole just like itself in you. It made you its son: the sun's son. You joined the sun in its strange life. The sun was an eye. It looked at you, wheeling slowly round you, looking at you all the while, and you looked back at it. It created a new eye for you to look at it with.

When dusk came he couldn't remember how many evenings had arrived like this. Was this the second? the first? had there been many? Did he always live like this? And what did 'live' mean? What was the darkness, and what was the light? What did 'day' mean? It meant: 'lie still and wait'.

Morning came again and the sea was much rougher

today. But the world was quieter. The reef had finally slipped away and gone where it wanted. The canoe was tipping right up, wriggling around, then tipping back. There was more water in it. He cupped one hand and found he could bail without moving. All he had to do was lift and drop the hand, tipping water over the side. Brown water, rust-coloured. Great heavy handfuls left the boat. He could feel the lovely weight of water like stones in his hand.

He manoeuvred himself on to his side, looked out, and came face to face with a blue rippled brow, which sank before his eyes, rushing under him, all in a rush and bustle, then the faint line of horizon swung into view. But only for a moment, until another mountainside of blue came hurrying in like a big housewife with all her shopping and her five children, hurrying down the high street. It made him dizzy to watch.

He tried the other side of the boat and saw the housewives heaving away from him, opening up gullies that yawned under the boat. His head swam. He caught another glimpse of open horizon. He looked past his feet, waiting to be lifted up high to get the view. The islands had all travelled away, leaving him alone.

That seemed right. It was right that he be here on his own. He only wished that the endless moving might stop. He closed his eyes and let his head sink. The bottom of the boat had become a sponge. Your belly gurgled and danced. Sometimes it slammed into your throat. Which hurt to begin with but he was used to it now. It was like having a thunderstorm within you. The thunder cracked and up came the lightning, into your mouth.

The sun nailed him to the board. Which was still again, a sheet of plywood that someone had painted green. Tap, tap, tap, went the sun, fixing you to the board so you couldn't move any more. This was fine. Never to move again. Only the silky rustle of your breaths like dark hills rising and falling, rising and falling. They were still permitted to move. But soon night would come and they too would be still. Then the whole world would be silent, transfixed by its own stillness, and darkness would whisper the last farewell to the last thing that moved.

Rogers was in the water. Silver water, with a shimmery blue-silver surface of mercury somewhere below him, or above. An animal, a grey creature, came up and nudged him in the side. A dolphin, he thought. Now he had broken out into a great bright cave. A dark triangle whistled past him, then came back travelling more slowly, quietly, then speeded up suddenly and shot past him close by.

Just a dog, a sea-dog: a shark. It had gone. Then there was its blunt grey nose again, drifting up to sniff him, asking to be stroked, its head a lump of gristle. He jabbed at it. The body flicked and span away. Part of it, the tail perhaps, caught him. He felt the knock on his arm. Then a moment later it was back again attempting to nuzzle him. He grabbed hold of it, got his arms right round and gripped tight, clutching his wrist in his fingers. He squeezed as tight as he could. The beast wriggled but he didn't let go. It hurried on in stilted spurts, carrying him with it. He felt it trying to thrash harder but he wouldn't release his grip. He could feel a panic wanting to rise in his lungs but getting waylaid. Who did it think it was, swimming up to him like that? He squeezed tighter, hoping to suffocate it, or at least hurt it. Then it dived. He clung on. His ears creaked and screamed and he let go. Some part of the beast knocked his calf as it vanished into the deep.

Then it was back and again he lunged at it, grabbed hold of it, and this time it pulled him streaking across the surface, riding the slippery mercury, then they were out in the broad bright cave again, knocking against a wall, the two of them, banging and banging against a sheet of iron. And now hooks had been sent down and were grappling with his arms, someone had hooked the damn fish with a great cable of a line, and dark big hands were reaching down for it, and for him, a boathook was under his shoulder, digging in his armpit, pulling him up out of the water, hoisting him into brightness. There was a hissing and roaring of water, and the silence had been broken now for good.

Road Movie

It was crazy, I know, but we didn't leave for the west coast until a whole month after my visa ran out. The delay was Carmela's fault. She was waiting for a sign. I'd already received two letters, certified delivery, and a week ago a friend in similar straits got driven out to JFK courtesy of the INS with only half an hour to pack. What more of a sign do you need? I asked her. But not until last Sunday, day of the new moon, did the stars finally say the time was right. (Carmela is an astrologer by profession, anyway by inclination.) Holy day, holy city, she said.

She wanted to wed in Santa Fe on our way west. She is part Taíno Indian and wouldn't do it on land desecrated by the blood of natives. Such as Manhattan.

So picture a stripped apartment, winter sunlight flooding in, piles of boxes everywhere. A woman with long black hair seated on bare floorboards smiles and weeps into the telephone. Behind her a man stares out the window. We swing round and see his face: clear blue eyes, reddish stubble on his jaw, almost a beard. He looks foreign. Perhaps it is his harsh, incongruously dark eyebrows or his soft, protuberant lips. He also looks anxious. We turn to the dusty window and follow his gaze down on to a slurry of commuter traffic glinting on a wide street . . .

Something like that anyway. The reality was a lot less orderly. Carmela did spend the last hour on the telephone but I didn't stand staring out of a window. I was too busy packing her multifarious belongings.

We will leave in painful sunshine, Carmela had told me in the oracular tone she adopts after consultation of cards and almanac. She was right. Nowhere in the world *does* a sunny winter morning like New York. That effervescent sunlight only the Hudson River knows how to throw off its back by the shovelful, the glistening fire escapes, each cross-street rosy on one side, plunged in shade on the other, and the cars still few – a yellow taxi gleaming like a beetle, a thunderous truck making a dash for a tunnel, a silver car with a jacket hooked against the back window gliding towards an office. It's hard not to love it. It is painful to leave. Especially when all the little breakfasteries, the delis and donuteries and muffineries, are rattling up their shutters and putting on the coffee to brew. Nowhere does a cup of coffee belong in your hands – the wisp of steam in front of your face mimicking the subway vents – like it does on a Manhattan morning.

Carmela's apartment was in one of those heavy buildings on the lower West Side. Down there the fashion in some clunky utilitarian spasm early this century was for blocks as near cubic as you could get them, constructed of bricks of a sobering shade of maroon. *Maroon* may sound fancy but imagine a three-hundred-foot wall of it. It's as uplifting as the grey gifts the Soviets left back home. I had perched there for four months up on the fourteenth floor (really the thirteenth: no one ever tells you how superstitious Americans are).

Imagine me hurrying along West Street beside the silver sheet of the Hudson, turning into a little office beside a U-Haul lot.

'Carel?' asks a tubby man behind the counter.

'Felix?'

We shake hands, grinning like long-lost friends. Felix is the rental man I spoke to on the telephone. He takes a long time preparing the paperwork, tapping away at his computer.

Meanwhile, a television chatters on the counter. A guy is saying, 'Well, Larry, this is gonna be the big one. We've got twenty inches al*read*y in Oregon, this baby is dumping it, and it's heading right on down to the Midwest.'

The Weather Channel.

'Mm-hmm,' Felix says, still tapping away. 'Sounds like you gonna hit some weather.'

The snowstorm of the year, they called it. Oh great, I thought. Sometimes I can't make head or tail of Carmela. If she wants to help me why she can't just say yes and be done with it, why we have to do it in New Mexico, why we couldn't leave till today.

I cursed inwardly then remembered what old Lepelski, chairman of the academy, used to say: a good director can use any weather.

Next shot: me and the doorman wheeling a trolley of

boxes out to a silver U-Haul. As we load up I'm frowning and jumping about like a character in a silent movie.

Carmela put on her dark glasses and marched across the lobby. 'Sometimes you've just got to go,' she said as she climbed into the truck. I could see her bottom lip trembling.

'If it doesn't work out . . .' I began.

'It's going to work out.'

We hadn't gone a block before she was crying again, staring straight ahead and shaking silently.

Cut to: the gleaming silver truck suddenly going grey as it passes into a tunnel. Green sign overhead: You Are Now Leaving New York.

On the road at last.

The truck, sprung like a boat, rocks and sways gently. One stick does everything – wipers, indicators, lights. Power steering, automatic: you drive with one finger, one toe. Its big engine hisses as it gathers speed. You ride high. I like that. Only the drivers of the eighteen-wheelers ride higher.

So a little about myself. I am a man with a beard: definitely more than stubble. I am a good film-maker because I am meticulous. If I hadn't got into the directorial side I could have made a great technician. I'm good with machines. I understand them, I like them, I am patient with them. I'm a good editor as a result. And I love my job, or rather my vocation, for it is not always a job. Isn't that the first thing you learn about film-making? You expect all this money to come showering down on you but even the big guys go months without work – lots of time to brood. What made me flee my native Czech skies? Suffice to say, what film-maker doesn't want to be in America? And as far as Hollywood is concerned, to be Czech is to be good. Eastern Europe and celluloid go together like burgers and ketchup. Let us hope.

But enough of that. There's something much more interesting going on outside the window: America!

All morning it was beautiful spring weather. The New Jersey Turnpike white under the sun clicked peaceably on its joins. The land looked sanitary. That was the real America, a place so clean you could eat off the suburban streets, a place people rinse their car tyres every week. I love it. Why do people moan about America? Even Americans do. Carmela does. She says the only place she ever wanted to live is New York. As for the rest, the towns are heartless, there are cars everywhere and all the states have the same McDonald's and Burger Kings.

So what! Give me McDonald's signs glowing in the evening by highway turn-offs. Give me quarterpounders. Give me quarterbacks and quarterhorses too. And quarters. Give me five-laners in the middle of cities and a hundred yards of parking between the stores. Give me suburban blocks with kiddieways under the trees because the streets are so dangerous, what with all those parents purring along at twenty. I like it, I love it, I want it. If I had just got here early enough, if I had gone to college here and married some honey-blonde whose father was an apple farmer, say, who led me down the rows of trees in the days of our courting and plucked the reddest fruit I had ever seen. We could have wooed in the orchards, honeymooned in the Rockies and settled in the suburbs. I *love* the goddam suburbs, with their quiet, orderly lives, the wives who work and bake and go to the gym and don't smoke. I'm through with the alcoholic smoke-rattly European whores too clever to be simple, too clever for happiness.

We roll south by west in self-assured yet delicate sunshine. The mountains off to our left, along Skyline Drive, turn from green to rust as the sun lowers.

Night falls. We just passed Roanoke, Virginia. Carmela is asleep beside me. I can talk about her now, *sotto voce*. Picture her there, a slim, even lanky girl in black jeans, white T-shirt, black jacket and beret, leaning her face against the window. Her cheek gleams in occasional headlights coming the other way. She is half Polish, half Puerto Rican, and wholly American. On two points her diverse genes agreed: she has heavy eyebrows and good cheeks. Otherwise they shared things out: a splendid arched Spanish nose, a pair of pale, Eastern lips, and a complexion that can seem pallid and powdery at times, olive-oily at others.

She likes to dress provocatively, where bordello meets hippie. She has a huge wardrobe of tiny clothes: glittery hot-pants and velvet miniskirts. It's something to do with her stance towards the patriarchy, all that student stuff we pick up and carry through life like excess baggage. Don't get me wrong, I'm no chauvinist, my only objection is to a life dictated by ideas. I knew her clothes were a political statement when I met her, which is why she let me take them off.

We met in Prague while she was studying numerology. All last winter I showed her my favourite haunts, the Slavia Cafe, the Blue Velvet, Plzenska, cheap places but real, and she got to see the underside of the city. We ate cakes on the Charles Bridge and kissed to the tune of a blind accordionist. We did the appropriate things but it was just an affair, a time-passer. I would have liked to take her to readings and screenings and so on but it wasn't worth the trouble of negotiating the faces that no longer approved of me. I did show her one of my movies, using my old projector and the kitchen wall, but she didn't understand the dialogue.

Life changes and with it your expectations change. After one failed marriage you realise love isn't what you thought it was. With Carmela I saw the possibility of an easier life. When she asked me to come to America I took a chance. We both wanted to marry. Why not? She may be ten years younger than me but she has reached an age where it's simpler to know where you stand. But ssh. She just gave the long sniff which signals that any moment she'll be stretching like a baby and waking up.

When New York is good to you it's very good. When it's bad it's worse than bad. Let's try this here:

A bleak, municipal office. A man in an ill-fitting suit snaps open a drawer of files, searches for one, slaps it down on his desk. He shuffles through the papers, jams the phone in his shoulder and reaches for an indigestion pill. He wears glasses and moustache – the faceless face of bureaucracy.

'This guy, this C. Hasek,' he says into the receiver. 'You ever hear back from him?' He frowns at the papers, stifles a belch. 'Uh-huh. Maybe it's time for a little visit . . . Absolutely . . . Downstairs in five.'

Cut to: a dark blue car. The door closes and on it we see a crest with the initials 'INS', and, just in case we still haven't got the message, up on the dash a plastic board: 'Immigration Officers – NYPD Parking Rights'.

Camera soars (crane shot). Far below, the car pulls into the shadow of that maroon block. Camera plummets, closing in on the officers as they press the bell of apartment 14F. The doorman emerges. The officers bend their heads sombrely, listening to him, then ceremonially shake his hand.

Next shot: Mr Glasses-and-Moustache is talking to Felix in the U-Haul office.

Felix shrugs. 'He said he wanted to take Route Sixty-Six. So I guess that's I-Forty? He was in quite a hurry.'

The officer nods. 'I bet he was.'

He climbs back into the sedan and as it pulls away from the curb a flash of sun on the windshield hides his face.

(You get the idea: ulcerous bureaucrat with a mission.)

The *Cracker Barrel*. This could be a montage unto itself.

A restaurant like a barn, with walls of chemically

weathered wood and a giant fireplace adorned with an iron pot of aromatic water. The manager, in tie and neat cardigan, pokes at the fire with a long rod, making the logs crackle, then stands his poker against the chimney breast and wipes his hands together, satisfied.

I liked watching that man. You could see what pleasure it afforded him to be immaculately clean yet engage with a wild, dirty element, even if it was at the end of a four-foot poker. I thought: that is America: all the comfort and hygiene in the midst of a wild land.

The menu was loaded with Daily, Weekly, Seafood and House Specials.

Carmela and I smiled at each other. It was sort of embarrassing – and sort of nice – for two city birds to be out here in the middle of Virginia in all this pseudo-rusticity. We both knew it was bad taste – after all, what is it to be urban other than to have acquired the principles of good taste? – but we both liked it. Carmela gave me a shy smile and wrinkled her nose. 'It beats Denny's,' she said.

'Denny's?'

'It's another chain.'

'This is a chain?' I couldn't believe it: a hundred identical fake barns strung across the country all serving the same Specials. I loved it even more.

When we knocked our two frosted mugs of beer together they clunked like they were made of clay.

After our sweet potato and pork with apple sauce all I had room for was a cup of coffee and a slice of one of their numerous apple pies, Dutch, French, Southern, Homestyle.

'Let's go,' Carmela said as I cast my eye over the list.

'Just one piece of pie.'

'But the truck.'

We had left the truck in the parking lot, lined up very correctly between its own pair of white lines. Carmela couldn't believe it was allowed there, among all the cars.

'The truck's fine.'

'Just imagine if we get towed.' Carmela is prone to sudden misgivings.

'Why should we get towed?'

She shook her head. 'Just imagine.'

I pointed out that even the drivers of the eighteen-wheelers have to eat, and therefore park outside restaurants. She scowled at me, tapping her fork on her empty plate.

Carmela is a non-rational being. Rationality offends her. She thinks the Western world went wrong with Plato. We used to argue – though of course to argue with a non-rational being is a ridiculous enterprise – but now I know this mood and don't bother, and we get along better. The apple pie would have to wait till the next Cracker Barrel.

In the motel over the road we watched fuzzy TV till we fell asleep.

Cut to: our immigration officer in his dismal office. He closes a file on his desk and drums his fingers. Then he reaches for the telephone. Frowning, he says into the receiver, 'I've got a runner, and I think we're talking west.'

He sits listening, muttering, 'Uh-huh.' He fingers the top of a bright pink bottle of Pepto-Bismol. 'Yeah, LA, with a stop in New Mexico or something . . . I-Forty . . . Oh, the visa ran out weeks ago.'

Gradually a smile spreads across his face. 'Cool,' he says. 'Excellent.'

He hangs up, takes a swig from the Pepto bottle then dials again.

'Juanita? Who's your man in Memphis?'

Picture the roof of our cosy motel. The 'Days Rest' neon sign glows in the night, the cars are lined up like horses outside their sleeping masters' rooms. The camera rises, revealing more and more of the black rolling land studded with points of light. Tufts of grey cloud flit across the screen, coming thicker and faster until they congeal into a blanket of fog. Which grows paler and paler, until blinding white fills the screen. On the soundtrack fierce winds howl hoarsely. The whiteness breaks up into flurries of flecks blowing about in all directions. Beyond them seems to be more blackness. It's hard to tell what's going on. Gradually the blackness becomes more visible, and we see the same points of light as before. We realise we are coming back down to earth in the middle of a snowstorm. We *are* a snowstorm. There's 'Days Rest' again, the motel roof, the cars outside. We focus on a strip of tarmac between two cars, accelerating towards it. Suddenly blackout. Silence. We have hit the ground.

Next shot: murky daylight. Our stubbled man in pyjamas opens a door, looks up at a white sky filled with snow. He takes a step with his bare foot, flinches. 'Ouch!' He has stepped on ice. The entire parking lot is a soft sheet of white. The cars have become mounds of snow.

Cut to bedroom. Same man getting into bed with black-haired lady, who is sitting up and holding a deck of cards. She shivers and pulls away from him. 'You're *cold*,' she whines as she carries on laying out cards on the bedcover. 'And don't move.'

He flicks through the TV channels, alighting on giant orange snowploughs with all their lights on, deep in drifts in a grey dawn somewhere on the continent. A man's excited voice says, 'Even Louisiana is getting it, Larry. This is really something. I hate to think what's gonna happen further east. All I can say is, I'm glad I'm not in Boston . . .'

Our man in bed says, 'Oh no.'

The woman turns over a card and smiles. 'The weather is going to help us,' she announces. 'Pray for ice.'

'Ice? We've got two and a half thousand miles ahead of us.'

'Ice is our friend.'

In the motel lobby a number of people pensively ate their breakfast. An air of waiting hung over them. Some said the highway was closed, others that they were salting it.

We sat down next to a big black guy who looked up and said, 'Hi,' then resumed the solemn eating of his cereal.

I sipped my coffee and stared at my donut. 'What are we going to do?' I feebly asked.

'We're going to drive, of course.'

Carmela went to fetch a coffee pot and filled both our cups and our neighbour's.

'Thank you, ma'am,' he said.

We got talking. He was a trucker with a fifty-three-foot truck of Chinese food. 'I got chow mein, chop suey, you name it.'

'A fifty-three-foot take-out,' I said.

He laughed, slow and deep.

'Where are you headed?' Carmela asked, picking at her donut.

'I don't know if I'm headed *any*where.' He raised his eyebrows preposterously high.

Carmela shrugged. 'Sure you are.'

'Thing is, I got bamboo shoots and beansprouts ain't gonna be too good if they sit here too long.' His eyebrows soared again.

'At least they'll stay cold,' Carmela said.

He liked that. 'Yes ma'am.' He let out another belly-laugh.

'And if we get marooned here at least we'll all have something to eat.'

He liked that too. He roared and shook his head and wound down with a lot of *mm-hmms*. I didn't know Southern black men really did do that.

'Tell the truth,' he said, 'I don't even like that Chinese shit.'

I loved him for saying that: people really say things like that in America! All you need to do in this country is keep your camera running.

* * *

We crawled along icy ruts in the slow lane. Carmela drove. Every so often her arms stiffened as a blizzard came thundering past, obscuring our view. In the heart of it you might or might not make out a wall of iron, a glimmer of a tail light.

We travelled through strange country: quiet and still, with small hills to either side looking jaundiced in their blanket of snow. That was Tennessee. The snow on the road retreated into occasional plates of silver, nowhere near as bad as on the television.

I had set my heart on a trip to Music City but we ran into a crawl of traffic and Carmela thought we should press on. All I saw of Nashville was a heart-stopping glimpse of grey-blue skyscrapers rising from a plain. *That* was a place to live. To be an executive high up in a downtown office, to get up from your desk with a city view open below you, to pull on your silk-lined jacket, snap shut your leather briefcase, and take a waiting taxi to the airport for the lunchtime flight to Atlanta, say, where you sign a deal with a CNN subsidiary. Then dinner on the plane coming home and guess what, the wife and kids have shown up at the airport to meet you. She lets you kneel down and hug the kids before approaching you with a special kiss. She's come straight from housework. No make-up, a sweatshirt bearing the name of your old college, a pair of jeans. But her eyes are fiercely clear. She loves you, and just then you cannot believe your good fortune, to be wealthy, in love, in America.

On we roll, on smooth asphalt, into the Tennessee night.

* * *

There are reasons they bother about me. Being a name back home, especially my kind of name, has its disadvantages. The INS wouldn't accept me as a political refugee. As far as Eastern Europe goes those days are over. When the regime fell back home things changed for me. People didn't want me. I have nothing against Havel and his gang but they have something against me. It's true I had not suffered under the old order. I had been allowed to make films and the films had not been critical of the regime, but why should they have been? Not every artist has to be a goddam politician.

Life is complicated and so is art but I believe in an artist's right to work. I wasn't about to go silent for the first ten years of my career just because of a hallful of boring old guys in grey suits. And when a hallful of slightly younger guys in blue suits took their place and said, 'We don't like your work but here, have a passport,' why would I refuse? Whatever they may say about me back home, everyone knows where a film-maker belongs.

I'm defending myself. It's a grubby habit but none of us stays unsullied. None of us is really fit to roam the apple trees hand in hand with the girl in white.

Memphis takes it during the night. We wake up buried in snow.

I lose a piece of skin off my thumb on the frozen padlock as I open up the back of the truck for Carmela. She insists on climbing in and rummaging through her boxes to find a particular astrology book. She had a dream in the night. Something about devils on a bridge. A *message*. She thinks we should avoid bridges.

'Carmela, why don't we just do it now?' I ask over breakfast.

She shakes her head.

I try telling her that New Mexico is hardly a virginal land, that sometimes a little flexibility goes a long way, but she has seen what must be. It's far beyond the pathetic reach of debate. And I know if I press it she could have a turn and I'll waste the whole day persuading her to climb back into the truck.

Then she discovers from the map there's a ferry service across Old Glory a hundred miles downstream, so we won't have to drive over a bridge after all.

'A hundred miles?' My heart sinks.

We navigated the bloated brown eddies of Mark Twain on an old-world ferry with iron chains and hooks and rings embedded in the deck. Carmela was in good spirits, leaning over the rail at the front and chatting to the crewmen. I sat in the truck nervously. I wasn't sure what lengths the INS might go to but kept imagining I could hear helicopter blades. Any minute I would see a great bluebottle of a machine whirring towards me over the restless water.

We headed south to I-10, which would drop us in the southern corner of New Mexico. It would mean not following the old Route 66, a switch that interested Carmela. 'Of course,' she chuckled. That was what the dream about demons had been trying to tell her: avoid

66. It was so nearly the devil's fixture, but she had missed the connection.

The snow got worse on the plains of Texas. Savage, unchecked winds drove the flakes across the road like water. Often you couldn't even see the edge of the paving. I had to slow to twenty-five, twenty.

After Abilene it eased up. Then there was just the cold. The plains were Siberian, barren, empty. The sky was a plain of blue-grey cloud every bit as flat as the land. Between the two sheets, one above, one below, our little truck trundled, rumbling and shaking like the first particle of life stranded on Creation's First Day.

We refuelled every four hours. In Midland there wasn't a car on the street except for a curb-crawling cop with his lights on. In Van Hom we stopped for dinner, then rolled on through the empty night. Carmela curled up and slept against the window then changed her mind and put her head in my lap. I turned down the radio, listening to the soft American voices filling the cab with their ghostly susurrus, debating Social Service issues and Domino Pizza's five million dollars of damages against CBS. Stories I had never heard, which meant nothing to me except that all was well in the nation.

We traversed the void and blackness, Creation's First Night: nothing but land and sky, a world yet to find a purpose.

Back in the INS office our officer is on the telephone rolling his eyes and asking, 'What do you mean, missed them? The traffic is crawling at ten miles an hour over the Mississippi Bridge and –'

The slow voice of Tennessee on the other end says: 'Mr Naturalisation, we got two feet of snow last night, the en-tire bridge is iced over and this may come as a surprise but your ve-hicle is not the only thing on our minds.'

The officer hangs up and dials a new number. Looking tired and fed up, he tears open a packet of Rolaids.

Now and then a big truck would show as a star in the mirror, far, far behind. It might keep me company for half an hour, gradually growing, then slowly draw alongside and pass me, aglitter with fairy lights, and gently ease into the distance ahead. Trucks went by in groups on the opposite side, festooned with lights like travelling carnivals.

At five a.m. we pulled into El Paso. I stopped at a Village Inn for breakfast (I've never seen anywhere less like a village inn). I chose eggs and Country Style hash. Carmela had Hot Cakes and syrup. We had twenty miles to go to the state line. That breakfast was a celebration. I didn't think anything could stop us now. And I was right. Even when the Border Patrol siphoned everybody off the highway for ID checks the soldier just squinted up into our cab and waved us through.

The sun came up on the biggest land I have ever seen: hundreds of miles of desert broken up by perfect miniature mountain ranges all laid out like one of those plastic contoured maps. We turned off the highway beside a line of mountains jagged as a row of rotten teeth, and drove into a town of low mud houses.

Carmela knew what to do. We parked on a square in front of a mud church. She took me by the hand and led me inside. We lit a candle from a rack of red glass jars waiting with new wicks and set it before a picture of Christ tearing open his chest. The painting reminded me of the art in churches of the eastern Czech Republic. I thought of the peasants back home and a wave of something like sorrow or pity hit me. I wished I could embrace all the simple folk of my homeland, kneel side by side with them in prayer.

Which is what I did with Carmela. Carmela says she is spiritual not religious, but she had already bowed her head and fallen to her knees. I did the same. I found her hand, cool and tender. We kissed. Her eyes glistened in the candlelight. I had never been anywhere like this town or this simple mud church. I was a newcomer to the desert. I couldn't believe this was still America. Whatever problems I had had it was clear now that I had outrun them. Nothing could go wrong in a land like this.

I whispered something to Carmela. My voice made a little, cool sound in the dark.

Outside in the early sunlight of the plaza Carmela said, 'You see? We were right to wait till we got here.'

Up on the wall of the church hung three crosses of cactus wood, stringy and warped. I imagined lonely homesteaders with a wagon, a cow and a hoe searching the dusty land for the straightest cactus they could find, having to settle for these. Again I was filled with longing and pity. I wanted to fall on the ground and bathe Carmela's feet with kisses.

Sometimes good things happen to bad people, sometimes vice versa, and some people are neither good nor bad, just lucky. That morning I wanted to let all America into my breast.

At quarter to ten in the Mesilla County Courthouse, the very courthouse where Pat Garrett tried Billy the Kid, a Justice of the Peace declares our couple man and wife. The judge is a young-looking man with a moustache who never takes off his sunglasses, not even to read from his clipboard, nor to type up the details on his computer after the little ceremony.

She looks beautiful in a minidress of white silk with daisies in her hair, her arms and legs smooth and dark, while he, our man, has finally shaved off his stubble and dug out his best black polo neck.

The couple stand kissing on the plaza. The camera wheels about, revealing as it does so a cop car pulled up in one corner, its lights flashing uselessly: too late. We rise up, spiralling higher and higher (a chopper here) until we can see over the mud houses to the desert all around. Higher still, till the little town is just a sprinkle of rooftops twinkling in the sun on that enormous land. Roll credits.

In fact Carmela did have a white silk minidress, but she never got to wear it. She only got as far as hanging it up in the room we took at the Holiday Inn. And her legs did look dark and fabulous that day – her Hispanic genes felt at home under the New Mexican sun. And we did go to the Mesilla County Courthouse to check in with the official there. He booked our wedding in for the only slot left the following morning. He needed our papers to log us into the system, and Carmela hesitated before handing over my passport. But I didn't think twice about filling in our local address on the form.

They came for me in the hotel. When the marriage clerk logged in our names he lit up the way for them.

I thought it was the maid knocking and shouted, 'Later.' They didn't like that. It was late enough. Two INS guys from El Paso, a couple of cops just in case. Carmela cursed them blind, breaking into Spanish, which I have rarely heard her do, and even into Polish, which I had never heard her do.

'Can it, lady, the guy's illegal,' they chorused.

She wailed and wept as they led me across the tiled hotel lobby out to the waiting cars.

MacIntyre, forgive this desperate and embarrassing plea but I never threw away your address at Paramount, sure that one day we could do something together. Now is the time. Remember your promise when we worked together in Prague? A short all my own? Well, here it is. A feel-good couple-on-the-run. *Green Card* meets *Badlands*. You have just read the treatment. The lawyer says that with a firm offer of work I still have a chance, but he can stall them only for so long. I don't know what will happen to Carmela if this doesn't work.

You can reach me at the El Paso Temporary Detention

Center. Which I must say beats a lot of apartments back home. I can't tell you what it means to have seen the American desert and to know that like in all good road movies something happened to me here. There is a spirit here – I can feel it even through these walls.

Carmela has brought me a candle in a jar with St Christopher on the side. I keep it burning and I tell my fellow guests: never let the flame go out.

Please respond by return.

Castaway

Harry Burton had had to get away from the island of Inagua. Ironically, the island's name was derived from *lleno de agua*: full of water. Inagua was full of water – inland lakes – but all of it was brine, seawater, saltpan. Salt, salt, salt. Not all the beer in Christendom could kill the thirst Inagua kindled.

And this bloody place, Blunt Island, next island in the chain, was no better. Pittstown Point Landings, the hotel was called. Harry had had enough of these itsy-bitsy names. Points, Bluffs, Landings – the Bahamas were full of them, yet the people who lived in the settlements were slow colossi, whale-like humans, ponderous, sleek beasts, gentle but vast in bulk.

Give him a decent name: Nottingham, London, Hull.

He opened his eyes and stared at the fan above which, infuriatingly, had a rhythm. Swish-swish, swish-swish. Bloody thing needed a service, it wasn't balanced right. He glanced round the room, which he had entered drunk late last night after four hours in the bar that formed the centrepiece of the bleak little hotel. Trudy, the manager, had walked him down the path to his 'cottage'.

It was nothing like a cottage, of course: a plain motel room, but without the air-conditioning. Swish-swish.

The sun was already up. A hideous shadow of a palm tree lay splayed on the blind amid an orange luminescence. He rolled on to his side. For a moment things seemed unbearable: to be hung-over in a bare white room on the tip of an island with a population of two hundred dreamy souls, surrounded, imprisoned by hundreds of miles of lurid tropical sea. To be here for a *holiday*, and all because he so desperately needed a break from that other island on which he lived, where he spent all day in a Nissen hut among mountains of grey salt, arguing on the telephone on behalf of the Morton Salt Co. (which couldn't care twice about its lonely Bahamian operation), and where he spent all his evenings drinking in the 'lounge' of the company guest house, a place like a giant bathroom, tiled on the floor and, in a bizarre misunderstanding of Western interior design, tiled halfway up the walls too. He had spent too much time in that lounge. Apart from three depressing prints of tropical sunsets on the walls, just in case you forgot where you were, the only adornment to the room was four motionless figures in the corner: whisky, gin, vodka, rum, standing there like sentries, reproaching you. Some nights he'd have company, though not company he would have chosen: a Japanese scientist visiting for a week, who communicated fine via graphs and calculations but spoke not a word of the mother tongue; an official down from Nassau, some heavy morose local whose office had only swollen his taciturnity; an American contractor. These last were much the best, it went without saying. They could put down a few and tell a story, were even on for the odd side-trip to

Topp's Restaurant for a touch of local life, maybe a bit of a flirt with Josey the tall waitress. Harry wasn't above sharing. Then the slump into bed to the roar of ancient air-conditioning mingled with the clatter of the town generator, a background of black noise that was the last thing you heard at night, and the first upon waking. Coffee and eggs served up by the hefty Viola or her equally hefty daughter, and a trip to the head – fruitless more often than not, with all the 'rice 'n' peas' they stuffed into you – and out to the Chevy Blazer, the one thing the job gave him with which he could say he was satisfied. At least he had a decent truck.

So Harry's work days went.

Check out Blunt Island, people had said, on your next leave. It real lay back, man, you go like it. It *fine*, man. Which meant highly desirable. But he should have known all the locals said that of anywhere or anything about which they had no particular reason to disapprove. He should have understood them, and it, and himself. He *needed* Miami once a month. The cars and streets and concrete buildings and traffic lights – just to remember that there was a real world out there, a world in which he, Harry, made some kind of sense. A world into which Harry could fly with his walletful of gold plastic, the hard-earned rewards of his years out of touch, beyond the reach of normal life, his years on rigs and mines, under tin roofs, in cots, in bunks, in canteens. What good was all that mounting heap if you didn't tinkle it around from time to time?

Pittstown Point Landings, Blunt Island. The only thing

that had ever *landed* on Blunt Island had been a few kilos of Cali's best, back in the days when the narcos still used the Bahamas.

Then an unexpected gust of generosity blew through him, as he lay blearily in bed. Give the place a chance. Go on, who's ever heard of Blunt Island? It's remote, they're trying. At least the beer is cold. He who expects nothing is never disappointed. You just might, he told himself, have a nice little stay here. And it's only three days.

He was thinking of Trudy, the hotel manager. She was neat and slim, with short, tidy blonde hair. American. She probably trimmed her pubes. All American women did, at least in the magazines. He would like that. The first thing she had said to him, when he checked in, was something about her divorce of two years ago. And she was hardly going to have met a new beau down here.

The thought of her gave him the impetus he needed to get to the shower, which turned out to be the same plastic cubicle as in the Morton company guest house, and sprayed out the same stinging froth. They were more like cappuccino machines. He had had hopes of a thick plunge of cold water, a stream to carry away not only last night's hours at the bar but the last few months of his life too, all the salt of Inagua.

Hopefully, with a new idea in mind, namely a dip in the fresh morning sea, he slapped a towel over his shoulder and opened the front door. For some blurry reason he was half expecting to feel a bracing morning chill. Instead there was only the uniform tropical warmth. It was infuriating. Couldn't the weather do anything other than warm or hot?

He stepped on to the concrete porch of his cottage and made his way down the path. Two lizards streaked across in front of him, and one, three paving stones away, crouched bravely, staring him down, its throat pulsing. The sea lay just a few yards off. As always, it was a vivid blue, with streaks of sickly green. But this morning it was more lurid than ever, as if a photographer had spilt the chemicals in the darkroom and come up with a grotesquerie of tropical colour. Feeble waves slapped themselves on to the beach, then gave a brief slurp, like someone sucking from a soup spoon, as they withdrew. He could imagine just how warm the water would be – like swimming in urine.

Ahead a palm tree was flapping about in a breeze that he couldn't feel, and sunlight flickered back and forth across his face. He felt giddy, and turned round. Depressed, despondent, feeling sorry for himself, Harry trudged back to his room and fell on to the bed.

A holiday. Week after week of work on a hot desert island, then three days off, a long weekend, and what does he do? Madly, he flies to another hot desert island.

Then he remembered that he hadn't yet started the day, and felt a little better: breakfast. First things first.

On his second outing he came across Trudy squatting in a pair of shorts by the side of the path.

'Hi,' she called, rather too ebulliently. The enthusiasm in her voice reminded him that he was the only guest.

'Morning,' he answered, with more verve than he intended.

'I'm trying to turn this damn thing on,' she said.

Sooner than he meant, before he had even thought about it, he had gallantly sunk to his knees beside her and was reaching into a drain, straining to open a stop-cock hidden inside a length of piping.

'I have to turn it off at night or the kitchen floor floods,' she said apologetically.

He got it open and stood up feeling much better, as if he had done something constructive for the day. 'There,' he announced.

She thanked him effusively. 'Come on, I'll fix you some breakfast.'

He followed her down the path, inexplicably struck dumb, watching her legs. They were a soft, creamy brown, as if new to the sun. She must have been forty, but she was well kept. Perhaps a little too well kept, too prim, altogether too *healthy* for his taste; he guessed she might be a Midwesterner. Yet he couldn't take his eyes off her legs and the twin shapes enclosed by her shorts.

He took a stool at the bar and waited for her to produce a cup of coffee and 'the works', as she called it, meaning eggs and bacon. Apparently the cook was coming in late today so Trudy was fixing it herself. He listened to her bustling about the kitchen. It was a soothing sound, and lulled him into a reverie of a home somewhere, a familiar home that at first he couldn't place, until he realised he was thinking of his student digs in Manchester. With a sudden chill it came to him that that was the last place he had ever lived that he could call home. Fifteen years ago. A surge of self-pity struck, at the thought not of his itinerancy, but of the innocent zeal with which he had travelled out to Botswana for his first posting. The roar of the yellow bulldozers, the clatter of the generators – sounds that had become the backdrop of his life – the dust-filled air, the strong sun, the beers with the lads in the hot nights – it had all thrilled him then.

Trudy came in to fetch ice from the bar's big refrigerator. When she opened the door, his eye fastened on the stacks of misty brown bottles inside, and another memory swept into him: he found himself remembering the bottles of chocolate milk they used to sell in Spain, where he had gone on holidays as a child. His father would buy him a bottle at the café on the beach, and the waiter would click off the top with his opener. At once Harry would catch the smell in his nostrils, a thick, malty aroma that filled him with excitement. He would watch the waiter glugging the thick grey drink into the glass, then he would lift it, ringed with froth, to his lips. He could taste it now. He felt his eyes moisten.

Trudy called, 'Won't be long,' in a cheery voice.

The coffee came first, then the eggs, and finally Trudy herself.

She sat down opposite him at the table she had laid, with her giant Koffee Kup in hand. Which was awkward. Much as he appreciated her friendliness, he knew himself well enough to know that breakfast was no time to practise his charms. He asked if he could borrow the newspaper at the front desk, even if it was last week's. She didn't take the hint.

'Did you sleep well?' she asked. 'I put you on the beach front specially. There's nothing like drifting off to the sound of surf, I always think.'

He nodded with his mouth full of salty bacon, while buttering a piece of brittle toast, which snapped under his knife. He forced himself to swallow.

'It beats the town generator on Inagua.' He laughed hoarsely.

'What's that?' She stared at him with an expression at once blank and uncomfortably penetrating.

He had to explain about the generator in Inagua. It fatigued him to have to spell it all out, first thing in the day. He lowered his eyes to the sunny eggs, and tore them open with his knife tip. A spasm of warm longing for their rich flavour ran through him.

'So what brings you to our lovely isle?' She raised her Koffee Kup, hiding her face.

'Holidays,' he said, snickering ironically. 'I thought a nice dose of R and R was in order.'

'You've come to the right place,' she said brightly. 'Nothing but R and R here. Unless of course you're a fisherman.'

Which he wasn't.

'Tell you what,' she went on, lighting up. 'I have some errands today, but how about a flying-fish fry-up tonight? I'll tell Maureen.' Maureen was the absent cook. 'Sound good?'

He hummed his accord, chewing a mouthful of toast.

It not only sounded good, it sounded, as far as he could tell, like a date. A faint anticipation stirred in him. He nodded. 'Wonderful,' he got out, pleased also because now that they had a plan for later on she might leave him alone with his breakfast. Moreover, he thought he detected the possibility of a long-overdue bowel movement.

Sure enough, Trudy announced, 'Well, no rest for the wicked,' pushing back her chair. She smiled at him in such a way that a smile was unavoidably summoned from his own face. As she walked across the room he resisted temptation for a moment, then gave in and eyed her buttocks as they moved away, encased by her shorts.

After breakfast he went back to his room to masturbate, then decided that he really must do something till lunchtime. But what? Perch on the scorching sand and watch the wavelets? 'Stroll' along a potholed road through the burning heat? Sit in a tin-roofed shack known as 'The Tea Room' sweating over greasy too-sweet coffee? And what about after lunch? He had the entire day to kill. In Miami it was easy. You could wander along the shore front, then take a seat at one of the sidewalk cafés and watch the models go by while sipping iced coffee. Or lie by the hotel pool, or take a stool under the palm bar. He could even finally have looked up, as he had been meaning to do, one of his old college acquaintances, who was living near Miami with his family. But here?

He felt another attack of his blues coming on. He had left home fifteen years ago, and arrived nowhere, and now it was too late to arrive anywhere. He was one of the cursed of the earth, doomed to roam the globe, passing wherever he went the houses and gardens and climbing-frames and family cars of the earth's inheritors. A decade and a half already. Twelve-, eighteen-, six-month contracts had eaten up his years, his chances.

Have a swim, have a swim, anything, something, but get out of this room, he told himself.

He walked around the hotel, following the paths among the twelve identical cottages. It was a sad place, every bit as impersonal and unloved as any motel on an Interstate. He guessed it would have been built in the sixties, in the Bahamas' heyday, when private pilots used to fly themselves and their girlfriends down to swinging clubs all over the islands. Now the place was graced only by occasional visits from sports fishermen. The coast of Cuba lay eighty miles away, and in between was the West Indies Channel, where the marlin fishing was said to be good. Harry sauntered into the hotel lobby and idly flipped through the register, still with plenty of pages to spare in a volume that went back to 1975. It was full of comments such as: 'Great fishing!!' . . . 'We'll bring him in next time!!!' . . . '352 pounds of pure fun!'

He changed into a pair of bright orange shorts and tried slipping into the warm ocean. He lay on his back under the blue sky. Wasn't there anywhere in the world where the weather was good but not so bloody hot? Somewhere like the English summers of his youth? He remembered long days cycling around the city park and down back streets with his long-lost friend James, then diving into the brown canal to cool off, and how the water used to have a warm film on the surface but cool dark depths beneath. He and James would kick about, sending up plumes of white spray, then swim slowly down into the coolness with their eyes tightly shut. That was good weather! Not this baking, sweaty heat above a bath-warm ocean.

He swam out thirty yards, took a breath, and let himself sink down into the sea till his feet touched the sandy bottom. The water was warm all the way.

He was grateful when a breeze got up and the palms rustled. He lifted himself from the waves to greet it.

The mailboat came in later on. Harry wandered into 'town', a handful of huts dozing among trees, to watch the boat unload. Every pickup on the island, all ten or twelve of them, had congregated in the shade of the great old iron vessel with its crumbling mildewed deck house. A crew in yellow hard hats were busy disgorging load after load of gas cylinders.

The locals, with and without pickups, had gathered in force. Some were evidently awaiting passage – women in their best straw hats and dresses beside old suitcases tied up with belts and string, men in slacks and white shirts, one old man wearing a pair of heavy black-rimmed glasses without lenses, as if glasses were part of a man's formal attire. Others watched the cargo coming ashore with a keen eye, awaiting goods. After the gas cylinders came huge string sacks of onions, potatoes, oranges.

There was something relaxing about the scene. It was hard not to like it – the rusty old ship, the twinkling blue harbour, the quietly excited crowd, the noisily bored ship-workers, all dressed in singlets, who kept up a continual shouted banter while they manned the derrick, guided the loads, loaded the pallets. Harry perched on a bollard at the end of the quay and wondered what it would be like to be one of the locals travelling away, up to Nassau and beyond. They'd see their little island become a tiny strip of green on the horizon, then vanish. Night would fall over the wide ocean, and they'd wake up in the Nassau Channel, flanked by a world of concrete and braying car horns. He wondered if they would be homesick or thrilled. He decided it would depend on their age.

He remembered, for example, his own first trip away from home, down to Lyme Regis, and the indescribable thrill of reaching a new town where his family would be staying for a whole week. It was like suddenly having a new home at your disposal, with all its streets and shops and walks and alleyways to explore, though it was better than a home because it was temporary, you could leave it if you wanted. He had felt a similar thrill when he first reached Africa. When the plane landed and the taxi took him through the bristling city, all sparkling under the African sun, he could barely believe his good fortune that this would all be his for a year.

New places were different now. They weren't so new. Harry found himself noticing the suburban homes, the satellite dishes, and whether there were one or two cars in the garage, a swing in the garden. All countries had turned into places to bring up children. Some were arguably easier than others, though it was largely a matter of taste. Harry was only forty-two, which wasn't old, of course, but more and more often the men Harry worked with were younger than him yet already had two or three children, and he noticed increasingly that wherever he worked people talked about the same things – schools, colds, the price of kids' clothes – whether he was in Accra, Aberdeen or Angola. It was as if there was nowhere exotic left. Exotic was just a memory.

Through the late afternoon Harry sat alone at the hotel bar nursing Johnnie Walkers. At quarter to six, bang on cue, yet another sticky tropical sunset began to spill across the world like undiluted orange squash.

Trudy walked in. 'Mind if I join a weary salt-miner?' she asked, pulling off a pair of yellow rubber gloves, which she draped over the back of a bamboo bar stool before climbing on. 'Must be thirsty work, huh?'

He removed the cigarette from his mouth and, in his suavest voice, amid a cloud of smoke, and full of gratitude for the distraction, drawled, 'I'd be thoroughly delighted. It's thirsty work just living in these parts. What'll it be?'

She fanned at her throat vaguely and laughed. 'Thoroughly delighted. You Brits. Only you can talk like that.' She glanced at her watch. 'Why, thank you. I'll have a beer. It is six o'clock, practically.'

She *was* a pretty thing. With her tidy, short blonde hair, possibly dyed, and her neat little shorts and tennis shirt, and that soft tan on all her slender limbs, she was altogether adequately desirable.

'Ahoy there!' Harry called out, towards the empty doorway behind the bar.

'Maureen!' Trudy echoed beside him, with a laugh, as if they were really having fun.

A moment later a slow island woman emerged. 'Yer call?' She stared at her boss implacably.

'Drinks, please, Maureen. Mr Burton will have another whisky, and I'll have a beer.'

Without a word, the woman set about the order. She lifted a great block of ice from the refrigerator and hacked at it with a screwdriver, sending chips of ice flying about the room, some of which landed on the bar top, where they quickly melted. Then she stooped, rather gracefully Harry thought, despite her bulk, to pluck the top off a beer bottle on an opener under the bar. Finally she unscrewed the top off a fresh bottle of whisky.

'Cheers,' Harry said.

They knocked their drinks together.

'Ever been our way?' he asked.

Trudy had a sip and wiped her mouth. 'You know how it is. Any time off, you head straight for Miami. But I'm dying to come and see the flamingos.'

Everyone had heard about the flamingos of Inagua. Inagua was nothing more than a ring of land encircling its great salt flats, where fifty thousand flame-pink birds fed and bred. They were about the only reason anyone ever visited the island, except for the salt-miners.

'The flamingos are a wonderful sight,' he said. 'And that's not all, you know. We've got five thousand wild donkeys, descendants of the asses of Roi Henri Christophe.' He pronounced the phrase with relish, having read it innumerable times in his *Fodor's Guide*, extracting from it every ounce of glamour it could yield.

'What?' she exclaimed, over-dramatically, not the reaction he had expected.

'As you may know,' Harry drawled on, 'Henri was King of Haiti. He shipped his gold over to Inagua when the French attacked. Donkeys carried it. But the gold was lost.' He swirled the drink in his glass, making the ice clink, thinking that it was deft of him to have introduced a romantic note so swiftly yet stealthily. Before she knew it she'd be dreaming of buried treasure and falling into his arms.

She was frowning at her drink. 'The donkeys *swam* over?' she asked, in a kind of whine.

He explained that they had been shipped across the hundred miles of sea from Haiti. But he felt irritated. She was too bloody literal. No passion.

'Well, what happened to all the gold?' she asked.

He shrugged. 'It's still out there somewhere, I suppose.' A solitary ray of golden sunshine found his left eye. He leaned out of it.

She looked at him and raised her glass. 'Well, let's go find it. Here's to Henri's gold. What are we waiting for?' She was smiling. It was a nice smile, sincere. He raised his glass to it. Maybe the old Burton magic was working after all.

He said, 'Tell you what, when you come over, I'll give you a guided tour in my Blazer. We'll find the blasted stuff.'

For some reason she found this hilarious and rocked back on her stool, knocking off her rubber gloves. He at once slipped to the floor and picked them up for her. He hadn't noticed until now, bending down beside her, that despite her trim figure she had a good bust. The words of an old Australian mining colleague ran through his mind: 'Mines beat bloody rigs. Pussy galore on shore, mate!' Harry let his face fill with a smile of modest gallantry, and carefully settled the gloves in the lap of her red shorts, folding the plastic lengths over at the finger joints.

She sat very still, clearly pleased, and said softly, 'Why thank you. I didn't know there were any gentlemen left in the world.'

'It's the one bloody thing Britain does still manufacture,' he said, seating himself again.

She gave him a look. He wasn't quite sure what it meant, but felt he should return it, which he did, with interest. It seemed to be the right thing to do, because she let out another peal of unexpected hilarity.

He answered with a low chuckle, a kind of snigger he had grown accustomed to using on Josey the waitress on Inagua.

'Well, we may not have any gold here, but we have got paradise. There ain't anything to do except enjoy yourself.'

Her accent seemed to have shifted. Perhaps he had been wrong in placing her in the Midwest; she sounded more like a Southerner now. Southern girls were a lot of fun, he remembered knowing from somewhere. They had the right attitude.

'I'm always on for enjoying myself,' he said. After a short but awkward silence, he added, 'So how long have you been down here?'

'Eight months, and *lov*ing it. Peace and quiet, getting away from it all.'

'Do you get many visitors?' he asked, though he already knew the answer.

She shrugged. 'People come and go. Suits me fine. But some time I'll be ready to move on. Move back, rather.'

Harry raised his eyebrows in what he hoped was a curious and mildly concerned expression. 'Back to the States?'

'Find me a little place in Arkansas, up in the Ozarks. A farm I can settle down in for the rest of my days. A place my grandchildren can visit.'

She tipped up her beer bottle. Harry tried to calculate how old she must be to have grandchildren already, but was distracted by the sight of her throat as she drank. He didn't expect her to have caught the sun under her chin, but the skin down there was golden in the late light. A nodule of bone flexed in and out complicatedly, turning out then reinstating a small pool of shadow. As he watched, a yearning grew in the pit of his stomach. There was something lovely about seeing the equipment of this human body doing its job so efficiently, and about being so close to it. But there was more. She stirred a vague sense of recollection, of recognition, as if they might have known each other long ago.

Perhaps that was what *he* needed: a farm in the Ozarks, a destination, somewhere to aim for, a cottage in the

Cotswolds, a farmhouse in Wales, a bungalow on the Wirrel. Somewhere he planned to end up. But he wasn't sure you could have that without a permanent woman. What could be lonelier, after all, than sitting by yourself up a rainy hillside in Britain while it got dark outside at four o'clock?

Trudy emptied her beer bottle and settled it on the table with a sigh of satisfaction. 'All *right*. Well hell, let's see how that fish is doing.'

She sidled off her stool and walked around the bar and into the kitchen with an eagerness in her carriage, her back upright and bust held forward. It was nice watching her. Harry decided he liked her. It felt good to like someone. They might see more of each other. It could become something regular. She on her island, he on his. There was no reason they couldn't meet up every weekend, for example. Two professional people out here, they needed one another's company. He could move out of the guest house and rent a villa, somewhere with satellite and AC and a big sitting-room where the two of them could unwind, joking, reading the papers, after their respective weeks of labour. It could turn out to be the perfect arrangement – a woman on the next island, not too close but close enough. They could have a real courtship, give each other plenty of time to get used to the change. He had fallen at that hurdle in the past – rushing things and then panicking and wanting out.

He pictured them in a white villa on a hill. There weren't any villas on Inagua, or hills for that matter, but where there was a will there was a way. Then, when they felt they had done their time in the Bahamas, they could see what the next step would be. With her American passport and his British they could go anywhere, once they were spliced. It would be the best reason for people of their age to marry: a practical reason, solid enough to spare them embarrassment, as well as the sprinkling of romance, of course.

Trudy re-emerged from the kitchen and announced, 'Maureen says it'll be a while yet.'

A loud hiss filled the bar, followed by the unmistakable soft click of a gramophone needle landing on a record. A loud chord, a drumbeat, a man gleefully singing out, *Ah feeling to wine on something* . . . It was the usual island music, which Harry heard interminably on transistors all over Inagua, only this time it sounded strangely appealing. It made you want to tap your feet, swing your hips and click your fingers. There was something about the strumming guitar, the hop-popping conga drums, the insistent cowbell, that infected your muscles.

'Another drink?' Trudy called.

She poured them both a whisky, then tore a packet of Marlboro out of a carton. 'We may be a small island, but we've got cigarettes, we've got whisky, we've got everything you need.' She handed Harry a fresh drink, clunking her own against it. 'Down the hatch,' she declared.

They danced. Normally Harry hated to dance, but before he could object she had whisked him out of his seat and placed herself in front of him, shaking her hips. She had learnt to move like the islanders, swinging from side to side. She leaned back and set her legs apart, either side of

Harry's thigh, just as the island women did. At first Harry was embarrassed – nothing was worse than foreigners who pretended to be locals – but she had a way of moving that brought a smile irresistibly to his lips. Her loins took on a life of their own, rotating and pulsing back and forth. Once she backed against him so he could feel her warm behind. Another time she held his neck in her hands and quite distinctly pressed her pubic bone against his. He started to shake his hips too, grinding himself against her. She whooped with delight, grinding back. Then she got into a kind of Latin dance, whirling him round and round. He laughed along and trilled his tongue.

Afterwards, seated at the table, Trudy leaned forwards and touched his arm. 'You're something, you know,' she said. 'Forget about mad dogs and Englishmen. Dogs and mad Englishmen, more like.' Her hand was hot on his bare arm, below the sleeve of the tropical shirt he had changed into earlier.

Maureen emerged from the kitchen bearing a platter filled with strips of battered, fried fish. She shuffled across the floor and deposited it on their table. 'Dinner time,' she said in a lazy, tired-sounding voice.

Trudy had been chilling a bottle of Chablis, which Harry insisted be put on his bill, but she wouldn't hear of it. While they ate, Trudy talked about Masterpiece Theatre and how much she had always wanted to go to England. Harry dropped numerous hints that he would gladly take her. After dinner she suggested a stroll along the beach. It all went like clockwork.

* * *

Who is Harry Burton anyway? A global man, highly trained, bulky, stiff, ruddied by tropical suns, he is glimpsed in airports, at poolside bars, behind the wheel of Landcruisers in hot countries. He long ago severed the ties that bind. He needed to break free, and having broken free finds himself not a citizen of the world, but no citizen at all. The world adjusts, and no longer needs him. When this troubling recognition dawns on him he ignores it: he's just a little low. Another night with Josey down at Topp's Restaurant, or with Marie over at Madame Nelly's, a decent screw, a night with the lads, whoever the lads happen to be, and all will be well. But after years of looking askance at himself, years of flinching at the sight of Volvos full of children and lights in living-room windows at night, Harry realises that the dream he set out to fulfil has become grim truth. The juice evaporates from the fruit and nothing can bring it back.

Harry stirs in his sleep beneath the swish-swish of a fan. A warm knee presses against his thigh. He rolls over and his hand grazes a pubic bush. At once he rolls back the other way. He cannot hear the woman's breathing, but thinks she is asleep. He slips out of bed and into the bathroom, assuming he needs to pee, but finds that he doesn't. His head aches. In front of him is the dark bathroom (he doesn't want to turn on the light), his dim, swollen shape in the mirror, and the familiar dissatisfaction with the day coming. He will have to sleep with her again tomorrow night, it will be impolite not to. Then he will be gone. He drinks from the tap. The water tastes like a swimming pool. He slips back into bed as quietly as he can and lies a long time staring at the fan overhead, waiting for sleep to carry him away.

Old Providence

'Oh *God*,' Rothman Case muttered as his daughter parked the car outside the gallery. 'This is ruinous, murderous. How did you ever persuade me?'

She switched off the engine. 'Stop being a prima donna. You'll love it, you always do.'

'I never do. And this is different and you know it.' He let out a long series of coughs. 'Oh good God,' he persisted, as if even now there might be some hope of getting out of the evening ahead. 'What if I got appendicitis again, for Christ's sake, or if the old liver finally gave out?'

She dabbed at an eyelid, peering in the rear-view mirror. 'Appendicitis *again*? Break a leg,' she muttered.

Rothman, a stiff man, bulked to the full by late middle age, though not obese, planted his feet on the pavement. 'Better get it over with I suppose,' he enunciated deliberately, adding 'Ha!' for no apparent reason, out of alcoholic bravado perhaps. He stood on the kerb and glugged from his flask, flipped the cap and had it back in his breast pocket before she finished locking the car.

He caught sight of himself in the glass doors of the gallery. The impression was of universal gleam. A gleaming face, a gleaming shirt, even his black trousers seemed to gleam. The glamour of the night was apparently upon him. He had stepped, it would seem, into the limelight that was duly his. He directed an imperceptible nod of thanks towards the mirage in the glass that was him, buckled up his mood, battened down the furies, storm-sheeted the miseries, and allowed the waiting doors to be swung apart on his behalf. His daughter alighted on his arm as he took the first step and he felt the two of them make precisely the entrance required.

Jackson Mitchell the critic was first to approach, gliding through the crowd, glass in hand as ever, cheeks flushed as ever. 'Oh but this is most *de*finitely the one we've been waiting for. By George.'

Rothman smiled involuntarily. But the 'by George' unnerved him. It was unlike Mitch the Bitch to euphemise his expletives, on or off the page.

'Paintings of Providence. Wonderful, wonderful. Want a little taste, eh?' Mitchell giggled in his high-pitched wheeze, pulling a programme from his coat pocket. The back page was covered in scribbles. 'Seldom has London,' he began in his incisive tenor, reading his own prose, 'had such cause for self-scrutiny as it did last night, at the opening of blah blah blah. Nothing shames the art world,' he delivered with Hitchcockian emphasis, 'like the arrival of a master.'

'Fuck off.' Rothman waved him away. 'Arrival?'

'Knew you'd do it sooner or later. Always did. You're a *force*, dear boy.' He uttered the word in such a way that Rothman could not help but smile, under pressure partly of flattery, partly of the man's absurd camping. 'And every single one of them gone already. A positive pointillism of red dots. By the way, who *was* she?'

Rothman raised an eyebrow and didn't answer.

'Well,' Mitchell glanced at his watch. 'I'll be out of here in five minutes to catch copy. That'll be in the morning edition.'

Then Chaim, the gallery owner, was at Rothman's side, along with Kachinski and de Jongh, and suddenly it seemed odd that Mitchell should have been talking to him *à deux*. Perhaps Chaim knew that Mitch was planning on kissing arse, had given him a minute to deliver the good news himself. Mend bridges, so to speak.

'Fuck off,' Rothman called once more over his shoulder as he was escorted into the main hall, aswirl just then with the well dressed and the ignorant, and with the delicious, reassuring scent of expensive women. For which thank God, Rothman reflected: in the end it was the old pleasures that held a man together.

Next thing he knew, cameras were flashing and he was caught in a scrum of naked shoulders, a shrubbery of champagne flutes and a blaze of light. Too much light. He bellowed out his daughter's name but she didn't hear, she didn't come, and meanwhile his shoes became light and began a two-step of their own, and the light grew brighter, and as it did so he grew more aware of the painting hanging to his right, he thought it must be *Maria IX*, a big dark canvas with the face looming out of it. The eyes in the face seemed to attach themselves to the side of his head and pull . . .

* * *

Maria cradled his head in her long Latin fingers. Such fine fingers the Latin woman has. What the devil was Maria doing here? They'd said their goodbyes long ago. Maria's eyes shone like the rain: like pebbles in a stream.

'An out-and-out triumph, old boy. Every single one gone.'

The older one got the more the asses felt it incumbent upon themselves to call one 'boy'. Who was this one now? Ah, Chaim. His daughter's fellow. Not half bad. Rothman attempted to let out a ribald cackle but it didn't sit right in his throat.

Where were they now? Somewhere dark, somewhere illumined, as far as he could see, by a phalanx of red candles whose light licked over a bowl of glossy fruit. Ah yes: the black mass of the groaning table, the still life of dinner: they were *dining*, of course, some eight or ten of them. A white tablecloth, a meal well in progress, an empty chair at the head, no doubt his, for he was slumped in an armchair, it would seem, unlit cigarette in hand.

'More wine,' he heard himself bawl. And: 'Where's my supper?'

Chaim, good egg, faced him on a dining-chair, straddling it like a cowboy, his elbows on the back. 'Wine for the maestro,' he called out.

Someone produced a brimming beaker which Rothman seized and promptly poured into his lap.

'For God's sake, Daddy.'

Ah: Virginia. Good girl. 'You're a good girl,' he might or might not have said aloud to his daughter.

'What *are* you doing?' she asked.

He looked up at her but not for long. She was a frightening sight: eyes with the glint of steel, of all-sobering clarity.

'You shouldn't be drinking.'

Chaim smiled up at her. 'I'm keeping an eye on things.'

No use carrying on like this, Rothman thought. Got to straighten the old self out, get back to work. The best days are the days we work, Maria used to say. Too right. They were the *only* days.

And Maria was beside him again, Lord knows how, stroking his cheek, explaining with the touch of her slender fingers that he had got it all wrong, it was all terribly simple, one just had to be humble and diligent, nothing else. Diligence was goodness. To live somewhere pure, with good air, good light, and to work.

Virginia got him home, scolding him on the way for being foolish and obnoxious, for drinking on the pills, on his ravaged liver: why couldn't he simply enjoy a night of success, why complicate everything? And Chaim was in the back of the car, coming along to help. The two of them would hoist the old fool to bed, have a little nightcap, compare notes, that sort of thing, and hey presto, the two-backed beast would be at work.

'I mean, Daddy,' she went on, 'why you can't just leave things be. All anyone wanted you to do was smile and say thank you.'

Outside his flat he said, 'I need to get away. You have to get me away.' But even as he said it he didn't believe it. After a certain point in life there was no getting away.

* * *

He was up early flagging a taxi to the studio, dosed with aspirin, sertraline, ribavirin and coffee. The high hall of the studio, with its great dusty window overlooking, if one could have got up a ladder to look out, the Piccadilly line at Barons Court, had never looked emptier. For once the place was tidy. Judy, his assistant, had evidently been in. The big table in the middle caked with decades of paint had nothing on it but a stack of art books. A fleet of rags hung bone dry, clean, over the sink. The two easels stood empty and the big armchair, cushions puffed, waited between them.

The pleasant sigh of morning traffic reached his ears. He sighed too. A subterranean tremor shook the floor as a tube train passed.

It was good to get the canvases out of there at last. Or was it good? The place was unnervingly empty. What was a man to do now? The only thing he could think of was to pull the flask from his pocket.

The new show had been his daughter's idea but had happened through his own carelessness. He was a fool to have listened to her. What was left now? His private store, his own little treasure chest, the one true store he had carried through life, was plundered, its lid unhinged.

Three months earlier, one late afternoon while finishing up his last series of *Chair* canvases for Chaim, Virginia had caught him at it. Alone in the studio, he had gone to one of the stacks, as he sometimes did, flipped up its curtain and pulled out the three canvases lodged there. Then he ripped up a strip of carpet on the bottom, inserted his finger in a hole and lifted out the baseboard.

Hidden under it were eleven canvases. He reached up to switch on the light overhead and peered in, finally lifting out two, studying them both in daylight, and replacing one. The other he carried to an easel.

The picture was straightforward enough. From a profusion of foliage the face stared out at you: a dark woman, her face a geometry of lines, bones, complexions, all suggesting a disquieting and more or less unfathomable mood, a mix of resignation, despair, hope. A deal made with passion, with disappointment too. A trad picture, but good, chock-full of the right stuff. A solid chunk hauled from the sump, authentic to its core. Marred only by a gauche stroke here, a jejune line there. No question: Scavello and the other dealers who had looked at it twenty-five years ago had been wrong, blinded by the fashions of their day, incapable of seeing true work when it stared them in the face.

Something of Frida Kahlo in it, he thought. And of Gauguin too, of course. But mostly it was him, Rothman, through and through. Or rather her, Maria. Maria as she had embedded herself in his mind, glaring at him from the profuse nature embracing her.

He went over to the sideboard, hunted for the right palette. Which Judy had cleaned and scrubbed the best she could. It would have been better if she hadn't bothered. He bent down for a box of oils, squeezed out titanium, chromium, returned with a pair of brushes to the canvas.

He began with a ghost of a stroke. By God, he thought, but the damn thing was done after all. The eyes were particularly good. Bright and sombre at once. Remarkable how they held the viewer. Rothman let out a cough that was also a sigh, a laugh, even a sob. Who the hell had done this picture? Who had that young man been? Rothman didn't know whether to laugh that such a talent had existed or weep at its squandering.

Then he had heard the door downstairs. Footsteps climbed the staircase. At once he picked up the picture, but before he was even halfway across the room he realised he would never make it to the stacks in time. He returned to the easel, angling the canvas away from the door just as the rising steps brought his daughter into the room.

'Oh it's you,' he said. 'Afternoon, dearest, or is it evening?'

'You're here late,' she said. Her hair was swept back and she looked good, fresh faced, touched with cool autumn wind.

'You didn't expect to find me here?'

She reached into her bag and tossed an attractively plump envelope on the table: his week's pocket money. If you couldn't run your life yourself you could do worse than have your daughter, if she was a capable woman, do it for you.

'What are you working on?'

It had been bad luck. But at the time it crossed his mind that perhaps it was good luck. Was he really going to keep these pictures hidden for ever? She came round the table towards the big window and stopped behind him. She said nothing for a moment. Then: 'Oh my. What is this? It's so unlike . . . Are there others?'

'Done before you were even born, my dear.'

'Let me see them.'

And it being a beautiful afternoon of late sun, and Rothman, having just finished the last of the *Chair* pictures for the contract with Chaim, each of which he knew would fetch a comfortable five figures, riding as it happened on the crest of a glorious daylong hangover, he had acquiesced. Why not after all? This was his daughter. What harm could there be? What exactly *was* he planning to do with them?

'But Daddy –' She was apparently speechless at the next three he took out.

A train rumbled past, trembling through the floor.

'I'm calling Chaim right now.'

'Whoa, hold on a moment.' Yet he couldn't help smiling.

'You have to come and see what Daddy's done,' she said into the receiver. And Chaim came straight over. They got all eleven canvases out, leaning them against the wall, propping them on books, up on the easels, until the whole studio was filled with Maria's dark face and the darker foliage of the island on which he had loved her, and with her breasts and torso, the perfect taut plateau of her stomach, her deep delta. Rothman's head began to spin. He was sick in the toilet.

Chaim stooped and peered and screwed up his face. He paced backwards and forwards, cocked his head, sighed, chuckled, hummed. He tapped gently here and there at clots of paint. 'Well,' he mused, and: 'Hmm,' and: 'Yes, yes, interesting.' Then he gave Rothman a big hug. 'Where have you been all my life? I'm putting everything on hold.'

Before Rothman knew what was what, it had all been

arranged, he wasn't even allowed to touch them up. 'They need nothing at all,' Chaim declared. 'I'm not letting you near them. What a departure. When did you *do* them? This'll be one in the eye for the critics, eh, who think they've got you pigeon-holed.'

It had been an accident waiting to happen. As the weeks went by Rothman felt worse and worse, drank harder and harder, until finally the night came and he collapsed in front of everybody in a ruinous, ridiculous, sozzled heap, as he would later put it.

The day after the show Chaim bought them lunch, Rothman and his daughter, at Little's.

'All gone, every blasted one of them. Time for a holiday, I think. Are you serious about going away?'

'What?'

'Last night you said you'd like to go away.'

'Oh that. Of course I'm serious. A man needs . . .' He trailed off, racking his brains for what a man needed.

'I've been thinking –'

'An island. That's what a man needs. A bloody perfect island.'

'Quite, quite.'

'Chaim's got the perfect place, Daddy.'

Rothman frowned.

'Unless you're working, of course.'

'Got to give the old eyes a rest once in a while.'

Why not? Yes indeed, he would go and have a haircut, buy some new clothes and off they could all go on holiday with Chaim.

'To every man's island.' He drained a tumbler of Rioja. 'To *away*.'

'Daddy,' Virginia began: an ominous note. He slumped in his chair. 'You can't go around collapsing on us, you know. I've made another appointment for you.'

He shrugged; he grumbled; he wanted no doctor but the alchemist, the alkahest, the ultimate dissolution. 'No need, no need. Thanks anyway. All I need's a holiday. Quite right.'

So it was that just three days after the Providence show opened Rothman found himself supine on a horsehair mattress in County Clare, falling in and out of sleep.

An owl was hooting somewhere out in the night. He could hear it when the wind went quiet. To how many creatures was it given to look behind themselves? he wondered. To the owl with its pirouetting neck, and to the long-necked ruminants, the slow cow, the jumpy horse, the skittery sheep. To how many was it not given? To the fish, with their sensitive tails, and the stiff-necked biped to whom had been given the inner eye, which was all he could look back with.

When he woke again, out of the window he could see the ewes in the field sitting down like a flock of birds. Broad daylight already, sunny.

Rothman studied himself in the bathroom mirror. Ringlets of grey and white hair framing the temples, the bald pink skin overhead, the bulbous shiny nose of his Hungarian forebears: a grotesque face. Hazel eyes that had become permanently untrustworthy. Grotesque because false – a half smile moulded into the cheeks kept the eyebrows raised. It was the face of a man who had been in the public eye too long, the mask of a *personality*. Which was what he had become. The Painter of Roads and Chairs and other Everyday Articles. One either had a personality or gave it up to become one. Of the many wrong paths an artist might turn down, success was the hardest.

He lathered up his cheeks. He was of the sideburn generation. Funny how some things stayed with you. He had journeyed right through life with a pair of sideburns, once brown, now silver.

Coming down the narrow staircase he glanced out the window again: green elbows and shoulders of land, a veil of mist driving across them, a muffled thunder of wind in the rafters. You couldn't hear the sea from here but you could see it, grey and boiling beyond the field. That was Ireland for you: weather that turned on a dime. It had been sunny just now, and already it was cloudy. A stand of reeds shimmered in beating wind.

A mistake, obviously: Ireland had never been *away*. Ireland was just more of the same, the same old axis of booze and rain and candles and landowners with flats in Eaton Square who bought, at least they bought. Ireland was just part of the grounds, even if you were flung up on the cliffs of Clare. No one around here had any idea what *away* meant. He couldn't bear to look outside. This was not, had never been, where he belonged. Pills and booze and good galleries got you by, and women too, of course, but they would not have been necessary elsewhere. His head hurt. There was a stone in his chest.

In the kitchen he mixed up a Disprin with a splash of Powers and a dollop of fresh-squeezed orange juice from a jug on the table. A farmhouse table at which were seated daughter, daughter's lover Chaim, and a lady wearing a blue scarf.

Chaim, curly-haired, bright-eyed – eyes somehow too bright, as if permanently made up for the stage – got to his feet. 'What'll it be? *Oeufs jambon*?'

Rothman didn't want to have to look at him. 'Whatever,' he growled, and thwacked the cork back into the Powers bottle.

'Daddy.' His daughter's voice.

'For God's sake let me die in peace.'

'You're not dying, but if you keep on like this you'll kill yourself. This is Mrs Williams.' She meant, he knew, the woman with the headscarf.

'Mrs Williams, how do you do?' Rothman didn't turn round. He drained off his glass. It went down awkwardly, stinging his chest.

'She's come to see you.'

He set the glass down. 'You mean, I think, that she's come to see *about* me.'

The poor woman buckled up in her scarf said nothing. Jesus and Mary, she'd be thinking, but this one'll be a handful and no mistake.

'From where do you hail, Mrs Williams? The out-patients wing at Lisdoonvarna Hospital? The Samaritans?'

'Cork General Hospital.'

He turned. She had eyes of the coldest blue, bearing straight at him.

'Cork indeed.'

And a sharp nose and no lips at all. She wasn't a nurse, she was a monster. What had happened to the exotic women in his life, the suntanned arms and long nails that he, being a man of mixed origin, preferred? You travailed through a desert of concrete, glass and stripped pine, and this was where you ended up, in terminal discomfort overseen by women without lips, with chips of ice for eyes.

He sat on the edge of the bed, shirt unbuttoned and lying around him like the petals of an old flower. Mrs Williams prodded and palped with cold, fleshy fingertips the blubber of decades that had settled on him like silt. When she hovered over his liver he jumped. Then she pulled out an ear-trumpet, at which he peered down his nose.

'Still using those things over here?'

She ignored him.

The wind rumbled, restless under the roof. The thing to do would be to sit on the black rocks and watch the waves come in. But even they lost their mystique eventually, they too suffered the ceaseless knock and rock of existence just like oneself.

'I suppose you'll be telling me we have to toddle off to hospital. Well, I'm not going, so put that idea out of your mind.'

Mrs Williams paid no attention but fastened the bell of her trumpet to his upper chest, where its cold rim sank into his flesh. She listened for a while. Her stiff dress rustled as she breathed. Then she straightened up, shook her head and tutted. 'And why not, might I ask? Lie down.'

He lifted his feet off the floor and tenderly introduced his bare back to the chilly counterpane. She raised up first one leg then the other, then did the same with his arms. Irish notions of nursing, apparently. Then she sat on the edge of the bed and looked down at him.

'You'd better stay put in that case. You shouldn't be up at all. I'm calling the doctor.'

She put her hand on his chest. And for just a moment in her palm's stone-like coldness he felt a flicker of peace. Snapped on like a light: quiet, stillness, a suggestion of joy: and off again.

Maria once more: Maria with her eyes like Marlene Dietrich, eyes that rested on you and saw through you. Maria understood him, always had. She looked straight at him and he knew full well what she was thinking, she didn't need to say it, she might as well have been shaking her head and tutting.

Maria had gone on and made a life for herself. Women were good like that, they knew how to settle for second best, for the bird in hand, understood as men never would the value of a suitable match.

'No, no, no, you fool, I'm not talking about Ireland,' he had trumpeted at Chaim over lunch at Little's. 'Who needs Ireland? Ha. The island. The Island of Providence. Home of the provident adventurers who put their bows to the west and their trust in . . .'

Chaim hadn't understood a word. It had been a mad idea anyway, that they might all troop off to a forgotten atoll in the western ocean. Chaim had gone and bought the tickets to Cork or Shannon or wherever they were. Tipperary, for all he cared. It was the wrong side of the ocean, wrong side of Cancer. That was the particular error of which his life had consisted: the wrong side. And now the demons who governed this side had come along to claim him, planting their pitchforks in his liver like the flags of the vanguard. Soon they'd advance to the spleen – or had they had that long ago? – and the kidneys, lungs and heart. What was left of it. They were taking him piece by piece, and he was powerless to resist. He had long ago given up his last toehold on firm ground. He had built on sand, and now the tide had come in, here it was, an iron-black tide carrying him off on the shoulders of its breakers.

This was not a place he could manage sober. He bellowed like a whale. What was he doing under a ceiling of white wood with the wind howling through it, the wind that had come from the right place, from far far to the west, that was hurrying to the wrong place, the lands of Tartar and Viking, of the unforgiving civilisations? The land of mercy was where he needed to be, in the western sea.

He bellowed his daughter's name.

'Ah God, thank God you're there. My dear, my dear.'

Mrs Williams had a sponge in her hand, she was sponging his brow. Stinging water on his brow.

'My dear you have to help me. I won't get through this you know unless, unless . . .'

Providencia. No one knows where it is. Isn't that a curious fact? They all think they do, and then if you ask where, they say: the Bahamas, Rhode Island, Cape Cod, anything but the right place. Old Providence, the locals call it.

In de Caribbean de very bes' is de beautiful island of Providence, the calypso men sang.

They were right too. *De very bes'*.

They had arrived in Maria's father's plane. Rothman had never forgotten the first glimpse of the island below, floating on the sea's brow. Was it really there? A hazy diamond of green, framed by the plane's wheel and high wing. His head reeled. The whole island was in view, a bundle of green hills, a sparkle of livid rocks in the luminous sea, a chipped nugget draped in verdure, incorruptible, preserved in a thousand miles of brine. Salt, the scourer and purifier, kept it safe. Then they were circling over white and black reefs, reefs like tears in a canvas, and over lagoons of an almost sickly turquoise, and beyond them the island became a lot of monsters tussling under a green carpet.

Providencia, Maria called it, being half Colombian. Gauguin had sailed past on his way to Panama. Rothman's stomach lurched as the little plane jumped off a rock in the air, freefalling until its wings snared in elastic.

Old Providence. Island of the provident souls who sallied forth from Plymouth soon after the Pilgrim Fathers to find a better world; and though blown off course by hurricane, driven south by storm, had nevertheless found their promised land.

Rothman was twenty-nine, had just had his first group show in New York. 'It's your Saturn Return,' Maria said. 'Everything coming together for a new dispensation.'

His fellowship from the Brooklyn Academy, his having left the stuffy Royal College for good, the dazzling new world of the New World, the broad horizon of post-abstract, post-pop, the white heat of his experiments in lithography – she was right, it was true, he was only twenty-nine but had touched his prime already, the flood would soon be full. And with him, beside him, Maria, the beautiful daughter of Colombian-American parentage who would be his wife. She was a daughter of El Dorado, of fabled wealth, giving her all to the starving talent of a man with eyes like dark stars, as she liked to say.

The plane wheeled. The island was a tumble of mossy rocks now. Above, the big grey head of the volcano brooded, the head that – pathetic fallacy be damned – knew what was what. That for now allowed the rivers of green to pour down its flanks and the villages' twinkling roofs to adorn its skirts but that one day would decide enough was enough and shake them all off.

So this was Old Luis's home.

'You know Luis?' she had asked.

'But of course. From Madrid. When I had that scholarship to the Prado School. He taught ceramics.'

'I forget.' And she gives him that smile of hers which melts his breast. She nudges his shoulder. 'But you have lived everywhere already. You're not old enough to know so many places, so many people.'

'It was just college, nothing more.'

'And how long will you stay with this one?'

'This one?'

'*Sí, querido.*' And she touched her own breast. 'Am I just college too?' Then she laughed and tapped his nose with an erect fingertip, hid her face in his chest.

'Let's start with a week,' he said. 'A whole week in bed.'

Which is what they had done. Her father's house, a Caribbean gingerbread of the old style, had a veranda, a porch and a four-poster pocked with woodworm. Rothman stocked the house with coconuts, bananas, guavas, mangoes, stalks of sugarcane, a loaf of sand-bread, and rum. A machete too, the island's universal tool. You could do nothing down here without one. And a flotilla of hibiscus and heliconia. They slipped the painter mooring them to time and for seven days drifted on their bed. The more they talked, the more they had to say. The more they loved the more desire flared. He rode her body as his own. They raped each other's mouths, talked with skin, tongue, limb. Meanwhile, outside, the savage sunsets and neon dawns came and went, and the night skies chalky with stars. The sickle of the new moon affixed itself to the sky's sheet. The sea turned vermilion each evening, then night-blue. He was a young artist in love, and he could already hear the canyons of New York clamouring for his work.

At the end of the week Rothman woke up and thought: Work, damn it. Time for work. And he stumbled up to the shed behind the house at first light, fuzzy-headed and heavy-limbed from the love-orgy, doped with her scent, and commenced to paint again.

It was all very well, this seeing things with the soul's eye, as the Colombians called it, but the more the soul's eye saw the less the eyes saw. To imagine was to be blind.

'At least let me get outside, for God's sake,' he wailed at his daughter.

'Mrs Williams won't like it.'

'Screw Mrs Williams. Wrap me up.'

Donegal tweed, that was the stuff. A hairy coat that weighed as much as a man, making a great prickly bear out of you.

An afternoon of wind and sun and rain. He sat on the black rocks with Virginia at his side watching the waves explode. Fifty yards away they flew against a ledge, sending up towers of spray like snow, which blew over the ledge and spattered down, then streamed off over the Irish turf in mist. They sat and watched, he hunched over his stick, she leaning back with her hair blowing about her face.

'Fifty-six,' he said. 'It's not a bad age.'

'You could have another thirty years if you wanted and you know it. Happy years too.'

He squinted at the walls of flecked water coming in, tumbling over themselves. The Irish Sea. The North Atlantic. It was a beastly, unfriendly sea, it had no time for people.

'Happy? I've used myself up.'

Even if she couldn't, he could see what he meant. There was only so much a man could do. There was no point pretending and letting yourself grow ever thinner in body and work. Better to stay plump till the end, assuming you had the choice.

He didn't know what to say. There was nothing to say. It was remarkable he had lasted this long, with so little moral ballast on board.

Soon the rain came once more and they got up to go. He had taken only a few steps back up the beach, kicking at the sand, when the hip seized. They had to get the car and steer him to it, then drive him up the track to the house. He sat in the passenger seat gasping.

'Ridiculous. A warm climate is what my bloody bones need, not this freezing rain and wind. Whoever thought of living here? We're not made for this kind of weather, none of us are. Whoever thought of this for a holiday? We're not Vikings, you know, not any more.'

'You should be thanking Chaim for having us.'

He tried to respond but couldn't. Chaim turned on the windscreen wipers. Whine-clunk, whine-clunk. The Britannic symphony. Patter of rain, whine of wiper. Why had he ever come back? Two good years he had had over there in the New World, two of the best, the only two good years of his life. What had the rest been? A ride half-asleep, half-drugged, swaying about on time's back.

The steaming palm trees after rain, the whole island giving up its cargo of fragrances to the trade winds, the old bus with its wooden seats and no doors or windows, no walls even, lumbering around the island first one way then the other, climbing in and out of potholes. And the islanders weaving along the lanes on bicycles, on mules, asses and ponies, with always time for a game of dominoes, a glass of rum, a healthy beer. And the straw-hatted farmers calling out their accelerating crescendo of '*Anda, anda, andale!*' to the skinny mules that plodded round and round the gears of sugar-presses, while the farmers themselves, long reins in hand, stooped beneath the spindly arms of the mills as they turned, feeding in the stalks one after another, making the brown juice splash into buckets. And the two of them, she and he, bending under the mill-spokes to where one farmer stood, and him whistling, *wheet-wheet*, and the horses stopping, and him dipping a coconut shell down into his bucket. 'Try it, señorita, what do you think? Better than Coca-Cola, no?'

And he, Rothman, drank too – '*Para el señor*' – and sure enough it was the drink of health and longevity and fortified the very soles of your feet.

'Lucky us,' she had said, clutching his hand on the beach as the sky turned lime-green and the sea blood-red and the sun zipped itself away.

Why were we doomed to make the fatal error? We were not. Doom was an excuse for stupidity.

Her father had bought the house long ago. He had been meaning to come down for years but never had time, too busy shuttling between his offices, mistresses and haciendas, between Bogotá, Miami, New York, Caracas. 'Just don't start importing anything,' he advised them. 'If you hunt about you can find all you need on the island. They're wonderful carpenters. What they don't have they'll make for you. But go easy on the island art,' he advised. 'It can be . . . *un poco fuerte*.'

High on a hill, with porch, peeling blue paint and red tin roof, the house had four rooms and a view over Freshwater Bay with its stand of royal palms. Now and then a boy on a horse might canter under the trees through the surf. With the shutters opened up, the trade winds fluttered through the house, rifling her papers (she was working on her thesis on Cortázar), rustling the sheets, stirring the festoon of mosquito netting gathered over their bed. Which they hardly needed, what with the breeze on their hill.

'If Gauguin had found this place on his first trip he would have done without the syphilitic South Seas.'

Maria shrugged. 'He was a young man, still curious. He would have left.'

'It could only have got worse. Curiosity is a euphemism for restlessness, which is a euphemism for incurable insatiability. He would have been a fool to leave.'

But sure enough he himself, Rothman, had left. And ended up a depictor of chairs. The *Chairs* had been Chaim's idea. Not a bad one, he had thought at the time. Shrewd chap, this. There was no end to the polysyllabics the asses could slap about when considering the *seat* and its absence, the implication of corporeality, the iconicity of the quotidian. Et cetera. What does a vacant chair *signify*? A kid with a dictionary could do it. The longer the words were, the higher the cheques went. But the truth was, you could no longer bear your own fatal humanity so you painted chairs instead, and idiots bought them and made you rich. You meant to stop getting rich, to go back to your true subjects, but truth was always just after the next show. Then gradually you got sick through and through, body and soul, and survived on a diet of pills until the pills themselves started to do you in. Then you took pills against the pills, and more pills against those pills, and pretty soon there was nothing left of your own biochemistry, your own metabolism, your own body; or, in fact, of you.

At least he had had the Maria pictures. Only pictures he had ever done from memory. Though of course it would have been better if he had never needed to do them at all.

Maria stayed boxed and packed, all eleven canvases of her, for twenty-five years. Later, he might slide one out now and then, when the studio was deserted, sit before it under the giant window, then shuffle over to the side-board littered with rags, palettes, bottles of turpentine and the five big jars of brushes, rummage about for the right palette, and maybe add a touch here and there. The eyes were the hardest thing, those dark eyes, like wet pebbles but dark, and shining with a stern compassion. How much you could find in an ordinary woman if you only looked. And she had made him look, she as no other.

They planned to build a studio for him higher up the hill. Meantime, he worked in the palm-and-plywood shed at the back of the house. Every morning he would unclip the bolts and fold back the entire wall, opening it up to the south-west, to the bay and the jungle tumbling down.

He would see the Black Sister out to sea, a granite rock where the frigate birds roosted. The little fishing boats would be scudding out under their scraps of sail to the reef. When the wind came from the west he would hear the reef, a distant thunder deep in the ear.

One morning he went out with two fishermen, brothers called Armando and Raimundo, who once they were near the reef threw their anchor-rock over the stern and uprooted their driftwood mast. Masked and finned they drifted down forty, fifty feet through the clear green water, swimming as slowly as astronauts until they touched the sandy bottom and began to gather shells. They'd come up as slowly as they descended, heads tilted up so the masks flashed with the sky's reflection, their green string bags bulging behind them. They taught Rothman to clear his ears and tip himself head over heels and swim down with them, though by the time he reached the sandy bottom he'd be bursting and have to swim straight up again, while they with their dolphin lungs got to work below.

Raimundo and Armando provided his first island set, a series of oils done each afternoon from sketches he'd made while out with them on the boat.

One time when he touched the seabed he scrabbled about in the sand and his hand closed on a clam shell. When they opened it they found a pearl attached to the flesh, a grey bead the size of a pinhead.

'I'm going to give you this,' he told Maria, unwrapping the handkerchief in which he had kept it. 'But not yet.' He had plans for it; to have it flanked with chips of diamond, set on a band.

Each afternoon looking out from his shed he would see the sky turn to flame as the frigate birds gathered like bats about the burning pillar of their rock.

And there was old Luis, a Spaniard of ageless middle age who back in Madrid used to talk about the islands off the Spanish Main, and one day had finally packed his bags and gone, taken up with an island girl. They lived two bays and three hills away, with a parrot and a three-legged dog. He sported a leonine white beard and gleaming bald head, and with his suspicious eyes fancied himself piratical. He even wore an eye-patch, referring obliquely to a fishing accident *en el mar.*

Once, Rothman showed up during siesta time and found Luis reading the paper with no patch to be seen.

'Have to rest the eye,' he mumbled, waving at his face. He called the girl. '*Conchita. Ven!*'

Conchita, clacking with braids, tall, black, clad in nothing but a loincloth, traipsed out on to the veranda. She saw Rothman, smiled at him and turned away. Her breasts, slightly angry with one another, as the French put it, gleamed in the sun. They looked like bronze. Rothman couldn't stop looking at them. She was a living sculpture, a miracle of form and function. No wonder old Luis had settled here.

She approached Luis from behind, bending over him in the hammock. She opened her hands, stretching wide the elastic of his eye-patch, announcing her intention with a kiss to the top of his bald head, and slipped the mask into place. Throughout the procedure Rothman was unable to prise his sight off those nipples, thick buds of chocolate, and the flesh that supported them. Her breasts looked firm like the *flan* they served down in town, firm and soft at once, magnificent.

Luis's house, a modern villa, was covered throughout with his own canvases, hurried daubings of virulent colour; the tropics had gone to his head. 'I paint, I read, I write, I make love,' he said. 'And I eat fresh fish, fresh fruit. This is the healthiest place on earth. Everyone lives into their nineties. It's the *Shangri-La del Caribe*.'

Inevitably, of course, Rothman had fouled his Eden. It was so simple a thing, so farcical he could hardly believe it would have had the potent effect it did. A pair of knockers knocked the tiller out of your hand and next thing you knew you were headlong down the face of a hurricane.

Conchita. One night she clacked out of the dark house on to the terrace, tipped back her head, making the beads in her headdress clack and shush, and smiled at Rothman with an emphatic sigh. It was hard to know what that sigh meant. Perhaps it was just a stray piece of island emphasis. The locals liked to be emphatic like that, speaking as if the language were a drum to beat. But perhaps it was more.

Night-time. Rothman had come out to suck on a Cuban and look at the moon. His bride-to-be and his old companion in arms were both inside at the table. He heard Luis laughing a long deep private laugh: an absurd man after all, but somehow inspiring, perhaps because he had truly cut himself loose from all ties. Though it hadn't necessarily been good for his work.

Conchita clacked up beside him and leant against the wooden rail. '*Dáme*,' she said. Give me.

She sucked deeply on the cigar. Her cheeks lit up in the flare of the tip. A lustrous red-brown, smooth as brass.

'You must let me paint you,' he said.

She demurred, inevitably, but it was equally inevitable that he should persist, insist, devise a portrait of the two of them, Luis and His Girl, in order to overcome her reticence. He made it a picture of that moment with the eye-patch. It was inevitable too that one day Luis would be too tired or lazy or gripey to stroll up the winding road to Rothman's shack, that she should therefore come alone. Nothing else could have happened but that she should stiffly, awkwardly, yet somehow passionately accept a glass of rum and crushed mint after the sitting, that under the pressure of his eyes and hands she should acquiesce, comply, agree, hike her skirt to midriff and sit on him, first one way then the other, and grunt and grind her way to a peak that caused a bloom of sweat to break out on her sternum; then that she, being an obliging island girl, should smear that sweat together with the coconut oil she had rubbed into her skin earlier, which her exertions had now brought to the surface again, into the valley of her breasts and sandwich him.

Which was when, true to farce, Maria appeared in the doorway. She had finished her day's work on Cortázar and gone shopping, and now came bearing a tray of fruit and punch, refreshments for the two toilers after art.

A little farce was a dangerous thing. It was Conchita who saw her first. She made no sound but bowed away, retreating with her arms doubled insufficiently round her. She fumbled through her sprawl of discarded scraps of clothes, bending double to pull them on.

Rothman lifted his head. One of his hands had already fallen listlessly to his bereft shaft. He said, 'What? *Qué?*' But he didn't need to go on, he could feel the trouble that had entered the room. He glanced back to confirm it.

Maria, after a moment's stunned hesitation, did the only thing she could: dropped the tray where she stood and ran out.

He was young, in his stride, not about to let her slip through his fingers. Fumbling with his belt buckle, shirt flailing, he skipped over the rolling mangoes and shattered glass and ice, raced out the gate and down the track.

Maria must already have reached the road, a fact he noted with surprise, and indeed as he neared the road barefoot and unbuttoned, he heard an engine pulling away: their scooter. She had already disappeared round the first bend.

Cicadas chirruped. The sun was hot still, though through the palms he could see a bloom on the sea as the afternoon eased towards evening. A cockerel crowed. A light breeze lifted itself through the fingers of a dead coconut frond at the roadside. The scooter hissed away into silence.

Rothman felt embarrassed standing there. That more than anything else. He was a fool. His eyes darkened, he felt the blood in his face. What could he do, though? He would have to wait for her, that was all. Had the bus been running perhaps he could have boarded it in the hope of finding her somewhere round the other side of the island. But she could be anywhere. And the bus wasn't running, it had broken down two days before.

Conchita's head appeared a hundred yards up the track, peering out of the yard. He realised what she wanted to know, and beckoned. She came shuffling briskly downhill in her sandals, elbows crossed over her chest.

'*Ay dios*.' At first it seemed she intended to walk right past him, but she stopped a pace or two beyond. Shaking her head (clackety-clack) she said, '*Ni una palabra a Luis. El me matará a mi. Ay dios.* Luis would kill me if he knew.'

She stepped to and fro, kicked a stone. Her legs the colour of wet sand. It was shameful to see such a statue of a woman reduced to the ridiculous.

'Enough melodrama,' he said. 'We're only human after all. We have our weaknesses, we live in error.'

'In sin,' she corrected. '*Pecado. Todo pecado*.' She looked into his eyes, imploring reassurance.

He said: 'You're lovely.'

Her eyes filled for a moment with the tenderness that had opened her legs in the first place. At least one thing might still be done decently: the farewell of these two briefly acquainted bodies: he stepped towards her and kissed her on the lips.

Head bowed, she scraped across the torn-up roadway and down a sandy lane to the beach perhaps wishing that she did not have to exit his life quite so soon.

Back in the house he removed the flowers from a pitcher, rinsed it and mixed up a lot of punch. He drank a couple of tumblers straight down and sat smoking on the veranda with a third.

The problem, he reflected, was not so much what he had done as Maria's actually having seen him do it. That was what would traumatise a Latina.

But if you fell in love with an artist what did you expect? He was a man of the senses. Yet he knew how it would wound her. It would be the ultimate betrayal. And even to suggest that it meant little, was just a stray cupidity, would be a betrayal too, implying that their own love-making was not the demiurgical undertaking that it in fact was.

The sun flared over the island and died. The night that followed was the longest of his life. What began as a gnawing anxiety grew into a wild panic that saw him confusedly rummaging through his clothes, pulling out a suitcase to pack, leaving it open, empty, yawning on the bed beneath the mosquito netting, which somehow in the course of the night fell into the open jaws of the case. Why a suitcase? By morning he couldn't remember; probably he had sensed somehow that she had already gone, leaving everything, passport, wallet, clothes and all, and fled to the mainland. And from there who knew where?

At first light he hammered on the door of the shack that was the post office (a yellow 'Correos' sign hung from a shutter). But Señora Carmen wasn't opening up yet. He slumped against the door, and when finally he heard her slide back the bolt and open the door he almost fell in. Then he found he had no money on him and she wouldn't let him use the telephone without a down-payment. She inhaled sharply and shook her head. 'No credit, no call, see the sign there?'

When he returned with his wallet he realised he didn't know where to call. He tried her mother's house in Long Island. No answer, why would there have been? Her apartment in Manhattan – also no answer. Then the island's phone went down.

Panic gave way to gloom. He thought of Luis, an older man, and could only imagine him devastated, were he ever to know. Would Conchita be able to pull off a lie? The island was her home, she had found a man here to appreciate her for what she was, to bring to her the aesthetic of the big world. Rothman had been playing for bigger stakes than he had realised. As the sun rose it was a sky of steel that arched over the little green island lifting itself from the sea. Love of such a calibre as his and Maria's could not be trifled with. When you had all nature on your side, as they had – all his nature, all hers and all the nature around them – you had to prove yourself worthy.

He drank rum for breakfast, then sat by their gate and waited and smoked and lied to himself that she would come back. But he was not a man who knew how to wait. She'll be back, said Armando and Raimundo. A lover's tiff, nothing more. A man must sometimes wait. *Un hombre tiene que esperar.*

But five months later she was married to a man who owned an Argentine bank; and Rothman, back in New York, left honest painting behind for good. That was the folly of youth: its dangerous solemnity had a power beyond its years.

Those first few days alone on the island he knew with a young man's melodrama that it was over. Hadn't this end been inevitable from the start? But life and work had to go on, they could not be stopped for long. The river of a life ran on, if not one way then another. A man was a man, an artist was an artist, there was no shame in fulfilling the desires of eye and body. Why then did he think of nothing but her face, her limbs, her fingertips, day and night?

This is no way to carry on, he told himself, and would briefly feel on top of things. It was in one of these respites that he decided: only one thing to do: paint her out of my system. No doubt while he was hard at work she'd walk in the door. He went into the studio with a saucepan of strong coffee and a box of paints. In five days he had finished a canvas and thought he was done, but no sooner did he begin to clean his brushes than another intention presented itself, a bigger one. In the end he worked for five straight weeks with hardly a break.

When finally he left the island he packed the paintings up and took them and himself back to New York. Which was no easy matter, without Maria's father's plane to collect them, nor the fare for a charter. He had to take a banana boat to the next, bigger island of San Isidro, an overnight journey, then a steamer down to Barranquilla on the mainland, where he waited five days for a third steamer up to Miami, where he boarded a train up the east coast. It took two and a half weeks. But it was a healing journey, he told himself. The young artist with his first masterly works in a box beside him makes his way back to the woman he loves, who surely will be unable to resist being won back.

But she was able. She had a moral muscle, denied to Anglo-Saxon women, that simply could not permit what he had done. 'I saw you,' she spat when finally he trapped her on the telephone in the Madison Avenue apartment.

He paused, surprised. 'But I know you did.'

'Ha!' At least that was what it sounded like, a shocked exhalation. 'You and your floozy, kissing goodbye.'

Maria had not gone down the hill but up. She had run uphill towards the grey head of the volcano. She had seen him kiss Conchita goodbye: that on top of everything else. She had gone up the farmers' tracks to the very crown of the island, then down the other side to the airport where a local air-taxi bore her away.

At that moment it all seemed ridiculous, excessive. Too much bloody earnestness, the phrase ran through his mind. His *floozy*. Surely she couldn't really mean that. That pitch of corn. But he fought back the feeling. 'Please let me see you.'

A long pause. Then: 'It's too late,' uttered in a soft voice, too calm.

That scared him. 'Too late?'

She sighed.

And of course the man in question was not an impecunious talent but a banker, or more than that an owner of banks, a man with his own plane and haciendas, a man from her own world, more or less, who would give her proper places to live and all the rest. Rothman called again the next day to ask to see her, but she had gone on a trip.

He didn't unpack the pictures for a week, just sat with them in the bare room of his shared apartment on West Broadway. Then he sent them up, still boxed, to Scavello's, and waited by the phone. A day, two, four went by. Finally he had to call himself.

'Hmm. Maybe a wrong turning here? This sort of thing is out of date, you know, you can't expect to attract the same attention. In this game to be with it we have to be ahead. To walk you run. That's why we did well before, in the group show. You were pushing the envelope, challenging our *concepts*, making us think about what art *is*. Carry on where you left off, I say.'

So he did. He boxed up the canvases and thought a lot and shipped them and himself back to London, where he embarked on his first tarmac images. 'The Road Show', they called it, studies of Britain's road surfaces. The show was his first big British hit. And at the opening he met Lady Daisy, the countess's daughter who would mother his one and only child, Virginia, then leave him for a rock drummer. Never again would he permit oils to seduce him.

Mrs Williams from Cork cleared the house of alcohol.

'What?' exclaimed Chaim. 'Have a heart.'

'If I didn't know better I'd think you were trying to kill him off,' Virginia said. 'What else can we do?'

'Let him down gently, for God's sake.'

'The man's not got long if he carries on the way he is,' said Mrs Williams.

All day Rothman sweated and bawled, then slumped into a dosed abyss. The next day he woke clear as a bell in a pool of lucidity.

Righto, he thought, pulling on his heavy trousers, making his way down to the kitchen in the early light. He made coffee, fetched his sketchbook, a box of charcoal, a rag, stuffed them all in his coat pocket and opened the door.

Outside was a world transformed. The gale that had been blowing the last three days had abated. Heavy dew lay on all things. The green sweep of fields sparkled as with wet paint. The sea, at last, had shaken off the turmoil of grey and was deep blue, speckled with white caps.

He levered himself over the stile and stumbled across the boggy field down to the rocks. Across the bay Ireland stretched away like a green shadow, ending in a little grey pinnacle. The horizon trembled like a taut string. A ewe bleated up on a hill.

I'm here, Rothman thought. I'm actually here. Meaning: alive, noticing things.

Squelch went his boots on the sodden grass. The breakers roared. Deep inside some blow-hole the waves thumped and gasped. And he smelled the tired old smell of the sea, of salt and stale seaweed, which instructed a man in a way he could not refuse to unloose his worries, lay down his burden.

Rothman sat on a broken stone wall. How much of his life, he thought, he had hidden behind a slab of paint, peering round the edge occasionally. Was it sad to have ignored the million daily calls to canvas in favour of one lode-stone from the past? At least he had avoided staking his name on junkie heiresses drooping in Bayswater light. He may have opted for Chairs and Roads, but he had not given in to the climate of fatal greyness that many had, had kept his little bottle of sunshine intact. Except no longer.

I am here now in a wet country by the sea, he told himself. This is my life. It scared him to realise how seldom he could have claimed the most rudimentary awareness of his surroundings.

Rothman heard a friendly *pop*. He opened an eye. Chaim was squatting beside him, Powers in hand.

'Got something for you.' He grinned, his face screwed up in a gargoyle-like grimace.

Rothman stared at him, groaned, and reached for the bottle. Cool in his hand, unreassuring, perhaps not quite what he wanted after all, but he'd be a fool not to accept a dose anyway.

Beneath all its packaging there was nothing *in* the Old World, that was the problem. Whereas within the New there beat a young heart which lent all newcomers its vigour, to which he had once been privy. Why had he turned his back on it? Crassness, self-deception, compromise. A wanton spilling of the basket of strawberries held out by the hand of a good woman.

Out on grey Westbourne Grove two weeks later, back in London, it was raining again. The taxis, the buses, the young couples went by, huddling under their umbrellas. *British United Providence*, one umbrella had blazoned on it. Under it a girl in a green mac clung to the arm of her young executive. She had blonde hair, a rain-washed face. The two of them huddled beneath the shelter of their mortgaged future.

One could do worse than that after all, Rothman ruminated. Get a mate, a job, a mortgage, then settle down and procreate. One couldn't hope for any kind of final fulfilment; just to get through life, as they, the streaming couples out in the rain on their way to lunch, under the shelter of BUP umbrellas, were doing, would continue to do, was no bad thing. Anything nice, ultimately, was better than whatever was not.

The tinkle of liquid poured over ice brought him back from the window. Chaim's sitting-room was big and deep, a room of low furniture and tall walls, hung all the way up with recent art. Rothman avoided looking at it. It was all junk, all the modern British trash of which he himself had been a prominent producer, with his Knives, his Shoes, his Foam on Beer Glasses, all his studies of the 'quotidian'. How little real content could you have: that was the game. The vacuous masquerading as the clever. The more vacuous it was, the cleverer it was thought to be.

'What they call a Dutch Martini,' Chaim said, handing him a glass. 'Genever and vodka. And a pickled onion.'

Rothman downed his in one. 'Disgusting,' he scowled. Then raised an eyebrow. 'The second always tastes better, eh?'

'That's the spirit. Screw those bloody hacks.'

Jackson Mitchell had printed another story, this time asserting that Rothman was past it, over the hill, in terminal alcoholic decline. His working days were over. All he could do now was salvage daubings from his distant past.

'The buggers just say what they like. Best thing is to ignore them completely, *n'est-ce pas*?' Chaim said. 'Anyway, it's time you and I put our heads together about your next contract, old bean. I've been thinking about "Brushes".'

It was while he was in the bathroom that Rothman noticed something unusual. All his Maria pictures were lying high up on a little gallery above the handbasin. A wooden ladder fastened to the wall gave access to the loft, and he climbed a few rungs and reached up just to make sure. It was them all right.

'What are *they* doing here?' he asked Chaim.

'They're on their way to the buyers,' Chaim answered. But it was odd: first the show had ended strangely soon. Now the pictures, long since taken down, were here in the gallery owner's flat.

'They'll be off soon.'

Rothman left feeling vaguely disturbed, to meet a gang in Little's where, while he stuck it out, someone commented that the pictures at his last show had been snapped up and out the door so fast people hardly got a look at them. It wasn't customary to pull them off the walls as they sold, surely. Rather a departure, those pictures, from what one heard.

'Not at all,' Rothman growled.

Next day he called Chaim for a list of the buyers.

'No can do, I'm afraid. But we've banked the draft all right. You'll be getting a fabulous cheque any day.'

Then he called Virginia. 'What's going on?'

'You've been drinking,' she answered. 'I'm not talking to you when you're drunk.'

It was true, he had been drinking, but he wasn't drunk.

'Will someone just tell me what's going on?'

She was silent at the other end. A warm, breathy silence in the receiver. He heard himself exhale, a soft rumbling in the earpiece.

'Chaim thought they'd be better off out of the way.'

'But they've been *bought*, for Christ's sake. Why are they all in his flat?'

'They have been bought,' she said. 'Yes.'

He was quiet a moment. 'So?'

'I'll come round.'

Which she did. To say: 'What does it matter? The things are sold, it's all above board.'

Except it wasn't. Rothman could see that a mile off.

'Who the hell bought them?'

'Some wealthy South American.'

'Of course they're wealthy. But who?'

'An Argentinian minister.'

In silence she watched him drink a glass of wine. He screwed up his nose. 'Argentinian?'

She sighed. 'He's married.'

Rothman stood up. He poured out another tumbler of wine.

'He didn't want his wife's body splashed all over town. And she wanted them too. She wanted to have them.'

Rothman began in a sing-song: 'Well why didn't anyone *tell* me?'

'Chaim was going to. She offered him a big bonus for getting them down fast. He was afraid you'd disagree, I suppose. And to be honest, everyone says how good it is that you've been consistent all these years. Chaim was worried about that.'

A mouthful went down the wrong way. Rothman gasped, spluttered and shook his head. 'Well, no more bloody contracts with him. I've done enough chairs or roads or bloody brushes for one lifetime. I'm an *artist*,' he said, but he couldn't help putting a sarcastic twist on the word.

Suddenly he badly wanted his pictures of Maria to go out into the world. Instead of which they would remain imprisoned in some basement in Buenos Aires. Chaim had never even done a catalogue of them. But they were his true representatives. Even at his age, with his name, Rothman was still stumbling around outside the citadel, begging to be let in. It was the wrong way round. It was he who had the power, who ought to be living behind the shining walls, while the likes of Chaim prowled at the gate. But he hadn't realised that. Too early he had made it his business to drink and dine with the enemy. Especially drink.

Downstairs, he opened the door on to a street just then enflamed by a brilliant low sun – a street of gold, with the silver cars rushing up and down it. He stood looking at it, just outside his door, with no idea which way to go, towards Hammersmith or away from it. As he waited there – or not so much waited (there seemed to be nothing at all that could possibly arrive to dislodge him from his static position) as wavered – he heard footsteps coming down the stairs behind him. He remembered that his daughter was still up there. At the thought of her, at first a habitual relief and gladness touched him; until it came back that it was she who had persuaded him to open up his private store, who had instigated its plunder. Even she was lost to him now. He couldn't forgive her. He was truly bereft.

'Daddy,' she said, stepping down on to the pavement and reaching for his hand inside his coat pocket. Her hand was cool and almost erotic in the warmth of the coat. He stood still, he wouldn't look at her. He felt the cool palm close over his fist.

'I've been robbed,' he told her.

'But they're paying massively. You can do what you like.'

He snorted. 'All my life. I've let them do it.'

A thought flashed into his mind: perhaps it was possible there might be one advantage to his having lost all that work; just for an instant he saw a glimmer of a kind of freedom, a productive kind, almost a desire to produce more work. Not only that but there was even a subject that suggested itself, a *real* subject, the first real subject he had thought of in decades. And as the thought of it, or rather the feeling, the clarity of need to pursue it, came upon him, he felt his limbs and torso wake up as they hadn't in so long, flushed as if with spring water, or as if lubricated with clear oil. The subject was his daughter:

he had never properly addressed it, just as he hadn't properly addressed any subject in three decades.

He turned to glance at her. She was looking at him. Her eyes were gleaming with reflected sun. It was like looking into luminous amber. Something jumped in his chest and he started coughing. He turned away, catching a glimpse of a western sky like a cauldron of gold before he doubled over.

Mortimer of the Maghreb

Charles Mortimer watched the rippled brown land wheel back to horizontal. He drained the last drops from the plastic glass of Johnnie Walker the air steward had given him, and decided: that's it, no more booze for a week. *Au boulot.* His former life, his real life, stitched together by the clackety-clack of the typewriter and the patter-patter of the laptop, and by the roar of jets, was coming back to him now. Once again he was baptised in the odour of jet fuel (which still made him sick), born again in the air, the medium of his real work.

They had been flying for two hours, deep into the desert. As the plane finished its turn for final approach, one of the Migs stationed at the El Zouarte air base sliced through the desert sky like a steel meteor. His heart tightened. The old feeling came back, the feeling you almost smelled in your nose which told you this was the one, this was the right place to be, you would find what you needed here – the feeling that guided you to the front page. Enough of those blustering columns on page twelve. How good that he had returned Mohammed Ahmoud's telephone call and gone to meet him at the Wolf and Whistle, that he had got away from the little office with its blue carpet and oversize computer terminal and private fax machine – all the perks just for him, the grand old man come home to grow fat and die.

'Welcome, Mortimer of the Maghreb,' a man in fatigues addressed him when he reached the bottom of the aeroplane steps. Mortimer squinted at the man, who was grinning broadly, by which Mortimer understood that he was to take the greeting as a joke. He chuckled back. Like his compatriot Mohammed Ahmoud back in London, the man looked like he would weigh very little. He introduced himself as Ibrahim. Mortimer noted a certain friendly roundness about his face, almost a clownishness. Men like that could be dangerous, Mortimer thought. They didn't care about anything.

'Welcome to SAR,' the man said, speaking awkwardly, with excessive emphasis, as if it was difficult for him to utter each foreign letter of his spurious nation's name. He hissed on the 'S'. The letters stood for 'Saharan Arab Republic'. A seriousness came over the clownish face as he pronounced them.

Mortimer followed the man towards a waiting Land-Rover. As he moved across the tarmac, away from the aeroplane, the wind caught him unawares. It was an extraordinary wind. He had travelled a great deal – in the Pamirs, the Balkans, the Caucasus, in South Africa, the Middle East, in Sri Lanka, all the world's trouble spots over the last thirty years – but never, it seemed to him, had he known a wind like this. Strong and steady, and so hot he felt there must be some mistake, someone had left an engine running, or opened a furnace at the wrong time. It scalded his face, burnt his neck. It came from nowhere, from everywhere. Mortimer looked round. Beyond the airstrip with the one jetliner there was nothing but flat, open desert, beginning at the edge of the tarmac and stretching away for hundreds, thousands of miles.

What a place to live. It was an unfinished world, not ready for human habitation. What a place for a war. He remembered his wars being in beautiful landscapes, among valleys and mountains and rivers. You would wake up to see the dew glinting on a gun barrel and feel the sun warming your back. You would eat your porridge overlooking a gorge. Or you would hike up a trail among fir trees. Or you might be staying in some dismal concrete city but from the hotel window you could see splendid dusty mountains. This was different. A construction site with no construction, an emptiness without end.

Mortimer had been here once before, over twenty years ago, but he remembered the terrain quite differently, as a glinting plain of gravel.

The Land-Rover sped off down a paved road that soon became a washboard track and finally a set of tyre tracks on packed earth. Beside the tracks ran an intermittent line of old oil drums, each painted with one white stripe. Finally the jeep passed several rows of canvas tents. The rows were very long. Mortimer couldn't see how long because far away the tents disappeared over a brow. This was the 'canvas city', as Mortimer had dubbed it all those years ago, where the Rio Camello guerrillas and their people lived, the vast tent home of the 'Nation-in-Exile', for whose homeland they had been fighting for more than two decades.

The jeep pulled into a compound of old buildings

covered in peeling yellow stucco, some French desert post from long ago. Mortimer was left in a high room with a stack of foam mattresses and a pile of blankets in one corner. He understood that he was to arrange a bed for himself, a comedown after the way he had been treated so far, in Algiers and on the flight. He pulled the top mattress off the stack and began unfolding one of the thick, hairy blankets.

A soldier interrupted him. '*Venez, monsieur.*' Then, not sure if Mortimer had understood, he added, smiling: '*Vamonos. Yalah, yalah.*'

One thing about these men: they really knew how to smile at you. Desert men were the ultimate brothers. Forget old-boy camaraderie. No men knew how to befriend one another like desert men. They held hands, they hugged, they sprawled by the fire with arms draped over one another's thighs like wild animals in repose.

He followed the man down a corridor, across the compound and into a canteen. He took a seat at a long bench, along with some fifteen or so others, most of them local soldiers, but one a man in a pale blue shirt with a UNHCR badge over the breast pocket. A soldier brought Mortimer a plate of couscous with some red sauce and a lump of tough meat. A glass of a sweet pink drink followed.

Mortimer was halfway through the meal when the man called Ibrahim appeared beside him, squatting on his heels. 'Are you ready?'

Mortimer was clearly still eating, but answered, with his mouth half full, 'Whenever.'

'Let's go,' Ibrahim said, as if eating were merely a way of passing time.

Outside, another Land-Rover, open-top, was waiting.

'Bring anything you need. We'll be gone four or five days.'

Mortimer wasn't sure what he needed. He went into his room and pulled a toothbrush and a new notebook from his bag.

The men wrapped a headscarf round Mortimer's face, laughing, until he was left with only a slit to peer out of. The material smelled of plaster dust.

'You have to,' Ibrahim explained. 'We drive fast.' A light chorus of laughter approved the remark. 'The wind here, the dust. They can make you ill.'

It was the most open a Land-Rover could be: not even a windshield. Just the bare bottom half of the body, with two spare tyres and two giant jerrycans attached to the back. The whole thing was painted a dusty desert brown, and all bare metal had been coated in matt grey paint. Mortimer noticed there was no speedometer. No instruments at all. Just the pedals and the various gear sticks.

The Rio Camello fighters were good with their Land-Rovers. They drove excellently and would long ago have had to give up their fight had they not. They likened the Land-Rover to the old Bedouin's camel, to the corsair's sloop, to Britain's Spitfire.

Thus, so simply, before he was ready for it, Mortimer found himself finally embarked on another war story, another front line, back in business.

* * *

Charles Mortimer, chronicler of wars and plagues and ruptured governments, interviewer of popes and pashas, had had columns set aside for his use in papers the world over. He had smoked a Cohiba with Castro, dined on a Maine lobster with Reagan, and had drunk beer with the mad Billy Fuentes, beer baron of Bolivia, commanding chief of the death squads. He had been the toast of London and Washington. Mother Teresa and the Dalai Lama had agreed to a joint interview with him. Noriega in his heyday had bestowed the Order of the Silver Stork on him, and the Queens of Norway and Tonga had awarded him honorary degrees. For twenty-five years Mortimer had ridden the biggest waves in the business. Embracer of causes, instigator of hunts, winner of media coups, Mortimer had redefined his profession.

He had done all these things, but he had done them five years ago, seven, ten, twenty years ago. Now was different. It surprised Mortimer, when he thought back, both how long and how short five years were. That so long a time could go by so swiftly, so emptily. Or not emptily, but filled with something so uncomfortable, so different from what had come before. Five years of doubt, drunkenness, regret. Regret, the great devourer, could swallow half a decade in one go. Regret was a terrible trap, people said. Stop it, don't think about it. You must look forwards, onwards.

Five and a half years ago Mortimer had risked everything on his biggest story. He had succeeded in gaining an interview with the Soviet President, and after exhaustive consultation of every source, he syndicated a story on the impregnable primacy of the Supreme Soviet. Contrary to all reports, he declared, the writing was not yet on the Kremlin wall. Everyone took the story – *Le Monde*, the *Zeitung*, the *Washington Post, The Times*. It was the coup of a lifetime. Except that just five weeks later the Berlin Wall came down, and six months later the Soviet Union was coming apart at the seams.

Mortimer had not just been spectacularly wrong, he *had* risked everything. It was as if every editor and source he had was implicated in his shame. A *Times* leader referred to him as a curiosity, an American paper alluded to his 'disgrace', and the *Spectator* cancelled his retainer. Of course most people were too caught up in the excitement of the new events to think about him; but he wasn't. After such a debacle, a man needed a change of identity. He needed to start all over again. Which was out of the question at the age of fifty-two.

Saskia, his wife, had argued with him about it at the dinner table. She had told him again and again that he was wrong, and she took their differences personally. Which was unlike her. Also unlike her, after his great misjudgement she started minding about his peccadilloes – the publicity girl at the magazine where he was an honorary editor, the assistant at *The Times* news desk. Their marriage had long been pragmatic, accepting of human weakness, elastic enough to contain his work, his erratic urges, his sudden departures and returns. But now Saskia talked to him only in public, at dinner. Otherwise, she slammed doors, left the house without goodbyes, and forsook for the spare room the matrimonial bed that he often forsook himself. Eventually, eighteen months after his great embarrassment, she left him.

By then he was already caught in a swift stream of forgetfulness. It wasn't that he stopped working – he dabbled with foolish columns in the *Standard* and the *Mail*, long inches in which he was free to scribble himself hoarse on any matter that piqued him: waiters no longer wearing ties, wine lists in which the Australian imports had squeezed the clarets into an appendix; the new 'Metro' taxi-cabs. The brash new world springing up around his ankles was ripe for stomping on. At three in the afternoon, with copy due for the evening editions, it provided an inexhaustible supply of annoyances for a man with a keyboard in his lap and a bottle of Pauillac in his belly, a man who would much prefer to have remained before his Camembert and gleaming glass than to have hailed a Metro-cab back to the grey-walled warehouse of an office where you were no longer even supposed to smoke. At least they allowed him that: a little box of a room all to himself, regarded, incredibly, as a privilege in that open-plan arena, where he was permitted to smoke up a fog as long as he kept the door shut.

Occasionally, in the office, Mortimer would look up from his column – *Mortimer's Monday*; *Mortimer on the Movies*; *Metropolitan Mortimer* – and sniff the air, test the ground: still foul, still tilted. When life went wrong, why didn't it right itself like everything else on God's earth? Five years on, the ground was still skewed. And while you waited for it to recover, the weeks turned into months, and once seven months had gone by, you saw that seventy-seven could do so, and before you knew it they nearly had.

The rushing chaos of these years could have gone on and on, he knew, until he found himself collapsed in a hospital ward with two weeks to live. Did you blame the drink? But he had drunk before, he had always drunk, except in Saudi or when he caught hepatitis. Was it Saskia's leaving? But he had never depended on her for his sanity or purpose. Things had gone wrong before she left, anyway. Was it really just his hideous error, then? But all men made errors. Editors knew that. They were willing to give him a second chance. He had only to indicate where he wanted to go, what war, what famine. Was it all these things combined? Why, every time he checked the weather, was it stuck on Stormy? All storms blew over. When, in short, would he no longer find himself churning out furious columns about newfangled menu items like arugula and pecorino ('What the devil is wrong with good old Parmesan?' he watched himself typing, like some foolish old colonel) and instead be back at work?

But it was a desperate not a hopeful question.

When Mohammed Ahmoud telephoned and re-introduced himself, they not having spoken for well over ten years, Mortimer had felt a stirring of old, good feelings – that simple enthusiasm, almost joy, of sensing that someone was about to do you a favour, and you would be able to return it, and together you would advance one another's causes. Twenty years ago Mortimer had first brought Rio Camello's war to international attention, though since then the story had stagnated and dropped from the papers.

Chuckles of reacquaintance down the telephone line. It was morning, fortunately. Mortimer was more or less sober.

'Something important,' Mohammed Ahmoud said. 'Can we meet?'

Mortimer and Mohammed Ahmoud met in the Wolf and Whistle in Pimlico. That was something new – lunch in a pub, not at a white-cloth establishment. It felt good. It felt like things ought to feel.

'A major new offensive,' Ahmoud said. 'We cut through their defences in many places at once. We reduce the Moroccan army to nothing. They're just boys.'

'When?'

They had to plan and arrange, Ahmoud said. Two or three weeks.

Mortimer watched the slight Arab facing him across the pub table, sipping his lemonade through a straw with his curiously big lips. Ahmoud moved slowly, with that desert economy born of unrelenting thirst. Mortimer liked that way of moving. It seemed more a way of being. Something in him loved a desert.

Sitting in the dingy Wolf and Whistle with the drizzle of Pimlico tapping against the window, Mortimer remembered how he used to feel in his heyday. It occurred to him that if he could still muster that feeling, then his heyday was not necessarily over.

'Can you get me to the front line?' he asked.

Mohammed Ahmoud put down his glass of lemonade

and tilted his head to the side, trying to conceal a smile. He shrugged. 'All things are possible,' he said, in the way of desert men.

Before they left the camp, the guerrillas drove Mortimer between two rows of tents for mile after mile. They were big square tents, canvas, UN issue. Women sat in the doorways, some dressed in the traditional robes, a few in fatigues with a scarf over their head. The Rio Camello were proud of their particular brand of Islam, which did not subjugate women, many of whom held staff positions in the guerrilla force. Here and there children in tattered clothes stopped to watch the Land-Rover pass. There was an air of slowness about the camp, as if everyone were living at half speed.

They drove past a huge old black Bedouin tent. Mortimer remembered such a tent from twenty years ago, when he had visited before. The guerrillas had held a kind of banquet in it for some delegates visiting the refugee camps. It had been like some bizarre folklore evening in a posh hotel, inexpertly rendered out here in the desert. They had slaughtered a baby camel, which sat, hump and all, on an ark of tin foil, being slowly hacked to pieces as the evening progressed, while in the corner a band wailed on primitive oboes and thumped frenetically on goatskin drums.

He had enjoyed that evening, drinking endless glasses of tea and smoking pipes of rough tobacco. He had just published his first story on the guerrillas, his initial report on the Great Wall of Africa, as he called it, a phrase that had been used in the headline and became general currency. The Rio Camello's enemy, Morocco, had constructed a thousand-mile rampart of sand in the desert to keep the guerrillas out of the disputed territory. It wasn't really a wall, just a bulldozed dyke with military posts strung along it, but it was still a remarkable story, and Mortimer had broken it. He had been riding high then. Everything he touched came out right. Memos went round the news desk referring to him as 'Mortimer of the Maghreb'. He remembered dancing along to the crazy music, flirting wildly with a pretty Saharawi woman who was a guerrilla colonel.

The Land-Rover passed a well where a throng of people had gathered. Further along, a water truck with a great green tank on the back crept past them, going the other way, dribbling on the dust.

Then they left the tents behind and accelerated on to the open desert. The day was cloudy now, and the desert stretched away as a sheet of grey sand, an endless beach without an ocean.

Ibrahim grinned at Mortimer and whispered, 'I could pick them off with my Kalashnikov from here.'

Mortimer believed him. He and Ibrahim lay side by side at the top of a mound, passing a pair of binoculars back and forth. Ahead of them, perhaps two hundred yards away, the top halves of three Moroccan soldiers showed as little figures above a long, low dune. This was the third time in one day that Mortimer had been asked to crawl up a stony bank to peer at Moroccan positions. He was tiring of it. He couldn't write a story about looking at soldiers. And it was uncomfortable. Little stones pricked his elbows and knees.

He nodded at Ibrahim and began to move down the slope. Ibrahim immediately started too, so that the initiative might seem his.

Back at the camp, Mortimer wrote: *The noisiest place on earth is not a pressing mill, not a rave, not an aircraft test hangar, but a war. War assaults not the ears but the bones.*

He closed his notebook. He was lying. This war was quiet. Now and then came the soft thud of a shell exploding far away, well off target, its sound absorbed by the endless desert. The enemy had installed a radar artillery system at immense cost and to little effect.

Mortimer had forgotten the strange matter-of-factness of war, the way you could be in the heart of a war and not even know it. Nothing really happened. You just drove about in an empty landscape. You saw no one. Occasionally you heard a distant boom, but otherwise nothing told you a war was going on. Except for something in the men, perhaps, a calmness born of danger, as if you could tell they were saving themselves for something big, like opera singers or rock stars on the day of a show, who might laze by a pool, say, or just sit around in a way that would bore anyone else.

Several times on his first day Mortimer heard the distant thud-thud of the Moroccan artillery, followed a few seconds later by a pair of brief whines, two soft crashes. The guerrillas had long since learnt to dodge the radar. Ibrahim pointed out a faint stick on the horizon once, between two hills. 'Radar antenna,' he said.

Mortimer nodded and felt he ought to take a picture, but he was buckled up in his jacket and headscarf, and it seemed like too much trouble.

In the evening and all the second day they travelled on the terrain Mortimer remembered. It was an amazing land, a rolling plain of gravel – real gravel, like on a drive in Hampshire or Connecticut. It went on for hundreds of miles. In the morning it looked like a beaten sheet of silver. At noon it shimmered like overheated metal. In the late afternoon, golden light hovered above it, blinding like the ocean. And for ten minutes just after the sun slipped down, it wheeled itself through the entire spectrum, beginning with a fiery red, ending in luminous violet. Under the moon it glittered like sugar.

Day Two. Saskia, I have decided I must write to you. I don't know of course if I'll ever send this, but you are the one person I want to talk to. Being here makes me think of you, I don't know why. I feel that I have been a fool, an ass, someone despicable mostly for his obtuseness. But let's forget about that. I think you'd like it here.

They stop every five minutes. What? Hello? A puncture? Carburettor trouble? An ambush? No: tea every time. Tea after tea after tea. I had forgotten all about this. We all pile out, someone lights a fire, out come the tiny blue pot, the plastic bags of mint and sugar, the tin of fierce grey 'chinois noir'. Six shot glasses carefully twisted into the sand. No warming the pot. They just pour in the water, add a palmful of tea, and set the whole lot on the fire. When it fizzes they drop in a great lump of sugar and the interminable frothing begins: pot to glass and glass to pot, back and forth in the highest arc you can manage. The idea is to get up a good sweet froth. But the first glass is never sweet. The tea is too bitter. You can hardly get it down, it's so strong. Bitter like life, they say. They always have three rounds. The second is better: they add the mint, and more sugar. Strong like love. The third is easiest of all. Sweet like death. A sentiment peculiar to the desert?

Tea helps a man who has just come off the bottle, no question. My fingers are settling down at last. Yesterday I had such bad shakes I could hardly hold the blasted glass.

Amazing men. They lounge by the fire giving half their attention to the tea, keeping half on the alert. You've never seen people so relaxed. And in the middle of the Sahara, in the middle of a war. Tolstoy was right: there's no laziness like a military life. You can spend weeks doing bugger all and feel fine about it because you're a soldier. You don't even get bored. Boredom is a child of guilt, and there's no guilt here.

Have I done the right thing? Too early to say. Is there a price? The thirst is intolerable. They ration water. I drink five times as much as anyone else. They have this way about them, like camels or snakes. They don't need to take anything in. My asking for water has become a joke. They call me L'eau. Yet I hardly mind the thirst. This is one of the damn things about life. Do the one right thing and everything else falls into place. But sit around doing the wrong thing and you can't handle anything. What makes you make the crucial move? That's the question. Thank God I don't have to worry about that for now. Just get on with the story. This must be the big one. The week that changed the Sahara. I believe it still, though so far we have done nothing but drink tea, and there's been no sign of an offensive.

Mortimer woke up disgusted with himself in the middle of the night. He got up to pee. The men were still sleeping, and as far as he could see no one was on watch. No sign of dawn yet, but you could tell it was close. A kind of plain peace hung in the air, a sense of ordinariness, which seemed to connote day.

His stream rustled on the dry ground. He was able to wonder why self-loathing had invaded his sleep. It was a strong, sad feeling, but it was possible it made no sense. It was possible that in the early morning on the desert such a feeling might evaporate.

Nothing had happened yet. He mustn't forget that. He had come down to give their cause the limelight as he had done once before, just as the tide turned, just as they swept across that Moroccan barrier in a flood of mortars and grenades and Kalashnikovs, in a modern-day Bedouin swoop. And after three days of rambling and camping, and enjoying it, there was no question he was going soft on the story.

His hosts carried on in their leisurely desert way: twelve cups of tea a day, hours spent in repose, hours spent driving silently across the wastes in order to fire off two rockets at some lonely stretch of the Moroccan wall, then all the way back for a bowl of couscous.

Mortimer liked being with them. There was nothing brash or macho about them. When men were doing the most manly things – fighting wars, sailing ships – they appeared most womanly, doing the cooking and washing, taking care of themselves with a fastidiousness beyond the scope of suburban man. They were modest too. They went about their chores good-naturedly: the building of the fire, the opening of giant cans of soup and pasta, all mixed together in an aluminium cauldron, the tea ceremonies, the spreading of blankets as if for a picnic, the handing out of enamel bowls of couscous eaten with a mix of ease and dutifulness, without pleasure. For they were never hungry. They showed up the Western obsession with food and drink, the compulsion to fill the mouth. Nor did they ever tire, or sweat, or sneeze, or even cough. They were hard to pin down.

The truck had broken down once. Mortimer watched the man who fixed it. It seemed he had no idea what was wrong. He stared at the engine a long time, then reached in with a spanner – he didn't even have to find the right spanner – and turned a nut randomly, it seemed, vaguely, dreamily. The Land-Rover started up at the next try.

Mortimer couldn't help admiring them. He felt himself become a little like them: perhaps that was what made a traveller. In Afghanistan, for example, he hadn't just laughed at the mujahidins' jokes, he had learnt to find them funny. In the jungle he had naturally squatted on his haunches and spat like the tribesmen. In logging camps he had drunk beer at eleven in the morning and enjoyed the feel of sweat spreading across an overtight T-shirt. In British country houses he developed a taste for port and cigars, for whisky before dinner. Now he remembered the taste and smell of other deserts, and began to recover a peculiar stillness of the mind which he had learnt from the Kalahari bushmen. A lizard mind: being still within the cave of your skull while looking out on the dazzling world. A useful way to be.

He felt better. Perhaps he was just a natural traveller, a man who couldn't live happily at home. Unless it was being with these men, who did not stand if they could squat, or squat if they could lie, who thought nothing of lounging by a tea-fire for half the day, nor of rising at two in the morning for a difficult and dangerous ride without food or even tea until the afternoon. They did not respond to comfort the way other men did. Once, years ago, Mortimer had shared a hotel room with one of their diplomatic team in Geneva. The room had two big beds. The guerrilla unrolled his cape and slept on the floor. What was the point of a bed? What, when it came to it, was the point of a house? Tombs for the living, they called them. Only they could claim an unbroken line going back to the apes. They alone of men had never stooped to sow seeds. Their daily life mapped out the truth of human existence: that our home on the planet could only ever be a transitory camp.

Day Three. The flies! You'd hate this. You've never seen anything like it. The absurd tea-pouring attracts them. They settle all over everyone's fingers, first the pourer's then everyone else's. Once the glass is in your hand they line the rim completely, like margarita salt. Wave them away and they ignore you. Only if you touch them will they move, and even then you have to push. Reluctantly they step on to their neighbour then angrily buzz away. You lift the glass to your lips. Inches from your mouth, there they are still. Just as you think: fuck it, I'm never going to be able to drink this. Or else: fuck it, I'm just going to have to swallow a couple of flies, they vanish. Lower the cup an inch and there they are again.

The desert is good for 'fuck-its'. Who can be bothered in this heat?

A funny thing: how I like it here. How it suits me.

About the guns. Men want clarity and simplicity and that is what guns offer. Guns make life simple. They feel right. Let me explain: guns clarify life. They give you a buzz of direction. They make a man feel loved. They justify him.

On the fourth morning, Mortimer looked through his notebook and wondered: What was all this nonsense? This was hardly the first time he had been in a war. Perhaps he had softened in the last few years; perhaps it was even a good thing. Saskia often said how hard he was, how he needed softening. He must surely be softened, if he thought softening good.

He wrote down: *Copy, you bastard. Enough bloody philosophy.*

They were lying in the lee of a dune, around ten o'clock. All trace of the morning cool had evaporated. Mortimer was having to resist the urge to pull away his headcloth, an action which they warned would make him thirstier. A trickle of sweat was making its way down his side. He remembered to lie still. The kettle gurgled as it heated. The man in charge of it opened the lid. He was a handsome man, the darkest of them all, dark as a Ugandan, with bottomless eyes and deep folds on his face.

'Ibrahim,' Mortimer called.

Ibrahim was busy stuffing a pipe with the foul powdery black tobacco they smoked. He inverted the instrument and lit it with a twig from the fire. Exhaling a stream of smoke, smiling benignly, looking high, he raised his eyebrows at Mortimer.

'The paper is not going to be pleased,' Mortimer said. 'There are many other places they might have sent me.'

Ibrahim rested his eyes on Mortimer in such a way that Mortimer felt easy about going on, in fact felt relaxed about his complaint, no longer especially wanting it acted on.

'I mean, at the very least I need an interview with Lamin Aziz.'

Lamin Aziz was the 'President', the guerrilla leader and head of the refugee camps – of the Nation-in-Exile. It was a toy town: toy government, toy politicians, even a toy government house, that giant tent of black wool, one of the original nomad tents. The intention was that one day all these toy institutions would be moved to a small dusty city in the disputed territory. It made one wonder about government and the machinery of state – it was all like a game at play school, not just here but everywhere.

Ibrahim shrugged and took another pull on his pipe. '*Vamos a ver,*' he said, breathing out smoke.

We'll see. Mortimer shook his head. These people. So

laid back. They didn't mind that their war was going on and on. In fact it suited them. They could carry on living in tents and scampering around the desert in Land-Rovers, just as they liked. What would they do with a country, if they ever got one?

All that day they stayed at the same camp, lying in the shade of the Land-Rover. Three of the men dozed beneath it, crawling out only to drink tea. Mortimer's impatience grew then dwindled, then grew again towards noon, as the strip of shadow he had been lying in became too narrow to cover him. He lay beside the hot brown iron of the vehicle, baking like a pizza, as hot as he had ever been, even in the baths of Siberia. Despair touched him: what was he doing here, wasting his time? If he was going to go somewhere, he could have gone to the oil spill in Greenland. The word 'Greenland' felt like a rebuke. He thought of fjords and ice and turf. What a fool. Here he lay, pressed to the ground by an immense heat.

At four o'clock they returned the teapot to the back of the Land-Rover, kicked over the ashes and climbed aboard with their rifles in their laps.

Mortimer had slept. When he saw the sunlight glittering on the plain like water, he felt better. The day was nearly over. He had survived. It felt like an achievement. They swayed and purred over the desert, then wrapped their faces for a long fast race across packed mud. At the far side the driver plugged the vehicle into four-wheel drive and picked his way between two gravel slopes, hidden from the world. When they stopped, Ibrahim took

Mortimer's hand, which surprised Mortimer, and made him follow behind on his belly as they slithered up a rocky slope. At the top Mortimer slowly raised his head. Ahead of them, some fifty or sixty yards away, four black dots showed at the top of a sandbank: helmets, soldiers.

No one else had come with them. Ibrahim pressed a finger to his lips. They were evidently to wait for something. He had an idea he was about to be given a graphic display of guerrilla tactics. They were showing off to him.

Two cracks sounded. Ibrahim sank to the ground and pressed a hand into Mortimer's back. He lay with his cheek against a rock. A moment later he heard a whine, then another, each followed by a thud. They came from somewhere behind them. Mortimer eased his head round to look back down the slope. The Land-Rover was gone.

Ibrahim kept his face to the ground and smiled. 'They know we are here,' he whispered. 'But you see? They don't know where.'

When they raised themselves on their elbows, the four little helmets had vanished. Mortimer felt uneasy. A clatter of gunfire broke out some way along the wall, accompanied by the whoosh of rocket grenades. Then there was silence, and another clattering of guns. Then some weapon made an odd noise, like a moan cut short. A little cloud of smoke rose up into the sky, faint and precious.

A few minutes later Ibrahim started crawling backwards down the hill. Mortimer followed. The Land-Rover had returned. In it sat two new men, wearing faded navy-blue caps. Mortimer could see at once that they were different from the others, though it was hard to say how.

Perhaps they were a shade paler. All the guerrillas climbed in and they drove off in silence.

That evening they passed a group of nomads. Their black tent was startling on the empty land. The nomads were apparently friends, and greeted the rebels warmly. The rebels left a jerrycan with them, and drove off with a small goat. One of them, sitting on the side of the vehicle, held it clamped between his knees. At first the animal attempted to stay upright as the vehicle bumped along, then gave in, realising that it didn't need to, the man's legs would hold it steady.

They made a detour across a dry wadi and pulled up beside a knee-high shrub. One of the men dug around the plant with a machete and excavated a small log of root.

They camped in the middle of an open flatness. The driver simply switched off the engine and let the vehicle coast, and wherever it stopped was camp. Everyone spilled out.

The two newcomers with blue caps sat in the circle of men, drinking their tea slowly and thoughtfully, staring at the ground. Mortimer pulled out his notebook and began describing them: *Young men, moustaches (like all of them), heavy eyebrows, quite dark . . . in short almost identical to the others. Maybe not as lean.*

He nodded at one of them and asked where he was from, thinking he knew the answer.

The man glanced at Mortimer then looked away. He must have been astonished by the question.

Ibrahim stepped around behind the circle and sat beside Mortimer. 'They're Moroccans,' he said. 'Fresh from the Wall. Prisoners. You want to talk to them?'

Mortimer asked them a few questions. Both were silent, unsure who this strange foreigner was, unsure whether they were being interrogated, suspecting perhaps that he might be a journalist and afraid of what might get back to their command. Mortimer left them in peace for the second and third rounds of tea.

He flipped through possible headlines. *Desert Rebels Stop for Tea. Tea on the Frontline. Desert Rebels Give their Captives Tea.*

From a little way off, outside the fire circle, came a soft, anxious bleating, then the sickly liquid sounds of slaughter. One of the soldiers fed the tip of the big root into the fire, building up a blaze.

Day Four. Barbecue tonight. First they flay the poor beast (a goat) then spread out the skin, fleece down, and use the slippery sheet as a butcher's block. They dismantle the animal and store the various components – legs, organs, skull, ribs – in piles at the edge. The first fresh meat in almost a week, but I have little appetite for it. Who cares? Eating is just something to do.

I keep remembering years ago when I walked from Timimoun to one of the little oases. While covering the Malian famine. There was nothing but sand, dunes for ever as far as you could see. It was a windy day. After half an hour Timimoun was lost from sight. We knew it would be a few hours before we could see the first palm gardens of the oasis. Just the compass to guide us across the ocean of sand, the Great Western Erg. What a place. The wind blew away our tracks. Can you imagine that? I can barely remember the sight now, but I remember what it felt like. It was a lesson. No tracks. No past. It was true not only of that journey but of everything, all life. All of it blows away. I mean that not as a metaphor but reality. We have no past. There is no going back.

They say the struggle for good and evil goes on in the human mind. Nowhere is that clearer than in the desert. This is the original tabula rasa, where whatever has been is erased.

This is embarrassing but I keep seeing you in the landscape, in the crevices between the hills, in the hill on the horizon, which lies there just like you do, still, sure of itself. I am beginning to realise how much I miss you. Sometimes I see suddenly that none of this makes any sense. I mean these last few years. Our situation. You were always right. You understood in advance of me. It has taken me a long time to see, to see myself, and you, and us and what remains to us. We must meet as soon as I am back.

The last time he saw Saskia, ghastly time, he took her to dinner at L'Escargot. Why there, of all places? He should have known better. The minute he held open the door and saw her sitting on one of the stiff little sofas waiting for him, he knew that it would not work. They had had to sit through an excruciating dinner. He should have had her over, if she would have agreed to that, or else gone to a Chinese or an Indian, even a pub. Somewhere informal. And why meet at night even, like a pair of dating undergraduates?

She had looked beautiful. He didn't have the habit of noticing her beauty. Seeing it that night, he felt excluded.

The old sadness rolled over him. Her blonde hair, pleasantly, outdoorsily grey at the roots, was pinned back the way he liked, sleeking her cheeks. She had lost a few pounds, she looked strong, lean. He recognised the beauty in her small frame. She seemed to have acquired shape. She sat very correct-looking, with her knees together, just showing beyond the hem of a black skirt. She had dressed up not for him but for the restaurant, he could see that.

What sharp intelligent eyes she had. She could look like some small, lean mammal, fiercely alert, sitting there hunched up and staring at you. Thank God, he thought to himself, that she had had children. Imagine if she had come to him childless, and he had kept her that way, as he would have done. Only one thing, in the end, could redeem any life: progeny. Not for him, of course, but for her. She could survive whatever love threw at them, because she had her future assured. Children mitigated death, he thought, as if reproduction really were the one thing we were put on this earth to accomplish. He would go naked into death with nothing to diminish it but age.

Was Saskia the love of his life? His first answer would be no. That was Clarissa, who had left him when he went off to Afghanistan on his first assignment, and who had never looked back. She was married by the time he returned, and she had made a good life for herself. Women were practical like that. But his second answer would be yes, of course Saskia was the love of his life, his actual life. The dream life might hang on, but in the end, he was sure, it would be the actual life that counted.

* * *

The prisoners were with them all the following day, silently doing whatever the party did – tea, drive, tea, eat, drive. They never looked at anyone, not even each other.

All wars were strange. You sat around a fire and chatted. The fact that your cousin or brother or friend was no longer at the fire with you made no difference. The fact that two of the enemy were, also made no difference. Still you sat and spat and smoked and drank tea and entertained the foreign journalist with little stunts. 'Fighting' consisted of endless sitting around. Clipping nails, picking at dry skin, rubbing stubble, musing, composing letters in one's mind.

Just now they were all sitting on a caked white mudflat. They seemed to make their own little stage around the fire. They had to have their own reasons for all of this. The surroundings could supply none.

'Ibrahim, this is the end of the fifth day,' Mortimer said. He had not showered since being down here and had lost all desire to. His skin and clothes had become one. 'Is anything going to happen?'

Ibrahim chuckled deeply. At times he had an incredibly deep, rather beautiful voice. 'No problem,' he said. 'Everything can happen.'

'I'm only here another day and a half. I have to leave with something. It's the *Sunday Herald*. Why won't Lamin Aziz see me?'

'All things can happen,' Ibrahim answered, with typical desert oracularity.

* * *

Day Five. We have taken two of the enemy. They seem nice enough. Life goes on. We all drink tea together. In the desert all men are brothers first, warriors second. It's a little like those Christmas truces in the trenches. Another tea, Maroc?

Night fell. The huge planet wheeled its flatness across the western sky, sending a band of deep blue shadow into the pale east. The band deepened and spread. The orange west became spangled with early stars. A sliver of a moon, a hair caught on a camera lens, shone luminously on the glazed sky.

The two Moroccans and two of the guerrillas had vanished. They had slipped away somehow. Mortimer must have been dozing. He got up to have a better look. All around, the plain lay flat: no sign of anyone. Yet they could not have gone far. The desert's apparent flatness contained hidden gullies and ditches, even small canyons that you saw only when you were almost in them, but still their disappearance startled him.

He heard something. A faint crack. A whine, a high-pitched groan. He stood still, staring into the silence of the coming night. Nothing more. Just stillness. A hissing in the ears. As he listened a wonderful feeling crept over him. His legs felt warm and fluid, his heart seemed to tingle. Good things would happen to him. They had before and they would again. His fate was to clasp the globe in his fist. Never in human history, perhaps, had there been a man of such wide experience.

Another crack, a moan. Both sounds were very faint. Mortimer wasn't sure if it was his ears playing up. It could be a desert fox, he thought. Or one of the birds. He had seen a bird in the sky the previous day.

One of the guerrillas fiddled with the knobs on a big cloth-covered military radio. He wore a pair of small hard-looking headphones. He raised a speaker to his lips and spoke softly, then adjusted a dial.

Ibrahim approached Mortimer. 'Get some sleep. We'll be up very early. Midnight.'

'Where are the prisoners?'

Ibrahim smiled. 'Sleep. The desert tires a foreigner.'

Mortimer lay on his back. He could still feel the glow that had entered his body. The stars dropped from the sky and hung just above his face, so close he could stick out his tongue and lick them. They were coarse like sea salt.

Mortimer understood that he had been playing it too much their way. He must stay awake, but so they thought he was sleeping. He was a journalist, a reporter. He had got caught up in the romance of things. Back to basics: the difference between what they say and what I see equals the truth.

The soft human voices in the emptiness were soothing. The crackles of the fire died down to a low hiss. The voices became big and deep, superbly resonant out there on the flat land. Mortimer listened, imagining at times that they were talking in French or Spanish, and that he would understand what they were saying if only he listened harder. At some point the Land-Rover left. When it came back there were a few hushed, concerned exchanges. He rolled on to his side and opened his lower eye. By the jeep's wheel, a cap lay on the ground. It belonged to one of the Moroccans. He decided to stand up and surprise them.

He did so. He yawned and shuffled off to pee, and saw what he needed: the two Moroccans bound back to back, lying on their sides in the back of the Land-Rover, slack as a pair of socks. The face of the man nearer him was covered in dirt. The mouth of the other hung open.

Mortimer's stream made a pleasant sound in the wide night. It drowned out the voices at the camp. He had a heavy feeling in his chest. He told himself: It's nothing to what you have seen, remember Eritrea, remember Cambodia, this is war, war is like this. But it didn't work. His stomach rose. He took a few steps forward, not as many as he had planned, bent over and puked. Strings of phlegm swung from his mouth as his stomach hardened into a knot.

'Too much for you?' came Ibrahim's voice. 'You've been to many wars, no?'

Mortimer didn't answer but walked with lowered head back to his sleeping roll.

The action that followed was hard to make sense of until it was over. In the middle of the night they dismantled the campsite and mounted the Land-Rover. They drove for an hour, then parked at the foot of a low hill. Ibrahim clutched Mortimer's arm, guided him halfway up the hill, then pushed him flat on his belly. What Mortimer saw from the brow surprised him. The whole area between the hill and the Moroccan wall was covered in bodies, and the bodies were moving. It was an eerie sight: an infantry attack of the old school, the oldest school. This was how the pashas' caravans had been ambushed: a knife clenched between the teeth, elbows nudging forwards over the ground. There must have been fifty fighters.

Then: thud-thud, thud-thud, sounding far away. A moment later the screech-booms rang out. There was another attack going on a few hundred yards up the wall. Mortimer stared but could make nothing out.

The snaking figures had risen up in a silent wave and were sprinting up the bulldozed dune. Then they were out of sight. This was the strangeness of war: Mortimer and Ibrahim still just lay there on the ground, and unless one knew, unless one actually made the imaginary connections, it might seem that nothing unusual was going on.

A clatter of rifle fire sounded out. Then silence again. Figures came back over the dunes: more this time. Soldiers kept on coming, more and more. Most of them held their hands clasped on their heads. Everyone was jogging, jogging and stumbling down the dune, across the open space, and up the hill, the nearest within thirty feet of Mortimer. It all happened in silence.

Mortimer slithered back down the hill. He watched the new prisoners being loaded into a waiting Unimog. He wondered how they would all fit in. Somehow they did.

The Rio Camello fighters dispersed. Mortimer found himself back at the Land-Rover with exactly the original band of six. Everything was as it had been before. It had been a good operation: slick, quick, and left no traces. Like a dream, the attack might never have happened. How would you know it had?

The two dispensed Moroccans were gone.

Day Six. Perhaps things are getting better not when the bad times are over, but when you stop thinking of them as bad times. When you can see good even in them. Heigh-ho.

For example? For example the locusts. Saskia, you have never seen anything like this. It changes you. I'm serious.

They passed the locusts on the way back to the camp. *Young locusts: lime-green, wingless, the juveniles draw up in marching columns hundreds of miles long.*

They showed as a black line, some geological feature remarkable only for being long and straight. The Land-Rover rode over it. Then Ibrahim called to the driver to stop and tapped Mortimer's knee.

The two men climbed out and knelt close. The insects were unaware of them. Ibrahim said the vanguard would already be in Mauritania, two hundred miles away. Every bit of them was bright green, the bent thighs, the heads and bodies, even the antennae, as if they had been dipped entire in green paint. They were at once horrific and magnificent. A thousand miles' marching lay ahead of them. Incalculable distance, incalculable number. You could just hear the rustle they made. Where were they going? What made them go? What made them that brilliant colour? They stopped neither to eat nor sleep. They belonged to a destiny vaster than man's.

Things of this magnitude, Mortimer wrote down, *require the whole sky in which to resonate.*

He put his pen back in his breast pocket and closed the notebook. His heart was racing. Had he been a fool? Had he failed to realise something perfectly simple? He thought all the trouble was to do with his work, but maybe it was quite different. Maybe he had nearly been doing the *right* thing these last few years, without knowing it. Perhaps he no longer wanted what he thought he did.

He looked at the locusts, and again his mind rang with a song to their magnitude. He didn't think: Famine in Mali, 120,000 refugees within the year, logistical nightmare, UNHCR, etc. He thought: The world is so big. That was all. His head hummed.

Then he wondered: All those years in which he had flitted from atrocity to atrocity and horror to horror, perhaps an overarching question had governed his ceaseless motion. He had been looking for a reason not to have faith. And he understood now that he had failed.

He must stop and rest. That was the injunction of the plains of gravel: rest, traveller, rest.

On his last day Mortimer had still not seen the President.

He understood what had happened. The Rio Camello fighters had tried to impress him with their first small capture, and failed. They had tortured their captives for information, and carried out the bigger raid. It would benefit them anyway, of course, but more so since Mortimer was there to report that Morocco's defences were at least partially ineffective.

But it was nothing like the promised offensive. Mortimer had been had. Or something had gone wrong.

War wasn't the way the papers reported it. It was all an act. Those Moroccan soldiers didn't want to be killed. They were recruits who had just left school. Of course they would do what they were told if the enemy had them at the end of a gun barrel. A war was a show, a movie. Algeria produced, Rio Camello performed. Meanwhile, Britain, France and the US bankrolled Morocco's side, pouring huge sums into the friendly autocrat's thousand-mile defence without any hope of return. What was in the disputed territory? A few thousand nomads, a barren sea-port clinging to the Atlantic coast with a few streets of crumbling concrete, some phosphate mines long ago abandoned because of the war, and a thousand miles of nothing.

Meanwhile, Rio Camello lived in tents, drove Land-Rovers, camped on the desert, just as they liked. They had a mission in life.

Mortimer was waiting in the same long, high room to which he had been delivered on first arriving. It might once have been a Legionnaires' barracks, he thought, though it had the air of a schoolroom. He had to wait until some time in the afternoon. The guerrillas had dropped him off that morning, and driven away with the minimum of goodbyes. Four of the foam beds had been made up. There were other visitors now. The same stack of blankets stood in the corner, shorter than before. Otherwise the room was empty except for Mortimer's bag, which sat open beside a pile of papers and books, his. He couldn't understand why he had brought them all.

He sat with his back against the wall. He was good at waiting now. In his lap was an open notebook, in his hand a pencil, but he was staring at the opposite wall where, just below the room's one window, a large section of yellow plaster had fallen away, exposing dusty brick-work. Something stirred in his mind and caused him to look up at the three big beams supporting the ceiling. It was a vacuum of a room.

He had been here three hours. He was covered in desert dust, but his appetite for what might have been a pleasure – washing off six days' dirt – had vanished.

Day Seven. I'm not sure how I'm going to leave here. I wish you could come and meet me at the airport like in the old days. I can see no reason to go back other than to see you. They killed our two prisoners. I was sick. Then they captured another batch. They want me to see that they can.

I leave this afternoon. There's no respite in this life. Not even in the desert.

A young reporter in Kabul once told me we were the reason people fought wars. Look at Lawrence of Arabia, he said. You know Lawrence was made by that American newspaper man. I thought he was crazy, but now I have to wonder if he wasn't right. I do.

Half an hour before he was due to leave, when his bag was packed and he was still sitting alone in the barrack room, Mortimer heard footsteps advancing down the hall. Ibrahim entered.

'*Yalah*. Let's go.'

Mortimer was surprised to see him. He smiled. 'I thought you'd be back at the front by now.' He zipped up the bag and lifted it to his shoulders.

'No, no,' Ibrahim said. 'No bag.'

Mortimer looked at him. 'The airport?'

Ibrahim shook his head. 'Important meeting.'

'The President?'

'Important meeting,' Ibrahim repeated, without trace of a smile.

Outside, another Land-Rover, dark green, hard top, waited. They drove Mortimer around the camp and away. At the side of a hill a set of unlikely steel doors appeared. They opened from within, and a guard spoke to Ibrahim through the car window. The Land-Rover entered a long ramp lit by intermittent bulbs. They drove downwards a long way, curving always to the left. As far as Mortimer could see, the ramp might continue endlessly downwards on its slow spiral beneath the desert. They stopped outside a grey metal door.

Ibrahim nodded. Mortimer climbed out and pushed open the heavy door. A guard within led him along a dark corridor into an enormous ambassadorial suite, full of huge armchairs and ashtrays. You could feel at once that it was a room large and comfortable enough to absorb fierce differences, and probably had done so.

President Lamin Aziz looked like a young man. He had a moustache and bright eyes and wore combat fatigues. He shook Mortimer's hand and pulled a pack of Marlboros from his breast pocket, along with a gold lighter, and offered one to Mortimer. His English, French and Spanish were fluent, Mortimer knew. He was an intelligent man. You could see it in his eyes. As the lighter flared at the tip of his cigarette a sparkle showed in them.

He lay back in an armchair, draping one leg over the chair's arm.

'Eventually he has to stop this insanity,' he said, of the King of Morocco. 'We won't stop. We are in the right.'

Mortimer took notes and fired off his questions just like in the old days, yet the more he wrote down the less he felt he had. As his pad filled, his hands emptied. Why was there a war? Sitting in armchairs and discussing diplomatic initiatives made no sense. Once you heard someone talk about it, war became absurd. What made sense was streaking across the desert in a Land-Rover, camping round a fire, sucking harsh smoke from a copper pipe and baking bread in the sand. That was what humans were made for.

'I know we can count on you to understand our cause,' the President said, blowing his smoke up towards the high ceiling. 'You know the injustice of the Moroccan position. You know he has violated the UN resolutions repeatedly. You know this must not go on. You also know how we can deal with two prisoners if it helps our struggle. You know how we can deal with eighty-seven prisoners also.' He paused, took a big draw on his cigarette, blew the smoke up again, following it with his eye.

'Eighty-seven?' Mortimer asked. He watched the President's face. It was rough, pockmarked, and shone with a contained excitement.

'From the other night.' The President didn't look at Mortimer for a long time.

Another man let himself into the room, also dressed in combat fatigues.

'Ah, Mohammed,' the President said expansively, waving his cigarette hand.

Mortimer nodded at the newcomer, who walked in smiling, took a seat, then asked Mortimer, 'So how was your stay?'

Only then did Mortimer realise it was Mohammed Ahmoud, the London man.

'What the devil are you doing here?'

He felt the floor move, as if beneath the ground one might actually feel the flat desert wheeling through space.

Mohammed Ahmoud could plainly see Mortimer's surprise. He smiled. 'I'm here to make sure everything goes well.'

'We need to know we can count on you,' the President continued. 'You are a respected man.'

Mortimer waited. The desert had taught him to wait.

'We know you support our cause,' the President said. 'Why does Britain still support Morocco? We must do everything to isolate them.'

'I'm a journalist,' Mortimer began.

'The struggle makes demands of us all,' the President interjected. 'I am a soldier by nature, not a politician. Look at Mohammed Ahmoud. He is a teacher by training, yet he must work as a diplomat now.'

Mohammed Ahmoud nodded gravely.

The President stubbed out his cigarette in one of the giant marble ashtrays. 'Think of those prisoners.'

'We can't trust anyone,' Mohammed Ahmoud added. 'We have been treated badly. By certain people.'

The President shrugged, smiling vaguely. 'You know our position is just. We do not like to mistreat our prisoners. It would be a pity if we were forced to.'

Mortimer saw that the glint in the President's eye was not humour or intelligence but zeal. He was a dangerous man. It seemed obvious now that something like this would be said. Mortimer had no doubt whatsoever that he would do what they asked. He would print whatever they wanted.

As Mortimer was driven towards the airport, out of the refugee city, a terrible nostalgia seized him. Everything seemed sad. The huge red desert, the two men who had died horribly and unnecessarily, the atrocities committed under cover of vegetation, and the brown rivers of ugliness and waste threading through the world, all were sadness incarnate. So too the gleaming airliners that ferried you back and forth among these places. He felt flat as the desert, and the flatness stretched on for ever. As he stood on the tarmac waiting to board, hearing the steel roar of the jet engines, his nostrils touched by the nauseous odour of jet fuel, he was surprised by the sudden knowledge that this was the last story he would ever do. He had crossed the wilderness now, the chariot had come to take him home, and he was going home. He would pay the warriors off once and for all.